THIRTY-FOUR

CA SOLE

Helifish Books

Published in 2021 by Helifish Books

Copyright © 2021 CA Sole

ISBN: 978-0-9954809-5-7 (Paperback)
ISBN: 978-0-9954809-6-4 (ebook-ePub)
ISBN: 978-0-9954809-7-1 (PDF)

British Library Cataloguing in Publication Data
A CIP catalogue record for this book is available from the British Library

I am sincerely grateful to my wife and others who have provided invaluable input to make this a better book.

THIRTY-FOUR

1

I am eighty-five, but for the last fifty-one years I've been thirty-four.
If this happened to you – what would you do? Would you trumpet your success? Would you hide away? Who would you trust?

IF ANYONE WAS looking for Andrew Duncan around midnight on that Saturday in August 2019, for a brief period they would have found him in a crumpled heap in a hotel car park. He was a man who valued his self-respect, but there was no sign of dignity in his body that night. It appeared he had dropped where he stood amongst the litter on the verge. His legs had folded as if they were rubber, and his left arm was pinned unnaturally beneath him. Mud stained his tailored clothes. His shoes, a half-eaten burger clinging to the right sole, were scuffed where the woman had dragged him across the tarmac.

The hum from the distant motorway never ceased, only lessened as the night crept into the early hours. A loud guffaw from the hotel was accompanied by a stream of laughter from other late drinkers. A light rain was falling, its drops swirling in the wind and sparkling under the harsh car-park lights. A black van had reversed up to the verge, casting a shadow over the prone figure. The woman stood at the front of the van, shivered briefly in the breeze and scanned the car park, waiting for something. She wrinkled her nose at the stench of rubbish, took a few steps to the rear of the vehicle and looked down at the body, but made no move to help. Prodding it with her foot to see if she could get a response – not a kick, but hard enough to make him wince had he been conscious – she gave a satisfied murmur.

Two men approached on silent shoes, their only greeting to her a raised open hand. One unlocked the van and opened the rear doors. The bigger of the two gripped the trunk under the arms, the other took the ankles. They looked at the woman. She nodded, and they lifted and slid me into the back of the van.

SAFFRON WAS my wife when I had my accident. Eleven years later, she endured a painful death, completely unaware of the long-term effects of that crash. Sometimes she interrupts my sleep in the depths of the night, even when I'm skin to skin with Alex. Her face is not the last, pain-ravaged countenance I remember, it's the pretty forty-year-old before her trials began. She mouths 'Andrew', but no sound reaches me. She follows my name with her kindest smile, and fades. I know why she still haunts me after all these years. She wants to ensure I'm happy and, from her vantage in a higher place, to see that no harm comes to me as a result of my condition.

I am happy; I have Alex. She's a wonder. Sometimes she follows Saffron in my head, even though she lies beside me.

These dreams are frequent, but that particular night stuck in my mind, because of everything else that happened. Saffron didn't come, but Alex's face appeared, though without her usual kind and amused expression. It came and went and came again. She was agitated and trying to tell me something.

It grew lighter. My eyes didn't want to open as consciousness returned. When they did, they were greeted by a white ceiling, moulded cornices, a smoke alarm blinking its tiny red light periodically – once, twice, three times …

This was not my room! Nor was it the hotel room I'd taken for the night. It was far from either. Where the hell was I?

My head wasn't spinning and it didn't ache. I had not drunk excessively the night before; I had not been smashed. I've had enough hangovers in my long life to know that this was not one. Yet my brain was fuzzy and incapable of concentration.

I was usually awake at five and would spring out of bed. It didn't happen that day. It was an atypical sluggish day, and relinquishing the warmth of the duvet for the toilet required determination.

Two open doors faced me. The left one was a spacious bathroom – almost as big as my bedroom at home. It was bright in there, the light streaming in from a high translucent window, which could not be opened.

Lever taps on the basin worked with a smooth, precise action that sent water gushing down a broad chute instead of a spout, conjuring images of a mill race. Above the basin was a shelf with a hairbrush, an electric toothbrush and toothpaste – all identical to mine at home. The paste looked, smelt and tasted genuine. You can't be too careful with things you don't know.

A shower, wide enough for daily exercises, stretched the width of the room and was separated from the remainder by a glass partition. The broad, square head, one of those water-falls that drench the body, power-wash the skin and seemingly cleanse the soul, beckoned. Had this been a luxury hotel, the toiletries would have been hand-made designer-label products with expensive names like Cetaphil or Bronnley. Only com-mon brands of soap and shampoo, together with a loofah, lay on the shelf – all the same as I normally used.

A shower would certainly stimulate my spaced-out brain. I craved it, but the entire flat had to be explored first. The bathroom alone showed there was too much in it that was familiar in those unfamiliar surroundings to allow me to relax.

Where was I? What was outside? Was the place a luxury apartment or hotel? The curtains would not open, and there was no cord to operate them. The entire wall opposite the window was blank but for two paintings. It was the wall where one would expect to see the entrance. It took a moment before the door's outline became apparent, because it was nothing more than a fine crack in the oddly textured surface. How come there was no handle and the door would not open? And why was there no spy-hole? Everything was wrong.

Beside the door's outline a remote control nestled in a cradle. Most of the buttons worked combinations of lighting, but I found one that opened the curtains, revealing a window that was not high but stretched almost the whole width of the room. The view gave me no clue as to where I was, but it was in the country. Opposite was a low hill with a copse of a dozen or so trees on its summit. A herd of cows was scattered over the rise, mostly towards the top. They were some way away, but the rhythm of their chewing and the odd swish of a tail were still visible. Two calves frolicked about near their mothers.

With my head clearing, my thoughts became more rational. I had to get hold of Alex. Where were the clothes I was wearing last night? Where were my things: my car keys, wallet and phone? I may have had no clothes on, but the lack of a phone somehow amplified my nakedness.

The other open door led to a walk-in dressing room with a full-length mirror.

'These shirts are just what I'd choose, and they're my collar size,' I muttered out loud.

A jacket fitted me perfectly. I left it on as my only item of clothing. My feet are broad – Saffron used to say they were gorilla feet – and few off-the-shelf shoes fit me. But those on the wardrobe rack were very comfortable.

An espresso machine stood on a counter above a minibar. Inside the fridge was a bottle of semi-skimmed milk and a selection of drinks and mixers, all of which were to my taste, with the exception of the Krug champagne. At the far end of the counter, beyond a bowl of fresh fruit and a plate with a napkin and a peeling knife, was a Highland Park single malt and a Hendrick's gin. It was too early for alcohol, and I didn't take milk. What I needed was the raw, bitter kick of a double espresso.

But for the jacket, I still had no clothes on. It was warm, and I turfed the thing onto the bed and took my coffee for a closer look out of the window. There was no one outside to see me, and the window was probably tinted anyway.

'*Bloody hell.* This isn't a window at all. It's a display, and what's playing is either a recording or a live camera view of …?'

I guessed it was the same concept as that to be used for windowless aeroplanes. Actual windows are to be replaced by a camera view to allow a more structurally sound and lighter aircraft. So the view out of the apartment 'window' could have been of anywhere.

What the hell was going on? It wasn't live. The cows were chewing and swishing their tails, but they weren't moving forward to fresh grass as they munched. Their calves were bounding about just as they had been before. It was a repeat.

It was better than a blank wall to stare at, but not much. They wouldn't let me see out – why? Would I identify where I was being held? Was the rural scene meant to calm me? It didn't; it reinforced my feeling of abduction and imprisonment. My world was suddenly much smaller.

The smell of the place raised its own questions. It had an odour of newness, a hint of fresh paint, of recently dried cement and nothing to suggest it had ever been occupied. It was also as quiet as a crypt, and a stamp on the thick-pile carpet barely emitted a muffled thud.

The paintings were not the average instantly forgettable hotel decoration. Instead, they were by Bruegel, Hieronymus Bosch and similar artists that I find fascinating because so much goes on in their work.

I was locked in and naked, a knight preparing for battle with no armour. Was I being watched? Cameras could be minute, much smaller than in my day, one could be anywhere. The ceiling was flat and smooth and the lighting discreet. In the smoke alarm, maybe? Or anywhere in the peculiar sound-absorbing wall covering?

'They know me. This room's been tailored for me. It's been designed as my home.'

I bit my lip to stop talking out loud to myself, because someone might be listening. All future self-consultations would be under my breath. 'Who are they?'

The beautiful polished mahogany writing desk had a leather insert. On it was a laptop. I knew for certain what was going to happen: it started when I lifted the lid, and it liked my password.

'How did this get here? And why is my phone missing?'

They had been in my house, they had learned what they could about me, taken the computer and brought it here. It had almost certainly been bugged or copied. They had probably taken control of the camera and microphone. Every time I opened it from then on, every key I pressed would be known to whoever was playing games with me – although no one was going to create a set-up like this as a mere game.

Beside my computer was a gold fountain pen, a Montblanc Meisterstück. It must have been worth over a thousand pounds. There was no clue from the writing paper as to my whereabouts; no letterhead, although it was faintly embossed with some pattern I couldn't make out.

My watch read 11.28, but was that true? Had reality gone out of that virtual window? Had I been dumped in another world for some unknown reason, by some phantom body?

Puzzlement and suspicion turned to anger. I had to think. For some weird reason, I think best when showering.

HOT NEEDLES of water stung my head and drove memories into my consciousness a few sharp pricks at a time. There had been a conference the day before on improving the survivability of helicopter occupants following a ditching offshore; technical stuff, but some interesting ideas were put forward. It was held in a hotel not far from my village, but the prospect of getting home, probably drunk, in the early hours, made me decide to stay the night.

Most of the colleagues and professionals at the conference were people I had known over the last five or six years. I certainly didn't expect to see Tony Hogg, who was a pilot with me in the Gulf fifteen years ago.

'*Andrew*,' he said, 'I didn't think you'd be here. Thought you'd retired ages ago.'

'That makes two of us.'

'Oh, I can't afford to give it up. As long as there's an income to be had, I'll keep at it. God, man, but you haven't aged a bit – still bloody young as ever.' He laughed. 'Please tell my wife how you do it.'

How many times had I heard that comment: 'you haven't aged …'? Dreaded words that kept reminding me to keep my distance from people, to cut a person out of my life before they drew attention to me. I'd had to do it often enough, but that didn't make it any easier. It meant, for example, not coming to this annual gathering until the current bunch had retired and there was no one left to remember me. A pity, because although never seeing these particular colleagues again didn't concern me, it has always been amusing to sink a few pints with the like-minded and join them in swinging the lantern over aviation exploits – as long as it only took place once a year.

But the drinking and reminiscing didn't explain what happened to me, nor how I ended up imprisoned in that room. A woman came to mind as the evening gradually returned to me – yes, of course there was a woman. She had nothing to do with the conference, we only met in the bar. Stunning, black hair halfway down her back, Mediterranean blue eyes. I asked her what part of the States she came from. Alaska, she said. I'd never met anyone from Alaska before and, as I picked apart my memory in the shower, I couldn't recall her name.

I had no intention of betraying Alex; never, but I did enjoy Alaska's company over a few drinks. I remembered nothing more, so I must have passed out. Questions flooded into my head. Had she slipped me a Mickey Finn? Did she get me to that sealed room on her own? What happened afterwards? How was it that these people – because it had to be more than one – knew so much about me? I must have been under observation for some time, otherwise how did they know I was going to the conference? They had been in my house – to fetch my computer, at least – and they knew things about me that no one else did.

What else did they know? They could have stripped my life bare after breaking in. And when was that? I had not needed my computer at the conference so I'd left it at home, which meant they had been there in the last twenty-four hours. So how did they get past Alex and Lupus?

The towel was thick and warm and dried me quickly. There was only one reason I was imprisoned. But how did they discover I was much, much older than they knew? Who had betrayed me?

LOST IN thought, I went back into the bedroom to find some clothes – and stopped.

She was sitting on the bed watching me with an amused expression. I remained still while her eyes held mine before travelling down my body and back up again. Too much water has passed under my personal bridge for me to be overly concerned about anyone seeing me naked, even beautiful, fully dressed women. Nevertheless, my slight discomfort must have been obvious.

'There's no need to be shy, I put you to bed last night.' She stood and took two steps towards me, holding out a pair of underpants.

I put them on as she settled into the armchair in the corner. 'Don't you knock before you go into someone else's room?'

She answered with another smile.

'Are you going to explain?'

'All will be made clear over lunch.'

'So why are you in here now?'

'There's really no need to be aggressive, Andy. I came to see if you're all right and have recovered. I'm sorry about that, but I wouldn't have been able to get you here without a little harmless potion.'

'You've abducted me. Who the hell do you think you are? Who are you working for? Is this a kidnap? If it is, you're going to be very disappointed.'

'You've not been kidnapped, I promise you. Nigel will explain everything over lunch.'

'Who the fuck is Nigel?'

She was completely unperturbed by my temper, which was even more annoying. 'Lunch will be served in half an hour through there.' A long, elegant finger pointed behind me.

It was so cleverly disguised. I hadn't noticed before, but when she showed me, the hairline rectangle of another door that looked exactly the same as the rest of the wall became apparent. Again, there was no handle.

'Where are my things, my phone? I need to call someone. They will have expected me home hours ago.'

'Oh, don't worry about that. She's been advised you'll be back tomorrow.'

Heat flashed to my face as if I'd opened an oven door. '*You what?*'

She must have felt my presence as I closed the gap between us, but she didn't turn and look back. The main door sprang ajar as she approached it, and closed behind her with a solid thump and click of the lock. Was it her, or did some watcher open the door for her in the nick of time?

2

MY TEMPER EASED. Was this situation a sequel to that odd meeting I'd had a couple of months previously with two representatives of a health resource organisation – or so they'd claimed?

It began with a phone call. 'Mr Duncan, Mr Andrew Duncan?' I couldn't place the accent – east European possibly.

'Speaking.'

'Mr Duncan, how are you? My name is Jakub Kowalski from UK Biobank. I believe you have participated in our research in the past, and are willing to continue to do so, is that correct?'

'Yes.'

'Well, we want to take a closer look at a certain portion of the population in order to learn more about the characteristics of this group, of which you may be one. I'd like to meet over a coffee at a time convenient to you. We can discuss the full nature of our research then. Would that be possible?'

UK Biobank is a highly respected source of knowledge, which is used by scientists across the world to research a wide range of serious and life-threatening illnesses. Back in 2016, I had thought it was a good thing to do to help and allow the company to follow my health. I had answered questionnaires and given them blood and urine samples, knowing that the procedures would be repeated several times in the future. It was therefore natural to agree to meet Kowalski. It never occurred to me that this was anything other than an innocent request. Although, I was curious as to why I had been selected, as I had always been fit, and no serious diseases had ever been detected in all my years as a pilot undergoing regular medical examinations. But I guessed that the organisation also wanted to study healthy people to find out why they didn't contract some of the disorders that others did.

It was early June, a warm sunny afternoon, and all the tables out on the pavement were taken. Some had umbrellas which hid their customers. I had no idea what Kowalski looked like; he would have to find me.

A tall young man scraped his chair back and stood as I approached. He waved to attract my attention and summoned a waiter at the same time. A glossy blue-grey suit with skinny trousers hung loosely on his coat-hanger frame. A narrow black tie and pointed-toe shoes completed his idea of being in fashion. His hair was cut short at the sides and swept back on top with something sticky holding it in place. Pale eyes crinkled in an insincere smile as he held out his hand.

'Jakub,' he said. 'It's good to meet you, Andrew. You don't mind if I call you Andrew? It's more comfortable to be a little informal.'

I nodded. His hand was hot and clammy, his grip limp. There was something slick about him, dishonest even. It was only a feeling, of course, but I'm rarely wrong about these things.

'Double espresso,' I said to the waiter, who was hovering and anxious to take my order.

'This is Sonia.' Jakub's other open sweaty palm extended to the woman who was rising to her feet.

'Hello, Sonia.'

After eighty-five years and a few hard knocks, cynicism comes easily to me. Sonia said little throughout the meeting, but smiled encouragingly at me and flashed meaningful hazel eyes whenever Jakub made a positive point. As she contributed nothing of substance, I guessed she was there purely to lubricate Kowalski's route to a successful outcome.

His English was excellent and only slightly accented. 'As you know, up to now we've been gathering samples from people and conducting surveys to determine lifestyles and dietary choices to build a picture of population groups and their propensity for certain diseases. The research continues for many years as we follow people through their lives.' He flashed a brief smile at me, which Sonia echoed with a slight forward push of her pretty head.

I nodded and acknowledged the waiter as he put my coffee in front of me. It was too hot to appreciate the full flavour.

'This research has highlighted a small number of people who are of great interest to us.'

'In what way?'

'It's quite harmless, of course. I'd like to ask you a few questions right now, if I may. Just to get some background. What is your date of birth?'

My antennae went on full alert; his chances for me to cooperate were dwindling. 'I'm sure it's harmless, but in what way are the people of interest? Me, in particular.'

'I'd rather not divulge that at this stage. Once you agree to take part in the research then of course you'll be fully informed.'

Sonia touched my arm. 'It's really, like, safe you know. Like, it's just a study, and it would be really useful if you could help, like with your date of birth.' She looked about to melt with sincerity.

'It wouldn't go unrewarded, of course.' Jakub winked.

I ignored him. 'What part do you play in this survey, Sonia?' I almost said 'charade'.

'Sonia will be your personal contact with us. Any communication you want to have – if you want to check on progress, find out results, et cetera – you will only have to call Sonia and she'll sort it for you, get you answers. There'll be short periods when we'll welcome you to our laboratory along with other participants. Sonia will see to your every need during those times.'

Sonia smiled with her head cocked to one side. Her eyes widened in a brief and not-so-subtle invitation.

I hadn't looked at Jakub since I'd asked Sonia what she did, but could sense him fidgeting to reclaim my attention. 'Well, what do you think, Andrew? Can we take it you're in? You'll be amply rewarded. Don't worry about losing time at work.'

'You haven't explained what you want me to do, or what you want from me. How can I give you an answer without knowing that?'

'Look, Andrew, this is all perfectly harmless and it's only to further Biobank's knowledge of the human genome.

There'll be other participants and you'll all give samples just as you did when you joined the research three years ago. We'll want to have you in our lab for a few days for detailed study as well, as I said, but those times will be few.'

'The place is really swish, like five star,' Sonia said. 'You'll love a few days holiday; like, I mean there's a heated pool, a gym, games rooms. I'm a qualified masseuse, so that'll be nice.'

'Sounds tempting, I must say, but I'm not agreeing to something without knowing more about it.'

Jakub's smile of understanding was clearly forced. He had oozed confidence to begin with and must have thought this would be easy, that he had the charm and the manner to convince me of his sincerity. His forefinger was trembling against his lips. I wondered if he had a commission waiting for him if he snared me, and he could see that fading away.

There wasn't much point in continuing the meeting. I drained my espresso; it had cooled and was strong and tasty. 'Who do you really work for, Jakub?'

His Adam's apple bobbed up and down his throat. 'I told you, UK Biobank.'

'I don't think so. They're a reputable organisation, and they don't approach people like this. I'm also pretty sure they don't pay people to participate, and they already know my date of birth.'

'Look, Andrew. I told you this is a special project and, as such, we're taking a completely different approach to normal.' He gripped my upper arm. Was it a threatening gesture, or one of solidarity, a statement that I could be a valuable team player, or was he pleading with me? 'Please take some time to consider the offer, you've been identified as a very valuable asset by the researchers.'

I took his hand to remove it, but he tightened his hold and his eyes narrowed. I wasn't going to get into a contest of strength over the coffee table, so I held his look with a bland expression while bending his little finger back as an easy and effective way to get him to let go. His jaw muscles were working overtime, his lips pursed.

'Sorry, Jakub, I won't be helping you. Thanks for the coffee.'

Sonia initially looked mortified, then smiled brightly. 'I'm so sorry you won't join us.' She slipped a card into my shirt pocket, letting her hand linger on my chest. 'If you, like, change your mind, just call me. Remember, I'm, like, your personal contact.' Maybe she was not as dumb as I thought; and she was certainly a good actress.

'GOOD AFTERNOON. UK Biobank.'

'May I speak to Jakub Kowalski, please?'

'Do you know which department he's in?'

'Sorry, no.'

'Please hold on while I look him up … I'm sorry, sir, he's not listed in my directory. Are you sure he works here?'

'I thought he did. Never mind. I'm sorry to trouble you.'

I had a pretty good idea what those two wanted. After all, I've been aware of my condition for at least thirty years and have taken extreme steps to hide it, because the implications of it becoming known are, to my mind, injurious to the future of mankind.

Who were they working for?

Whoever Kowalski and Sonia were, they didn't bother me again, and I put the meeting behind me and essentially forgot about it for two months. During that time I became aware of being watched, perhaps followed. It wasn't a daily suspicion; I would sense another presence at significant moments, such as when I went away, or had to undergo a flight medical examination. I had no clear sighting of anyone, it was purely my intuition, but it was a strong feeling, and as time went by it became stronger still. I wondered if I was being paranoid. But sitting there, in that luxury apartment with the evidence in front of me – the clothes, my taste in art, my computer – I knew I was right: I had been under close observation.

The time had come, once again, to undergo another makeover, to kill my current personality and adopt another.

But it was too late.

3

BORED WITH RUMINATING cows and frolicking calves, I was relieved when the side door opened with a slight swish. With her head at an angle and a friendly smile – which belied the fear she must have felt when I almost caught her at the door – the woman beckoned me. She left the door open after I passed through, glowering at her on the way. What the hell was her name?

Four men were talking on the far side of a long, highly polished table. This could have been a corporate boardroom or a large dining room, it was hard to tell which, but the table was laid for six people eating four courses. The men did not appear to have noticed me. On the sideboard lay a silver tray with decanters of, I supposed, sherry, brandy, Scotch and port. An array of crystal glasses of appropriate types was alongside.

A gentle feminine cough alerted the men. They turned to look at me as if I was some freak of nature, which maybe I am.

'Ah, Mr Duncan Andrews—' A southern American accent, not as rich as Louisiana or Alabama; Texan, possibly.

'Andrew Duncan,' I corrected him.

'Pardon me.' He was a large man, very large. Heavy-jowled and six foot five at least. But maybe some of that was his polished and decorative Western boots – pointed toes and high heels, real 'shit-kickers', as they call them. He was standing with his legs spaced wide apart – dominant. If he'd brought them together, he'd have the centre of gravity of an inverted cone and be just as easy to topple. His trousers were strapped up by an ornate hand-tooled belt, which stretched round and under his heavy belly as if to prevent it slumping to the floor.

An enormous paw was thrust forward for me to shake. In order to do so I would have to move five paces towards him, and he wasn't going to budge. I was pissed off, so I stood where I was. His eyes narrowed for a second, and he dropped his hand.

'Andy,' the woman said, 'this is Nigel Pettigrew, president of—'

'Actually he's Nigel Pettigrew the Third, the chief operating officer of NiPetco. His father, Nigel the second, is the company president.'

Nigel's expression hardened even further. 'You know stuff, huh?'

'I have shares and have seen your financial report, with its glossy photos of the board.'

Nigel recovered his composure and grinned as if to say, 'Shares – y'all's one of us'. But he turned sour again at my next comment.

'Do you realise your corporate logo is incorrect?'

'Huh? Whadaya mean?'

'The two serpents twisted round a staff is the symbol of Hermes, the Greek messenger god, or his Roman equivalent, Mercury. It's called a caduceus. The symbol you should be using is the Rod of Asclepius, the Greek god of healing, which uses a single snake wound round a staff. The mistake lies with your military, I'm afraid. You'll find most professional medical bodies in the US use the Rod of Asclepius, but your military and some commercial organisations such as yours incorrectly use a caduceus which, appropriately in some cases, is associated with liars, thieves and alchemy.'

Nigel looked about to burst. It felt good to score a few early points.

He shot glares at each colleague, spitting out his words, as if it were their fault. 'Is this true?'

A short, neat man said it was. Nigel calmed down in the silence that followed. Suddenly, he perked up, cast off the bad news and threw out an arm. 'This gentleman is Don Cripps, our chief financial officer, the doctor-looking guy is Paul, our chief biologist, and the little guy with the big grin is Hymie Green. He makes sure everything we do is legal wherever we are in the world. Right, Hymie?'

'Right,' said Hymie, who had demonstrated his correct knowledge of symbols.

Don was a severe, heavy-set individual with thin lips and narrow eyes. He was much the same height as his boss but only mildly overweight. He was immaculate in a blue suit, a white shirt and a black string tie. Before I saw them, I knew he also had to be wearing cowboy boots.

'Amy you know.'

Amy … of course. Last night's flirtatious looks – *Alaska is warmer than you can ever imagine, Andrew* – and inviting smiles – *come and visit, you'll have a great time.* Deceiving bitch.

Amy offered me a drink. The men all had whiskies by the look of it.

Would a stiff drink have settled me? Yes, it probably would have done, but it was better to keep a clear head until I knew what was going on. 'A juice will be fine, thanks.'

A door on the far side opened and a smell of cooked meat drifted across the room. A couple of waitresses in blue uniforms with white pinafores brought in hot dishes and put them on the sideboard. Blue and white were the corporate colours. Nigel demanded we eat and took his place at the head of the table. Amy pulled back a chair for me at Nigel's left and sat next to me. Don, Hymie and Paul were opposite. The waitresses served the soup then put the tureen back on the sideboard and departed. Not a word was uttered while they were in the room.

'Bet ya hungry,' Nigel said, and slurped from his spoon.

No one else spoke until the soup was consumed. The silence was tense, to me anyway, but I wasn't going to start a discussion to ease it. This was their show, and I would only respond if it suited me.

Nigel dropped his spoon into his bowl with a clatter. 'We don't want them ladies back in here till we're gone, so y'all put your dirty plates up there on the counter and help yourself to whatever's next.'

Amy was the first to move and offered to serve me. I declined and watched her lift the lids off the main course.

Nigel was playing with his cutlery. 'Duncan—'

'Andrew.'

'Yeah – Andrew. You're a mighty interesting fella.' He waved his knife at me, almost under my nose. 'Our guys have been checking up on you.'

'I noticed.'

'Yeah. Too bad, but necessary. I'll tell you why. You're one of a kind. You may be the only guy on this planet with your condition. You know that?'

I did, but didn't reply.

Nigel carried on anyway. 'How old are you?'

'Thirty-four.'

'Nah. I don't think that's the truth, Andy. I have evidence that you were born in 1934 in Haywards Heath. That makes you eighty-five. Don, is my math right?'

Don had tucked his napkin into his shirt. His fork stopped in front of his mouth and dripped gravy onto his bib while his head inclined his confirmation. 'Dead on, Nigel.' His slow drawl conjured images of a taciturn cowboy issuing his only three words of the movie.

'You're eighty-five, but you look thirty-four. You're tough and fit and slim as a gymnast – wish I was.' Nigel gave a silly laugh. 'Your brain is sharp. You ain't old, but you're eighty-five. How come, Duncan?'

'Andrew,' said Hymie.

'Yeah, whatever.'

When you're in your eighties you've lived long enough and done enough to deserve some respect. I have to forgive people for thinking I'm much younger, but even so, it rankles when some treat me as a commodity, which Nigel, from the perch he'd built for himself, seemed intent on doing. On top of that, I was brought up in an age when good table manners were the norm. Cutlery was for eating with and was put down if it was not being used. Waving it and gesticulating, especially when food was stuck to it, was extremely rude.

'I don't know what you're talking about. I was born in 1985, that makes me thirty-four. Right Don?'

Don glared at me. Obviously I wasn't supposed to take the piss.

Nigel didn't notice. I suspected a little narcissism there. 'Hymie, you explain the situation to Du–, Andy here.'

Hymie was British; his accent was from somewhere round London. He had to be pretty sharp. To be a legal adviser to a massive international pharmaceutical corporation and know US, British and EU law meant he wasn't stupid. But he was a slimy little bugger.

'Andrew, we know everything there is to know about you. On January the 15th 1934 you appeared in this world, courtesy of your mother, Doris. Your father, Henry, was in the navy, but tragically lost his life on an Arctic convoy in 1942. It must have been terrible to lose your dad when you were eight.'

'What a fascinating fairy tale.'

Hymie ignored my sneer and gave me a benevolent smile. 'Wasn't it hard growing up during the war and in the fifties?'

'It must have been with rationing, no luxuries, bombed homes, cold homes … That generation was much tougher than we are.'

'You had a chequered career as a youth, various low-paid and worthless jobs such as…' He ran his finger down a paper on the desk and looked up at me. 'Groom – there's a bright future. I presume you were at a loss, which is why you joined the army – nothing better to do.' He looked up for an answer, got none and shrugged.

'Oh, and a helicopter crash in 1968. Was that terribly traumatic? Were you badly injured?'

I shook my head and kept a straight face. *If you only knew how close I had been to death, you lot, you would not be wasting everybody's time with this theatre.*

The next of Hymie's revelations hit on the most sensitive areas of my past. 'Your marriage to Saffron Crawford and her subsequent death – my condolences. You have been associated with a number of women since then, but stuck with none. We can make an intelligent guess as to why that was. Your current lady, Alexandra, is she aware of your condition?'

He wasn't happy with the look I gave him. 'No, then. Are you going to tell her?'

The less this lot knew of my true situation, the better. 'I don't know what you're talking about.'

'Andrew, don't take us for fools, please. You have something in your DNA that stops you ageing. Do you have the remotest idea how valuable that makes you?'

'I don't need to listen to this rubbish.' My voice came out louder than I intended. 'You people have abducted me, you have broken into my house and found out as much as you can about me. You know things about me that even my wife didn't know. You have most likely hacked my computer so you can monitor me. You have given no apology for this, and now you sit here spewing rubbish about an impossibility. I want to leave. Right now.'

Hymie sighed. He expected this reaction, of course. 'Andrew, please hear me out before you go.'

Nigel was chewing on his steak with his fork pointing at the ceiling, but that didn't stop him interrupting. 'You need to hear what Hymie has to say. Yeah, we kinda forced you here, but no harm was done. Y'all's free to leave after you've listened to our proposal. I think you're gonna like what we're offering.'

Amy, on my left, put a hand on my arm. 'Andy, why not relax and enjoy the lunch and listen. It costs you nothing.'

'Andrew, not Andy,' I snapped.

She jerked as if I'd slapped her. 'Oh – sorry.'

Hymie, getting no reaction from me, glanced down at Paul and went ahead. 'Humans age at different rates, as you know. We think this is due to telomeres, special sections of DNA at the end of chromosomes, which are within our cells, as I'm sure you're aware. It appears that the longer these telomeres are, the slower the ageing process. People with short telomeres age quickly, people with long telomeres age slowly, but we all age. Anti-ageing creams and remedies are focused on preserving telomeres. However, it's also agreed that this is not the whole story. There must be other factors at play in the ageing process and every company is working to find out what they are, because when someone finds the magic formula, it's going to be worth a fortune.'

'Megabucks,' said Nigel, who was returning to his seat with his second helping of steak.

Paul nodded his confirmation of the facts. He was a small, scrawny man with a pinched face and round, wire-framed glasses that magnified pale blue eyes. His hair was yellow and thinning prematurely. He was the caricature of a Nazi doctor in a death camp. He didn't say a thing.

'But,' Hymie carried on, 'you are different. The whole world, humans, animals, fish, trees and insects, may be ageing at different rates, but you're not ageing at all. Whatever it is about you, is not about telomeres or whatever other elusive element everyone is looking for. You are stuck at age thirty-four, and that's a whole new ball game.'

Don's slow drawl came from deep within his chest. 'Why thirty-four? What happened to change you then?' I had a strong feeling that those were the most words Don had issued in a week.

You've no idea of the severity of that accident, have you? In fact, you have no knowledge of my other identities either, my alternate lives spent on causes close to me all in order to avoid vultures like yourselves. Well, those are things for you to find out. I'm certainly not going to tell you.

Paul looked at me as if I was the juiciest heifer in the pen. He couldn't wait to experiment on me.

NIGEL HAD consumed two large steaks and little else. Half his chips, smothered in ketchup, remained on his plate. He waved his small knife under my nose; a crumb of cheese was sticking to it. 'Let's cut the bullshit, Andy. We know and you know you're a thirty-four-year-old guy born eighty-five years ago. We don't know how this works, but we're gonna find out. Now, I'm gonna put a proposal to you which you will be a dumb-ass to refuse. Hymie, you ready?'

'Ready, Nigel.'

'Go for it.'

Amy leant slightly in my direction. Her hand went up to my left shoulder, but I ignored it and it went away.

Hymie studied me in silence for a moment, a thin forced smile on his lips. The prosecutor's unfriendly eyes were dissecting me, until I remembered Hymie was not a criminal lawyer but merely the legal adviser for NiPetco. 'He oils his way around the floor' came to mind.

'In broad terms, Andrew, we want to study you. Everything will be at our expense throughout your stay. You can have anything you want provided you allow Paul and his team to examine you over a period of time. Obviously they will take samples of your body fluids, your DNA and any-thing else they might need to determine what is going on.'

'What does "anything else" cover? Surely everything you need will be in the samples you've mentioned? Do you want to remove my liver?'

'Ha, ha. No, God no, nothing like that. Sorry, it was just a slip of the tongue, a poor choice of phrase.'

'And what is "a period of time"?'

'Well, that depends on what they discover. It could be a quickish or a longish period. We can't say until they have a chance to examine you. Once they're satisfied, you'll be able to live your normal life. We hope to develop a treatment for general distribution. That's going to take time, of course. So, under the contract we, you and NiPetco agree on, we may need to call you back from time to time to verify results or take more tests. You know.'

'No, I don't know. And what, Shylock, do I get for sacrifi-cing my pound of flesh?'

Hymie gave a silly, weak snort of laughter. 'NiPetco will pay you half a million pounds a year after tax for life. Infla-tion linked.'

Don did not raise his eyes to me, but his knuckles round his fork were white.

That was ridiculous. 'For life? If you stick to your word, that will be a significant expense. On the other hand, you could save yourselves a lot of money by killing me.'

'Hey, cowboy, rein it in,' blurted Nigel. 'We're in the business of saving lives, not takin' 'em.'

Amy the honeytrap put a calming hand on my thigh. I left it there and gave her a quick grin. If I pretended to fall for the short-term pleasures she offered, they might be lulled into a false sense of confidence that I could take advantage of.

Don's eyes were still down to his plate; he clearly didn't want to look at me. 'You can take a lump sum, say fifteen years' worth instead.'

'It could take you ten years to develop the treatment and get it through your FDA, and you're going to want me around until it's proven, which is going to take even longer. I reckon seven and a half million pounds is not worth it when I could be getting an unlimited sum, since, according to you, I'm not going to die.

'And you're talking nonsense anyway. If I agree to provide samples and you find nothing you want, what are you going to do then? And what happens if I refuse to cooperate? I mean, you've abducted me and held me prisoner for a day. How can I trust you? Are you going to force me?'

'We'll drive you home and won't bother you again.' Hymie's lies were transparent. 'But you won't get a tax-free income of five hundred thou a year for life.'

'However long that may be.'

Don, still staring at his plate, was gently shaking his head.

Nigel gripped my right shoulder. 'Don't be so cynical, buddy. This is a genuine offer from a reputable international corporation. It'll be laid out in a legally binding contract, of course. Won't it, Hymie?'

'Absolutely, Nigel.'

'You know, Andy, you cain't afford to pass up an offer like this. It ain't nothing more harmful to you than a small loss of your time. Your present income is about eighty-five thousand. My senior executives are earning four times that, but they've got big responsibilities. We're offering you one and half times what they're getting for doing nothing – guaranteed for life. You cain't beat that.'

'True, but I don't want to be a guinea pig.'

'Think of yourself as aiding research for the benefit of mankind,' said the lawyer.

Amy's fingers gave my thigh an encouraging squeeze, which almost led me to believe she was on my side – almost.

'It is tempting. I need to give it some serious thought.'

'Sure. Make yourself at home in your den through there.' Nigel waved a hand under my nose towards 'my' room next door before clasping my shoulder again and shaking it in a firm, confidence-building, we'll-make-a-great-team, gesture. 'Amy will see you have everything you need. You can call her any time to tell her your decision, but I reckon we should meet again for breakfast, huh?'

'I want my phone, keys and wallet returned.'

'We got those? Hey, that ain't right. Amy will get them back to you. Right, Amy?'

'Right, Nigel.'

AS AMY closed the door on the dining room behind me, her fingers briefly linked into mine. She smiled. 'Can I pour you a drink now?'

'Scotch, please. I'll do the water.'

She poured it, and one for herself, obviously intending to stay a while. She was wearing a black wrap-around calf-length skirt that overlapped at the front. When she sat on the bed the split fell apart to show her thigh as far as her stocking tops.

As one gets older and gathers more experience, surprises diminish and cynicism rises. If the situation hadn't been so dire, I might have laughed. Did Amy, or even her management, imagine that a night with her would convince me to sign my life away? It was such an amateur approach, unless cameras were to record it all, of course, and I was to be black-mailed.

Amy sipped her drink. 'Mmh! This is better than the smoky ones. What do you think? That offer sounds great to me. All that money and never having to work, I would be on permanent holiday, have servants, a great house. I'd travel lots. I really want to see the world, there's so many exciting places to visit, spend time at. What will you do if you say yes?'

'Pretty much the same, I suppose. I like to keep busy, so I'd have to find a purpose, especially if I'm going to live forever.'

She thought about that. 'Yeah, I guess you could get bored eventually. But think of all the girls you could have.' She laughed and patted the bed beside her. 'Sit with me, Andy – Andrew.'

I shook my head. 'I need to stand after that long lunch, and in any case I need to think. This is a momentous decision.'

Amy looked disappointed, but smiled anyway. 'Okay, I'll call back later, before dinner. You and I can eat next door. Nigel and the others are attending some event tonight, so they won't be here.'

'You won't forget my phone and keys, will you?'

4

SUNK IN THE comfort of the armchair, I nursed a Scotch and mellowed, letting random thoughts flow freely.

This was not the first time I'd considered the implications of my condition being known. I'd run through them often, but being abducted and pressured by NiPetco had brought things into sharp focus. My future did not look good, because this bunch were not to be trusted any further than a crocodile.

Amy was due back before dinner. Another drink, more enticing words and more exposed thigh were going to be used to convince me how good a deal I was being offered. And at breakfast the following morning, the mafia were expecting an answer.

They thought they were onto a massive windfall by ana-lysing me. If I turned them down immediately, in spite of Hymie's assurance, it was a safe bet they would stop me leaving, by force if necessary. They would immobilise me somehow and take whatever samples they needed. Worse, they would hold me until their research was over, which could be years away.

If I agreed to help, they would probably start their harvesting of my body straight away. What, actually, were they going to take from me? Blood obviously, but what else?

I had to convince them I would cooperate, but delay the start of things. With a bit of time secured, I'd escape, which was not going to be easy.

The cards appeared to be stacked in their favour, but I had a great deal more life experience under my belt than any of them, and I was spurred by anger – on top of being abducted, being called *Andy* annoys the hell out of me.

Amy was able to open both the doors to the room, yet neither had a handle. She must have had a proximity tag or something like it to activate the locks. So I needed to take the tag from her, because she was unlikely to help me voluntarily. If I used force to immobilise and search her, I might find it, but there was more than a good chance that the room was bugged and had hidden cameras. They would be on to me immediately.

It couldn't be helped; Amy was going to have to be dealt with in a heavy-handed way. I don't go around abusing women, I've never laid an aggressive finger on one, ever, but Amy was in the other camp and she was guilty of drugging me. However sweet she was being, she was not to be trusted. I had misgivings over her being physically weaker than I was, but I didn't give a damn that she was female: she was an enemy, and she must take what came if I was to escape. Not only that, but she kept calling me Andy.

Amy returned around six o'clock. She'd showered and smelt good. She'd changed into a pair of skimpy and fashionably tatty denim shorts, and a red blouse that plunged to tummy level, where it was fastened by a single knotted tie, leaving a broad V of bare flesh, no bra. The message was clear.

We had a pleasant conversation about nothing of importance during dinner. Afterwards, putting a smile in my eyes to show that I thought the episode amusing, I said, 'How did you manage to get me here, and where are we, anyway?'

She hesitated and bit her bottom lip. 'I'm sorry, really I am.'

'It's okay, Amy. It's history, don't worry.'

My hand on hers seemed to calm her. 'The powder they gave me to put in your drink wasn't strong enough for you. Don't you remember? You wanted to go outside to get some fresh air. We walked around, and the air must have kept you conscious. You were supposed to have collapsed by then.' She gave me a string of details as if it would help, then a long, searching look. 'You don't remember that? I had to give you an injection to put you down. Two of the guys put you in a van and brought you here. I'm sorry. Do you forgive me?'

'Of course; I've put it behind me, even though someone must have kicked me, because I've a nice fat bruise on my ribs. Not to worry, it's the here and now that's important, don't you think?' I touched her hand again, and we were back into seduction.

We didn't mention the contract for my future, we focused on boosting our relationship. That was fine with me, because that night might be the only chance I would have to escape, and the cosier she thought we were getting, the more her guard would fall. I didn't even make an issue of her forgetting to bring my phone back. With a bit of luck, the mafia would be breaking their fast alone in the morning.

I played barman; I wasn't going to let her slip something into my drink as she had in the hotel. We had a whisky each. Amy was probably a nice girl. Well, she might have been if she wasn't working for Nigel and co. We got on famously, but she was still my enemy.

'Let's get comfortable,' she suggested, and went to the dressing room, returning with two robes, one dark and one light blue. She tossed the dark one at me before going to the bathroom.

In the dressing room, it took a couple of seconds to strip and put on the gown. Two belts, one black and one brown, along with four ties and two handkerchiefs taken from the cupboard were enough for my purpose. I put running knots at the end of the ties while my hands were beneath my robe and out of sight of any camera. Amy was still in the bathroom, so I grabbed the little peeling knife from the fruit bowl and shoved it and two of the ties and the handkerchiefs under a pillow. The belts and the other ties got pushed under the bed on the same side.

Even though it wasn't my first choice, it was probably best to join her in drinking champagne – more romantic. The cork came out of the Krug with scarcely a pop, and just in time, as Amy came back into the room and dropped her clothing on a chair. There could be nothing beneath her robe.

I handed her a glass of champagne and raised mine towards her. 'Cheers again.'

'Cheers.' She sipped and smiled enticingly over the top of her glass. 'Your good health, Andy. Here's to a long life.' And laughed.

It didn't take long before she was pulling me towards the bed. I pretended to be rough and ripped her gown off. Her eyes flashed, and her lips curled up, baring her teeth. My robe was open, and her nails clawed at my chest and scratched down my belly. It made me squirm, but had the desired effect.

She was surprisingly light and easy to throw onto the bed. I shed my robe. Diving under the covers, we slithered naked body to naked body. Firm breasts with hard nipples poked into my chest hair and resisted my weight.

A slippery slope. I was sliding too easily down it into her trap. I had to grasp at a fixture, haul myself back up and out of it – I had to think. Alex. She was at home. She was waiting for me – Alex. Focus: I had a job to do.

With the duvet pulled over our heads, we were enclosed in our own little world. Light filtered into our cave, but no one could see us. I found the handkerchiefs and tucked them beside her ear. She didn't notice. She was past noticing much anyway, the way she was performing.

The duvet still covered us. If anyone was watching, all they would see would be heaving bedclothes as two bodies engaged in passion – with a bit of luck.

The tip of the little paring knife pricked her throat. There is no way that stinging pain could be associated with sex, even rough sex. Her body tensed, her eyes opened, alarmed, and met mine just inches away.

'Don't move, don't scream or I'll push this all the way in.'

She began to tremble. I slid the knife around her throat, dragging it against her skin, not drawing blood, just letting the friction terrify her. Round to the front, over the larynx and slowly up under the point of her chin. Her eyes were wide, unblinking, as if losing a split-second's contact with mine would make me shove the blade in.

'Now, Amy, if you do as I say, I won't hurt you. I want you to open your mouth wide. Wider, wide as you can. Good girl.' And I rammed a bunched handkerchief between her teeth. She gagged slightly, but kept still bar the trembling.

I rolled her onto her stomach and knelt on top of her. A tie round her head and tightened over her mouth to hold the gag in made her panic. She tore at it, but the noose in the other tie slipped over her wrist and tightened easily. Was the duvet still covering us? We had to stay hidden. What were the watchers thinking?

With her hands secured behind her back, the other ties and belts from under the bed were enough to strap her feet together, and her feet to her hands. With all this upheaval beneath the covers, with one amorphous shape moving from the head to the foot of the bed and back again, any watchers' grubby imaginations must have been running riot. I lay still on top of her for a minute in imitation of a post-coital collapse.

There would be time to laugh about it afterwards; I needed to get out of there – fast.

STILL WORRIED about cameras, I slithered out from under the covers and headed to the bathroom, scooping up Amy's clothes on the way. There was no tag in her pockets. In case it was integral to the clothes themselves, I felt in the lining and the hems but couldn't find anything strange. But there was something small and hard at the end of the tie of her blouse. The stitching ripped under my teeth, exposing a disc the size of a shirt button.

'Swiftness is of the essence,' one of my teachers used to say, seventy years ago.

Amy was still trembling under the duvet. Did she imagine I was going to hurt her, even kill her? She deserved a smile and a 'One good turn deserves another'.

Out loud for the benefit of any listeners, I told her she should get dressed and dumped her clothes on the bed.

The most practical wear in the dressing room was a pair of charcoal jeans and a blue shirt. A green jacket that looked waterproof and a pair of trainers completed my outfit. Time was slipping by and was of increasing essence. The watchers would get suspicious if Amy didn't get up, and once they saw me at the door the alarm would be raised. The tag did nothing when I moved it around the area where the lock should be. This was taking too long.

It was at the end of her tie. I tried to picture where that would rest on Amy. Moving the tag to that height caused a click and the door sprang open a few inches. A long corridor stretched out in front of me. It was the sort you would find in a hospital with a polished vinyl floor, not a thickly carpeted hotel passage as would match my room. A CCTV camera covered the entrance – it pointed directly at me. Glancing back, it was almost impossible to make out the door I'd just come through. A hairline crack in the camouflage of a forest mural was the only evidence, just like the door to the conference or dining room.

Walking briskly down the corridor, I tried to look as if I belonged, but there was no one around to see. Windowed doors led off on both sides. The view through them was of sterile environments, with microscopes and centrifuges and biosecurity cabinets where samples could be tested by scientists who put their hands into long gloved sleeves. Another passage joined from the right. It was empty, but the sound of running feet – two pairs at least – echoed along it. Another camera was watching me. Don't look at it. Keep moving as you are. Don't run, you'll attract attention.

What day was it? It was after nine o'clock; only people on night shift and security should be in the place – if they worked nights. Where *was* this? Was I even in England?

The passage ended and the only way was left. It was devoid of people, but there were voices off to the side. A window, a real one, lay ahead. The virtual scene in the room gave a more pleasing view than what the street lights illuminated below: ugly roofs, empty pallets, a van with a flat tyre and two over-full refuse skips. No wonder they showed me happy cows and calves.

This was the first floor. Where were the stairs?

At the bottom was a reception area with a lift and double doors to the outside. They were locked. What was there to break that lock, or was there a window to open?

Elevator doors slid back ahead of me; I heard them before I saw them. Two men were deep in discussion and were slow to leave the lift, giving me a few precious seconds. The space under the stairs was cramped and dark. Something dug me in the ribs as I squeezed deeper into the recess. The men disappeared through a door, and I was able to emerge.

Running footsteps and two more voices sent me back into hiding. Their tone told me these were men on the hunt. The object that was trying to bruise me was again in my way – a fire extinguisher. Would a hefty blow from that break the lock on the door? It wasn't worth a try; it would make too much noise and probably wouldn't work, even if it did in the movies. It would be a good weapon, though.

A sign on the other side of the reception area advertised a male toilet. All I had heard had been men's voices, making discovery in there more likely. The female loo was on my side of the foyer. The door squeaked. Extinguisher in hand, I locked myself in a cubicle. A window was high up the wall.

I'd be able to fit through it without being slashed if I cleared every little fragment of glass.

Standing on the toilet with the extinguisher above shoulder height, it was easy to smash the window. It was harder to use the cylinder to clear the fine shards of glass that were stuck in the frame, though. They were certain to cut me or shred my clothing when I squeezed through.

The toilet entrance door squeaked. The safety pin would have come out of the extinguisher trigger with a sharp tug, but it would make a noise. I worked it free in silence.

'Security,' a man shouted.

'Security,' repeated another, as if no one had heard the first one. But I suppose he had to have his say.

Cubicle doors were flung open one by one. The guards were getting closer. Mine was rattled. 'Ma'am, answer please.'

'What do you want? This is the ladies. Go away.' My female voice was not convincing.

The cubicle door split under a heavy kick. A mean-looking guard got a blast of dry powder from my extinguisher. He fell back, choking. The other man reached for a baton and got his squirt. He was still reacting, so I gave him another at close range. Their uniforms were ruined, their faces white, they were choking their guts out – they were useless. I had never realised a fire extinguisher could be so effective.

Getting through the window was a squeeze, but I made it without bleeding all over the place. Past the skips, past the dead van. It had a British number plate, so that was one query settled.

I had to get to Alex, but the first place they'd look would be my house. I had no money and no phone. How was I going to contact her? And where the hell was I?

5

THE ROADS OF the industrial estate were deserted. A couple of pantechnicons were parked, one behind the other under a street light. One of them, with a Romanian number plate, had curtains over the windows. Sounds of snoring escaped the cab.

Time had left me behind. What day of the week was it? The conference had been on a Friday, so it could be Saturday or even later. Unless I had been out of the loop for forty-eight hours or more, it was the weekend.

The road ended in a cul-de-sac. I wasn't keen on going back the way I came; they could have been following me, even though there was no sign of pursuit. There was no option, though, since steel palisade fences, about eight feet high, on either side protected the businesses from thieves, vandals and lost fugitives.

I was almost running; the quicker I got out of the immediate area, the safer I'd be. The end of the road was a T-junction. The only way was right, because left led back to

NiPetco. A short while later the street joined a main road, and a glass-sided telephone box was on the corner – ideal. The charges could be reversed to my house phone, although what the number was to get an operator to do that escaped me. The idea was shot anyway: one glass wall was cracked, the handset was hanging from its cord, and the screen had been smashed.

There was a bus stop further along, under a light. The timetable should have provided a clue to where I was, but scanning down the list, I had no idea where those stops were. The final destination, though, was Reading and the last bus had been and gone, not that I would have been allowed on without the fare. Depending on where I was in Reading, it could be a five-hour walk if I couldn't get hold of Alex.

Was it 100 or 200 to dial to get the telephone operator? It was one of those, but first I had to find a call box that hadn't been vandalised. Although I'd slowed to a more economical pace, I was still walking quickly and soon entered a residential area with large, pricy semi-detached houses.

Why was there no sign of pursuit? Surely they were not going to let me go so easily? Were those two guards I left choking in the ladies the only security people around? NiPetco had put a considerable amount of effort into capturing and housing me securely in a luxury room with all facilities; a room that had been specially constructed, disguised from view and had electronically controlled doors with no handles so I couldn't escape. That they had taken that trouble meant they must have been confident they could hold me or trace me. They had taken my clothes and supplied others. Were the replacements fitted with a tracking device? Patting myself down revealed nothing. Still walking, I felt my way around the jacket. It held nothing that could do the job, not even a zip toggle.

The next house was in darkness and had a chest-high hedge bordering the pavement. Within the garden and using the hedge as cover, I stripped off the shirt. Unless it was a button, there was nothing there. Jeans next; the only possibility was one of the rivets on a pocket. Would they bug every item of clothing to ensure I chose one with a tracker? Surely not, but the one garment anyone would wear no matter what the outer covering was underpants.

A couple were coming down the road, arm in arm and laughing, and there was I, skulking naked in suburban bushes with the jeans, shirt and jacket hanging from the hedge. I squatted down out of their sight, kept my head down, and felt around the boxers.

Why does being naked make you feel so defenceless? Was I being watched? Was someone peering out of an unlit first-floor window? 'Mrs Jones', behind me, if she was there, must have thought I was making a horrible mess of her garden and was probably phoning the police.

Sure enough, there was a hard, button-sized object in the fly seam. I had to go, but, to use army slang, Mrs Jones was welcome to the shreddies as her evidence for the police.

There was a pub on the corner – how many White Harts are there in Britain? They would have a public phone, or they'd let me use theirs, wouldn't they?

The place was humming. The smell of fish and chips smothered that of alcohol. The barman didn't speak, he merely raised his eyebrows at me.

'Sorry,' I said, 'but I've been mugged. My wallet's been stolen and I need to use a phone – reverse charge of course.'

He gave me a suspicious look. 'Reverse charge only, all right? And I'm not getting you a drink if you can't pay.'

'I don't want anything, I just want to contact my girl-friend to come and pick me up.'

He pulled a phone out from under the counter and put it in front of me.

100. *'We are sorry, but operator service is busy at the moment. You are number … five in the queue.'*

I drummed my fingers on the counter. The barman was watching me, but I wasn't talking and shrugged to show that nothing was happening. He gave me a last sideways look and went back to work. Across the room was a couple at a table. The man was staring at me. He obviously said something, because the woman twisted round to see. They both looked away when I made eye contact, but he picked up his phone and dialled. He gave me little surreptitious glances as he spoke. It was time to leave.

The operator answered at last. My home number rang and rang and rang. Come on, Alex, answer. I need you.

'There's no reply, sir.'

'Please let it ring a bit longer.'

An audible sigh carried down the line, but she didn't argue.

The man across the room put his phone on the table. He moved so his head was almost hidden from me behind the woman's, but he was flicking one eye in my direction all the time. An amateur, he hadn't the control to be natural when he was spying on me. What mattered was that he had made a call to someone, and it was certain I was mentioned.

Come on, Alex, pick up.

Why wasn't she answering? I gave up and thanked the barman, who nodded at me and greeted another customer.

The couple had their heads down, desperately trying to avoid looking at me as I turned to leave. Big Nigel's boys were probably well on their way to pick me up by now, and if those people were hoping to see their efforts rewarded, they were going to be disappointed.

IT WAS a beautiful, clear night. Cool, but at least it wasn't raining. My ancestors wore kilts with nothing underneath them, they say. They must have been hardy men because it was definitely chilly down below in trousers and no underpants.

It would've been stupid to thumb a lift and find myself in a NiPetco car. Someone gave me directions and, once clear of the town, I took a cross-country route using public footpaths. Utmost care would only need to be taken when I was near to home. Even so, trying to see if anyone was following me in the faint light of the moon was a strain.

Saffron and I had walked the first footpath I came to several times, and I had often done it again over the years. It led across a meadow, between some farm buildings, then followed the edge of some fields and into a wood. Forests: the trees have closed in around me ever since … They steal the light and take me back over half a century to the day the jungle claimed me and changed me forever.

It's not that being in the woods scares or worries me, in fact I find them fascinating and homely – sheltering even. The memories of that day don't haunt me, but they've never receded. Is that because deep down I know that's where my condition originated? I'm not sure.

Through the wood ran a river. Standing on the footbridge and gazing down into the black water whose ripples twinkled in a patch of moonlight, I was transported back a further two years.

Saffron and I stood on this very bridge, arms around each other, and I asked her to marry me. She was twenty-eight, and I was a thirty-two-year-old army pilot. We didn't consider having kids at that stage, there was too much living to be done before settling down. It happened that there was always too much to be squeezed out of life and, as a result, we never had any children. Two years later, in 1968, I had my accident.

Several years after that, I suspected I wasn't getting any older. I held the same fitness levels I'd had aged thirty-four, while my peers had lost pace. On the rugby pitch, climbing hills or running through the Malaysian rubber plantations, I was as fast as the young bloods. But it was only an impression, until Saffron commented.

'Were your ears burning?' she asked after a beach party. 'The other wives were discussing you with some relish.'

'Oh God.'

'Seriously. They're watching their husbands sag and spread out like apples and pears, while you stay in youthful shape. They used more colourful words, some of them.'

It took a lot of thought over several months before I eventually accepted I had definitely not aged since the accident. The consequences of this impossibility would be dire if the wrong people got to know of it. It had to be my secret, mine and Saffron's alone, forever. To protect it, we had to move on, to break contact with people we'd known for years, people who had noticed and commented on my age.

It meant leaving the army. That was hard: the army was my life.

I never had a chance to tell Saffron, because in '78 she began losing weight she could not afford to lose, and once the diagnosis was made and the shattering prognosis given, I thought it best not to worry her and kept my secret to myself.

Over the following year what age I didn't gain, she tripled. Her features became drawn, pain slowly and inexorably invaded her body, and she resorted more and more to bed. Only her eyes retained their sparkle.

Near the end she said, 'I'm going, but you will have a long life. Something's different about you, Andrew. You'll not die of natural causes.'

They did their best, but it wasn't enough. Her suffering was thankfully short compared to many cancer victims, but it was still painful, sapping both her energy and mine.

Death affects people in different ways. I cannot speak for anyone else who has been in that situation, but for me, Saffron's ordeal left me with scars that have affected my life and my attitude to others ever since. To protect myself, I rejected close contact and kept prospective partners at arm's length.

When no end to life is in sight, the incentive to get things done loses emphasis. There's no hurry, and no bucket list is necessary. Realising that my goal of reducing the world's population growth was impossible, I could only do my best to keep my condition a secret. Unable to pursue my long-term objective, I focused on short-term targets.

I began a career flying civil helicopters in several countries, each one using a different identity. The helicopter community is relatively small, and I had to be careful which identity to use and who to meet. My choice of jobs was based on the help I could provide, and the danger and therefore the stimulation they gave me. It became an exciting and unsettled life: Charlie Maxwell was contracted for anti-poaching activity in Kenya, Jim Connors for disaster relief in Nepal, Harry Bennett was good at firefighting, and Dan Peabody was experienced in operations he was not allowed to talk about. Different passports, all fraudulent, and different licences supported these activities. But although the work was valuable, I could never bring myself to get close to the people I helped, nor my fellow contractors.

By the time NiPetco began to interfere in my life, all my friends and loves, those I would help in a crisis and on whom I could count if in trouble, had either already died or were knocking at the door. Except for Alex and one or two others, no one else concerned me. What was the point of wasting emotions on people with whom I could make no connection, or the faceless who could be living on another planet if, when you admit you care, they go away, or turn their backs, or die? I've been described as unfeeling and cold, one for whom other people mean nothing. Saffron's death was my turning point, and how those that know me today describe me is mostly true.

The reminiscing had to stop. The current situation had to be dealt with, and thinking was best done while walking. I sniffed, blinked the moisture from my eyes and set off after first checking back to see if anyone was following me.

Alex was the ideal person to check on NiPetco and on Pettigrew himself. She was good at that sort of thing; it was her job – investigative journalism. But in telling her, I would have to reveal my condition, which was going to be difficult to do having spent years hiding it. My secret would inevitably be laid bare at some stage in our relationship, so it might as well happen in the course of these events and under my control.

Once she knew, would she want to leave me to find a man with whom she could lead a normal life as she grew older? I couldn't guess, and I didn't know how I felt about it either. I would not be happy knowing the age gap was growing, and for Alex's sake, the sooner she knew, the better.

She usually trusted me with a broad outline of her investigations, and we would discuss them at length. She used me as a sounding board, and my questions would spur her into unearthing greater detail. But she had been unusually reticent about her latest research, which was something to do with child sexual exploitation. With her being so secretive, I suspected it was dangerous, and she didn't want me involved. Her reports brought in her only income, which was good but irregular and unpredictable, so she had to work hard. Would she be able to find time to help me?

Closer to home, I had to think on how to approach the house. I've sold it since – a detached building set back from the street near the edge of the village. A further two properties and the lane enters farmland. On the other side of the road opposite the last house is a primary school, and every day in term time a crocodile of kids and young mothers would run, skip and scooter their way past my gate. It was peaceful and pleasant, and crime and violence had not found a place there.

But this predawn was different. How many of NiPetco's men were watching my home? Were they covering all the angles? The best way to approach was to pretend to be a neighbour and enter the wrong property, say the next but one. It belonged to Henry, who was also eighty-five, but looked and acted it. He wore fish-bowl glasses and a hearing aid, which he would adjust so he could be selective and ignore you. He wouldn't be wearing it at four fifteen in the morning.

My pretence was to be drunk and in desperate need of relieving myself, so I adopted the pose. The view over the hedge from inside Henry's garden was of an empty street with a single familiar car about five houses down. There were no street lights, so I couldn't see if anyone was inside.

Round the back there was no sign of life either. It was hard to believe this crowd weren't waiting for me. Why? Surely they weren't still occupied with a futile hunt for a pair of used underpants?

Looking along the side of my own house from the back, my Volvo was just visible in the front. What the hell …? I had left it in the hotel car park. The bastards must have driven it here. Were they inside, waiting for me? What had they done with Alex? *Jesus!*

They had my house keys. Was I going to have to break in? Alex could be absent-minded over locking up, so I tried the back door before breaking some glass.

It opened with a gentle push. It didn't squeak and, because it was silent, it was easy to hear a faint whimpering.

6

I REMOVED MY shoes. Doing so left me feeling disadvant-aged and unprepared for attack or even flight, but if any intruder was in the house, an additional light, or the slightest squeak or click, might alert them. Soundless steps through the kitchen and along the passage towards the front of the house, avoiding the squeaky floorboard, meant the only sounds were the strange spasmodic whimpers ahead of me. Those, and my heart.

The glow from the lounge doorway had never been as dim as it was then. The hall carpet was rucked, and dark spots disrupted the pattern on the floor. I flicked a glance up the stairs, but no one was about to pounce. The horror of what lay ahead grabbed my attention.

Lupus was stretched out at the foot of the stairs with blood oozing from a slash to his left shoulder. My stomach lurched – my precious dog. What? Who? Was someone still there? The poor animal was in pain, but he was alive. His head didn't move, but his eye watched me as I reached down to give him a comforting stroke. His breathing was rapid and shallow. He needed urgent attention, but the place had to be secured first.

Where was Alex?

A lamp, the sole source of light, its shade bent, was on the lounge floor and almost hidden behind an upturned chair. The couch had been slashed with a single cut. Shards of porcelain littered the carpet on the far side of the room. Paint had chipped where it had hit the wall. It was the vase that had stood near the door.

Alex! Who did you fight? Where are you?

Not there. I slipped my shoes back on and stepped over Lupus, giving another quick one-handed stroke to his head. 'I'll be back.'

Looking up the stairs from the hall, all I could see was a forearm drooped over the top step. Dark red dripped off dangling fingers. *Christ!*

How many steps can one take at once? Alex lay on the landing, one arm stretched out, the fingers pointing down the stairs. I've seen enough bodies to recognise when one has no life left in it. She had no colour, and her hair lacked its normal lustre. Her eyes were wide and empty and had lost their hue. Her other hand lay across her throat. Congealed blood had seeped between her fingers and run down the underside of her outstretched arm, hesitated at her bangles and dripped onto the step below. The carpet was soaked in it. There were more wounds to her chest and stomach, and the handle of a knife protruded from her midriff. Every detail crossed my eyes, but I didn't register them all until later.

My stomach heaved, and bile burnt my throat.

Common sense fought with my irrational compulsion to hold her and breathe life into her. It almost overwhelmed me.

No. I must not touch her. Instead, I reached for the knife handle. If I get that thing out of her, she'll come back to life, she'll heal. No, you fool. Don't touch it. Instead, I grasped her cold and waxy hand. It did not return my grip.

The upstairs phone was nearby. Tears welled un-ashamedly in my eyes as I gave the operator the details.

Stepping over my dearest love in forty-two years as if she was a pile of clothing, I accepted there was nothing I could do for her. But I had to do what I could for Lupus before the police arrived.

With the dog's wound temporarily dressed to stop the bleeding – he would have to go to the vet – I unlocked the front door and sagged onto the bottom of the stairs with him cradled between my feet. He must have tried to protect her.

What bastard …?

Stroking Lupus gave me as much comfort as it did him. His eyes locked on mine, which were freely shedding tears. 'You'll be all right, my boy. You'll be fine. I'll get you to your vet and he'll stitch you up, and in a week or so you'll be off chasing squirrels again.'

My mind wandered. If Saffron was the wife of a lifetime in a different era, then Alex was my most wonderful partner in the current generation. Sometimes I tried to compare them, but it was pointless and too difficult. They were very much alike, but they lived in different times and had different points of view. Alex wasn't even born when Saffron died. I had always worried, because one day Alex would want to know why I wasn't getting older like she was.

We had met nine years before. I was seventy-six then, but she thought I was thirty-four, because I looked it and I told her so. I had given up telling people how old I really was a long time ago; it caused too many questions and, frankly, disbelief. Having accepted my condition, it became easier to maintain the pretence than tell the truth.

I should never have let the relationship get as far as it did, because the cut of its ending would go deeper the longer it continued. It would come with our age difference. I would be a thirty-four-year-old toy boy to an eighty-year-old woman. Not a recipe for a faithful relationship, especially if it was repeated over and over. Consequently, I had been wary of such ties for decades. But Alex was too special. She captured my soul and wouldn't let it go.

A heavy knocking rattled the front door. A uniform, distorted by the glass, moved to the side to be replaced by a grey jacket.

'Come in, it's open.' In looking up, my gaze crossed the hall table. My car keys, phone, laptop and wallet were lined up beside Alex's flowers.

They'd abducted me, brought my car back, and killed her. A premonition rose in me, and it was bad.

'YOU SAY you didn't kill her. You say you didn't touch her. Why, then, is there blood on your hands?' The detective's attack pierced my vulnerable shield. Was I being overly sensitive in believing that in his mind I was the first one on the scene, lived with the victim, and therefore I had killed her? Never mind that I loved her and would never harm her in a million years.

I was stroking Lupus, who had calmed but was still whimpering with pain occasionally. 'The blood is the dog's. I dressed his wound as best I could, but he needs to get to a vet urgently. Take samples, but be quick.' I wanted to skirt around the problem of Alex. I could take refuge in looking after Lupus to avoid confronting it. After all, the dog was alive, and there was nothing I could do to help my Alex. But the detective wouldn't let me.

'One of my men will take him. Me and you are going to the station for a long chat. We need to get out of the way of the forensic team.'

'Are you arresting me?'

'No – not yet.'

'Then I'll take my dog to the vet and come to the station as soon as he's settled. You can send an officer with me if you want, but the dog needs me. He obviously tried to defend his mistress and deserves better than being left with a stranger.'

His jaw muscles were working as he debated the wisdom of this. He must have felt something for dogs, though, because he called one of the uniformed men outside. 'Willis, take Mr Duncan to the vet and bring him to the station as soon as the dog is treated. Maximum half an hour. Got it?'

'Sir.'

'In the meantime,' he said, turning to me, 'I shall be questioning people in the local area.'

'What's his name?' I asked Willis as we drove to the vet. 'He did tell me but I wasn't listening.'

'Payne, sir. DCI Payne.'

THE VET, who was initially grumpy at being called out so early on a Sunday morning, said the muscle was cut. It was a deep wound, but it would heal in time. She used a Latin word that meant nothing to me. I left Lupus with her to be stitched and bandaged and to rest overnight, at least.

The constable who drove us to the vet had been keen to help with Lupus. 'Lovely dog, sir. He'll be all right won't he? We'll get the bastard who did it, don't you worry.'

'Thanks.' With Lupus in safe hands, my attention was forced to my loss and what to do next.

Hermione was Alex's closest friend and had to be told the news before it made the media. Fortunately, no reporters were in evidence yet, but the drama would be all over the TV in a couple of hours.

But first I had to give a written statement to DCI Payne. This was not easy, as I couldn't tell him I'd been abducted and escaped before walking home, because I'd have to explain why I was abducted. I wrote that I'd lost my car keys and some kind person must have found them and delivered my car for me. Payne made it obvious that he didn't believe me, and that, of course, made me more of a suspect in his eyes.

7

HERMIONE OPENED THE door at my knock, her swollen belly intruding into the space between us. Her welcoming smile was always genuine. 'Hello, Andrew. This is a surprise. I was just making coffee, come in. Are you okay? You look awful, to be honest.'

Mark came into the hall and reached out to grab my hand. 'Andrew. How are you? What brings you round so early?'

In spite of his bonhomie, Mark was my antithesis. He was an amateur dramatics enthusiast, an extrovert, considered himself hip and embraced new tech as if it was the saviour of humanity. The internet of things fascinated him – it was the only way to go: smart fridge, smart TV, Alexa his virtual assistant, smart doorbell and camera, smart flushing toilet, apps to tell him when to take a rest or when a dull patch was coming up in the movie and he could use the moment to take a pee – apps for every conceivable thing.

I had scoffed at him and tried to convince him how insecure and unnecessary these things were. The system would rob him of his privacy, record his wants and needs so Amazon, or whoever, could tailor ads to convince him to buy more stuff he didn't need. I told him the world had always functioned and was still functioning perfectly well without a smart environment, and was he really happy to let the tech giants know so much about him and exert some control over his life – and that of Hermione and future child?

In turn he scoffed at me, telling me, not knowing how right he was, that I sounded like an eighty-year-old. I said at least I could hold my head up and say I could think for myself, was in control of my life and had not handed it over to an algorithm.

Since then each of us regarded the other with a degree of contempt in spite of our overt friendliness for the girls' sake.

What role was the actor playing that day? An ebullient pub friend up for a laugh, perhaps? Other than his reliance on high-tech gadgetry, I'm not sure I had ever known the real Mark, since one moment he was a politician or a senior banker, and the next he was a postman or a butcher or something. He was very good at this role play, but his frequent switching of personalities spelt insincerity. Whoever he was, Mark was usually cheery. He was harmless enough, but he was a nothing-person to me, his only merit being that he supported his wife.

Hermione reminded me of a long-departed girlfriend. Celia was a good person, and we had a fun relationship, but she became more and more homely, baking scones and cakes and insisting on darning my socks, apparently trying to show me what a wonderful wife she would make. Unfortunately for her, there was no future worth living in that environment for me. After all, I was toying with the idea of putting my military experience to use as a soldier of fortune. Good money could be made from such a varied and exciting life, I thought.

Hermione was a sweet and harmless woman in her own right and, as Alex's great friend, she was someone I valued and respected. For her sake alone, Mark had my backing when necessary.

'Hermione, Mark. I've some terrible news, I'm afraid. You'd better sit down.'

It was a good job they did, because Hermione went white and toppled sideways off her dining chair when she understood what I was telling them. I was still standing and just managed to catch her before she hit the floor.

'Give me a hand, Mark.'

He didn't make any move to help. Instead, he stared at me, stupefied, mouthing silently like a fish.

'*Mark!* Help me with her. Lie her on the couch.'

He managed to pull himself together, and we got Hermione comfortable.

I told them what had happened, omitting what I had been doing prior to arriving home and, of course, the gory details. Hermione was due shortly, and I had no idea what effect an emotional shock would have on her. Wide eyed, she was shaking her head in disbelief at the news.

Mark was different. For once, he was not acting. A mature, intelligent man, a solicitor, he should have been more in control of himself. Instead, he repeatedly sniffed, wiped his nose and dabbed at his eyes. His lips were tight – so tight they were trembling. I raised a mental eyebrow – this was a bit over the top, Alex hadn't been his wife.

I made the coffee, adding more sugar than they normally took. I was keen to get out of there; I needed to think. So much had happened in the preceding hours that I hadn't had a chance to go over things for myself, to come to terms with it all. But I couldn't leave straightaway: because Mark was being so useless, it was up to me to support Hermione on my own. Weeks later, he claimed I coped better because I'd been through the death of a loved one before, with Saffron (which he thought was just before I met Alex, not decades earlier). But this was worse, because Alex was murdered. I didn't know why that would make a difference, but it did.

Mark only moved when I got up to go. He showed me to the door, barely able to speak. Head down, unable to meet my eyes, he mumbled, 'I'm … I'm so sorry, Andrew.'

He closed the door as softly as he could, as if the noise would be a shock he couldn't take.

THE VET had recovered from her early-morning call-out and was cheerful when I went to check on Lupus. 'He'll be fine. He'll have a limp, but at least he'll have four legs not three. We'll keep him here for a couple of days to recover under supervision. You can come and see him any time.'

She held up a small plastic bag with a narrow strip of cloth, about an inch long, inside it. 'Whoever did this might be in pain and have bled. This was in Lupus's mouth. He must have been too shocked to manoeuvre it and spit it out. It's probably been in there too long to be of use to forensics, but you never know. Give it to the police.'

'Thanks, I will.' And it was the first thing I did before going home. I had to get some overnight things and fresh clothes, before booking into a hotel for a few days – until Lupus was out of hospital, anyway. Home was the last place I wanted to be and, while ducking under the police tape at the gate, my heart was making itself felt and my stomach had a hole in it.

They let me in to pack a case, with every item inspected and listed by a watching officer. I wasn't thinking clearly and was indecisive about the clothes I would need.

'I've a navy jacket somewhere,' I said as I sorted through the cupboard. I wasn't actually talking to the constable, the announcement was irrelevant to him, but he shrugged anyway. 'It seems to have vanished.'

I searched through the cupboard again with a bit more care. 'No, it's not here. Maybe she took it to the dry cleaners.'

The officer scribbled in his notebook. 'Maybe, sir.'

The hotel bar opened at five, and the barman set his things in order under my impatient eye. I was in the mood to drink a lot, which meant it would be better to stick to beer to get the quantity without getting a bit worse for wear and sobbing my evening away in a dark corner.

The first pint went down, not in one gulp, but three. As I started on the second glass, my phone vibrated on the table.

The voice was rough, rasping and quiet, like something out of *The Godfather*. 'I'm sorry for your loss.'

Who the hell was this? 'Uh, huh.'

'Me and me partner was parked near your house last night. We saw you getting back about ten forty or so. Not sure of the exact time, 'cause we was occupied, if you get my drift, but it were definitely around a quarter to.'

'Rubbish—'

'Blue Volvo, right? The thing is, the police was asking for witnesses this afternoon, and we reckon it was our public duty to come forward. On the other hand, for a small remuneration, like, I mean, ten grand, we could forget all about it – didn't hear the announcement, if you get my drift.'

'It's not true, you're talking rubbish. Go away and leave me alone.' Putting the phone back on the table, I took a long, slow draught of beer and sat back. This was worrying, because even though it wasn't true, if this guy did report me, it would be cause for Payne to call me in for an interview and possibly arrest.

8

TO MY TROUBLED mind, separating scrambled egg into its original parts would have been simpler than dealing with the matters clamouring for attention: the killer, the police, Mark, Hermione, my house, NiPetco and its mafiosi … Plus Alex's bloody corpse refused to recede. The only contributor who would not intrude, my sounding board who would actually help me put some meaning to all of this, was Lupus, but he was in hospital.

I had to get away from the vicinity of her death for a short while. It was not a place to make sense of this host of thoughts. There were too many associations to Alex in everything I saw or heard, touched or smelt. I needed a wide-open space with the only sounds those of nature. On leaving for the coast, both my phone and the car radio were silenced.

A fair breeze off the sea was pushing a heavy swell. My seat was a log halfway down the beach. My mind was blank. I couldn't seem to summon thought, so I stared out over the Channel, mesmerised by the regularity of the waves. One approached, building in height until it became so steep that the crest broke and toppled forward to pound onto the shingle. Another backed it up; was it bigger than the last? The seventh wave is said to be the biggest, but I lost count. How could I lose count before seven, for heaven's sake?

The wind whistled past my ears, and each crash of a wave soothed the turmoil in my head. As happens when grieving, precious moments resurface to be treasured once more. Early on in our relationship, Alex had thrown back the covers of the bed and traced the outline of my scars with a gentle finger. 'These are terrible injuries. Were they painful?'

She was taking me back to when I was thirty-four, before she was born. 'Only at first, before they filled me with morphine.'

'Tell me what they are.'

'Bits of helicopter stabbed me, some ribs were broken and one punctured my right lung. So there were internal injuries, and there's a couple of surgical scars as well.'

'And? Come on, I want the whole story.'

The accident is one memory I'll never forget. Not only was it traumatic, not only did I look death in the eye, but I'm convinced it was the cause of my condition.

I missed Lupus that day at the beach. He would have pushed sad memories to the side, and I would've been throwing driftwood for him. He'd have bounded after it, worried it and chewed it and brought it back over and over again. My shoulder would've tired long before he did. He'd have had a whale of a time. I knew this because that's just what Alex and I had done a short month ago. But why was I focusing on Lupus when my great loss was Alex? The thing was, I could do nothing for her, but I could look after my dog, and concern for him took my mind off my mutilated lover. Lupus was a mechanism for pushing the greater problem into the background, but until he was out of his hospital and recovering at home he'd remain the focus of my attention. How badly was he injured? How well would he recover? Would he regain his enormous energy and agility?

After an hour doing nothing but absorbing the rhythm of the sea, rational thought crept back into my mind and I knew I had to change my next project. I, Charlie Maxwell, was due to go back to Kenya to rejoin the anti-poaching effort, but that would have to go on hold until I had the answers to some fundamental questions. Who killed Alex? Was it NiPetco, or was it whoever she was going to expose in the child trafficking ring? Or was I looking at the same person?

Not only would learning who killed her prove me innocent, but I owed it to Alex to see that her investigation was completed. Whatever she'd discovered was big. It wasn't a giant leap to assume that the people involved would want her silenced. No, but it was a bit of a stretch to imagine NiPetco would kill her to get at me. And why would they do that when they needed my cooperation? On the other hand, NiPetco knew where I was and had the keys to my car. They had to be involved somehow, and if I had to expose the organisation to prove it, I would.

If I was going to complete Alex's investigation, I had to learn what she'd already discovered.

I headed home, or rather back to the hotel.

Tiredness dragged at my eyes. There had been no sleep for me at all on Saturday night and not much on Sunday. Is there a worse feeling than struggling to stay awake and have your head keep falling forward? You jerk it up to concentrate, shake it violently in a fruitless attempt to revive yourself, but two seconds later it crashes forward again. To drive in that state was crazy, I was looking for an accident, and there was another hour at the wheel ahead of me.

I took the next slip road and soon found a lane with a wide field entrance. Before anything else, I had to relieve myself, and stood by the fence. The only creature about was a horse that was ripping at the grass a few metres from the gate. Even though my eyes were drooping, I could not resist a chat with the animal. He plodded over, sniffed my hand and nuzzled at my jacket.

'What are your problems, big fellah? None. You should be thankful you're not human, your life is so simple.'

We had a comforting few minutes while he listened to all my woes. I've always got on well with horses and have seldom met one that failed to respond to a soft voice and a gentle touch.

I didn't bother to turn the car around, just wound the seat back as far as it would go. That was all I remembered.

9

1980: DAN PEABODY was born from a phone call one night after I'd left the army. Saffron's death a year earlier had left me at a loss as to what to do with my life. I was drifting along, looking for a direction, for any opportunity that would spur me into action and drive away the demon of depression that lurked in the recesses of my mind but never quite showed itself. I needed my blood to race, to feel the adrenalin surging. I craved danger no matter what the cause, be it through conflict or reckless activity with safety going to hell out of the window. Dan came into being at just the right moment.

An American voice belonging to someone named Carl asked if I would consider a little well-paid irregular work in a foreign country.

'It depends,' I said. 'Where, how much, doing what, for how long and why me?'

Carl wouldn't tell me where and would only say that the work was flying passengers. The pay was unbelievable, and secrecy was paramount.

'Sounds good, but why me?' I asked again.

'You've done this kind of work before, and you know the jungle and the operating conditions. You know what you're in for.'

'So have hundreds of ex-Vietnam war pilots, Americans.'

'Exactly. You're not American.'

Carl's people gave me my first alias, complete with a real British passport and a foolproof history of Daniel Roger Peabody to go with it. Based on that experience I created three more false identities for myself. The passports weren't a bad effort, bought on the black market, and in the early eighties good enough to pass immigration in the developing world, but they weren't up to the standard that Carl produced.

DAN PEABODY is sitting on a camp stool in a tent somewhere in Southeast Asia. He's not supposed to know where, but he's worked it out. A trickle of sweat runs down his back, and the first evening mosquitoes have smelt his blood. Another half hour, it'll be too late to fly and he'll be free to sink the first ice-cold beer.

The only other person in the camp is the Filipino helicopter engineer. He has his own tent and, although they make a satisfactory team, they don't get on, so they keep to themselves. A man arrives from somewhere in the forest armed with food three times a day. He's also from the Philippines so the food is Philippine. He and the engineer chat away and ignore Captain Dan most of the time.

This trip began with a flight in a light aircraft from a flying club outside Bangkok to a grass landing strip surrounded on all sides by dense jungle. From there he was driven for two rough hours in a Mahindra 4x4.

Now, visible from his tent is a camouflaged hangar housing a Bell 205 helicopter, the civilian version of the iconic

Huey of the Vietnam war. The machine has no registration (a legal requirement in every country). Dan has checked the aircraft's data plate to find out when it was made and the exact model number. That the serial number does not match the model causes Dan to shrug. 'That's no surprise. What I'd like to know is whether this clandestine operation is a political secret or a legal one.'

As Carl had said, Andrew had done this work before; it was what he was doing when his engine gave up all those years ago. Inserting specialist troops deep in the jungle and pulling them out weeks later. There was a low-key war on then. There isn't supposed to be a conflict in this region any more, but the Americans are doing something they'll never admit to, so they're employing a British pilot, a Filipino engineer, and an aircraft that doesn't exist – outside the CIA, that is.

Dan knows the reason he's being paid so much is because, unlike before, there'll be no help, no rescue operation if he goes down in this jungle, or gets shot up – he'll be disowned. It's of no great concern: the money's good and it suits his current state of mind.

This took place years before satellite navigation was in use. Instead, a messenger would arrive in the camp and give Dan his briefing for the day, plus the maps, or sections of map, he would need. All place names have been removed from the maps. His base, the camp, is always marked as well as his destinations, which are only shown as points A, B and so on. They've made it impossible for him to read the co-ordinates of his landing zones, so where these places actually are is a mystery.

He's done seven insertions and three extractions so far, and the passengers have all been similar. Three Caucasians, and the remainder had the eyes of the region above their masks, but whether they were Cambodians, Vietnamese, Laotians or Thais, he doesn't have a clue and prefers not to know.

Dan understands they need him for a year, but after four months he's told there'll be a break and if they need him again they'll be in touch. Dan is flown into Bangkok, and Andrew is taken on to London. His offshore bank account is looking extremely healthy, but he wants to know if he'll have to go back to the forest again. If not, he'll take on other work – but there is no way to contact Carl. So Andrew puts Dan's professionally made false passport in a safe, saving it for some future use, not necessarily for his secret employer.

RESOUNDING BANGS on the car roof shattered my dream of the past. What? Where was I? Who? An angry, ruddy face at the window brought me to my senses. 'What you think you're doing? This isn't a bleeding parking area. I'm trying to get into my field. You're blocking the gate.'

An enormous tractor towered behind me, one of those four-wheel-drive monsters fitted with bale spears, the tines threatening to drive a hole through my rear window. 'Sorry, I had to sleep. I didn't mean to intrude. If you go back a bit I'll get out the way.'

'I'm not reversing that lot up the lane, there's a bloody great trailer with ten tons of hay behind. You go forward and let me pass, then you can get out. If you get stuck, you'll have to wait till I've finished unloading. I've got a lot of work on.'

I didn't get stuck, but only when I was back in the lane did I realise that it was seven on Tuesday morning, not Monday night.

Driving back, I tried to understand why I had dreamt of jungle and covert operations and men with assault rifles who hid their faces, when I had much more important things on my mind.

Dan had appeared when I needed to drive the grief out of my system. He gave me some purpose for a while, but he was no use any more; too much time had passed. Unless Carl called again, Dan was finished; he belonged in Saffron's era. Charlie Maxwell, on the other hand, would live for a long time and would serve to ease my pain over Alex. His was a good life; he made a difference and got great satisfaction from hunting poachers and helping to protect wildlife.

I would become Charlie again – as soon as I had found Alex's killer.

REFRESHED, HUNGRY but still feeling down, I grabbed a late breakfast in the hotel before heading to Hermione's house. Parking was often difficult in their street, but I struck lucky with a vacant slot in an angled bay at the kerbside. It was a squeeze, and as I took time to extricate myself without scratching the adjacent car, another cruised by looking for a space. The driver, a dark unrecognisable head and shoulders, peered at me, perhaps to see whether I was leaving. Further down the street, beyond Hermione's door, were two more empty spaces. The other car drove on without stopping – so why did he stare at me?

Hermione looked worried. She was rubbing her belly and shifting her feet. There was an atmosphere in the house I had not previously experienced. Mark was at home, but was dressed for the office. He had a cold and had decided not to go in, he claimed. It was more likely that he felt he had to guard his wife in case I, the cold-blooded killer, decided to appear. At first it seemed he wanted to take his miserable health out on me, but it wasn't his virus that was the problem.

He retreated to the far side of the room. 'The police are looking for you. I said I'd call them if you came here. Where have you been?'

'Why, what's going on?'

Hermione flopped onto an upright chair. 'Haven't you seen the news? Your picture's on TV. The police asked for witnesses who might have seen something on Saturday night, and someone has come forward.'

What did the blackmailer want to achieve by going through with his threat, unless he was the killer and was diverting attention to me? 'I don't know what's going on. That's not possible. I told you, I had to walk back from Reading. It took me five hours. The witness must be mistaken. I'll go to the police straightaway and clear this up. Hermione, please believe me, I did not kill Alex. Why would I? I loved her. You know that, and I gain nothing from her death.'

She nodded. I had the impression she was torn between believing me and listening to her husband. Mark, judging by his expression, had found someone to blame. If the police thought I was the murderer, then I must be guilty. This was a strange attitude from a solicitor, but then Mark didn't deal in criminal cases.

Actually, I didn't care what the little nothing-man thought, except for how his opinion might influence Hermione. I gave him an intense stare. 'Mark, I did not kill her.'

He glanced back, then dropped his eyes, anger and pain in his expression.

Hermione scraped her chair closer to the table so she could lean and rest on it. Sadness, lack of sleep and worry dragged her eyes down. 'You look like you need some coffee, Andrew. Mark, please make some.'

Clever thought – he needed something to do to defuse his attitude.

Mark made three coffees, handed the first to his wife, took one himself and retreated to his position far away from me. My mug waited for me on the counter.

'You should not go to a police interview without a solicitor present – golden rule,' he said. Mark confused me sometimes. This offer of advice: was his attitude wilting, or was he being professional?

'Can you help me with a name, please?'

He shook his head. 'Oh, I don't know any criminal lawyers. They're a different breed.'

'Of course you do,' Hermione said. 'What about that woman you're always saying is so good?'

'Who? I don't … Oh, her. I suppose she'll do.' He turned back to me but avoided eye contact. 'Kirsten Pearman is a barrister with an excellent record in criminal cases. Using a barrister will cut out the intermediate step of a solicitor when you go to court. I'll call her.' He took a route round the far side of the table from me to reach his phone.

'And if she can't help me, is there anyone else?'

'I can't think of anyone else.' He took his phone into the next room.

'Don't mind Mark. He's quite upset about this.'

'So are you, Hermione. And you've every right to be, even more so. You were her best friend, but you're not preparing a noose for me.'

She shook her head. 'How's poor Lupus?'

'He'll be all right, he's still in dog hospital.' A sudden thought struck me. 'Just in case, if I have to be away for a short while, would you look after him, please?'

'Of course we will, don't worry. But I'm sure it'll all turn out all right.'

'Thanks. Any news on your big day?'

She gave a brief smile. 'I'm already at forty weeks and I haven't had any twinges of labour. Doctor Richards is talking about inducing it next week if there's no progress. Mark is fretting over it more than I am.'

Mark came back. He said to the floor, 'You're in luck. She has a gap. She'll meet you at the police station in an hour. You'd better be there,' he added, as if I was going to go on the run.

'I'll be there. I'd appreciate it if you don't call the police. It's important they see me as reporting in voluntarily.' The look on his face did not fill me with confidence. 'We've known each other a long time, haven't we. Long enough to trust me,' I said, knowing I was trading on an association which would not have existed were it not for our women.

'That's not an excuse to protect a criminal act.'

'*Mark*.' Hermione was shrill and wagged a finger at him. 'We won't, don't worry, Andrew.'

Mark glowered at her. Could I trust him? He was reacting as if Alex had been his sister or his wife. He made me feel as if I, as the most deeply affected person, should be showing more emotion. Was he in love with her? I should have made allowances, since he was also stressing about Hermione; but he could stew in his own misery if he insisted.

KEEPING AN eye out for officers who might detain me before I had a chance to hand myself in, I made my way to the police station. My phone vibrated in my pocket and began its signature call for my attention as I was passing the park. The pavement was busy with people hurrying in both directions. I stepped onto the grass to get out of their way.

It was the blackmailer. 'You didn't cooperate, so I told the cops and they're now hunting you.'

'So?'

'You're going to be deep in the shit when they find you – witnessed to be on the scene of a murder and avoiding arrest.' He dropped his voice and, in clearly separated words, added, 'Did – you – enjoy – stabbing – her?'

I must have registered shock somehow, because a couple of passers-by stared at me.

'Was it good to feel that knife going in again – and – again? They say it takes more force than you think, is that true? You can tell me.' Cruel words designed to upset and weaken me.

The memory of Alex's bloody corpse welled up in front of me and forced an involuntary swallow. Sick bastard obviously didn't know I was handing myself in. It took a great deal of willpower to remain calm. 'You know I didn't do it. What do you want now?'

'We could be persuaded that we was mistaken and in the wrong street. That would take fifteen grand. That's nothing to get away with murder.'

'*Shit*. That's robbery.'

Hoarse laughter. 'No, mate, it's a little exchange of favours. Think about it: life for murder, or fifteen thou. It's a no-brainer in my book. We've got more to tell the cops to clinch a conviction as well.'

'Let me think a moment.'

'Five minutes, that's all.'

I could have braved it out, told him to get lost and trusted the truth to win out in the end. Or I could have agreed to pay, got dummy cash and tried to catch the bastard at the handover. It had to be the killer that was doing this to deflect the investigation away from himself. Was it NiPetco? In which case, were they setting a trap to capture me again? Either way, the chance to meet and possibly identify the killer would give me a chance to prove my innocence.

I was going to be late at the police station, so trotted the last couple of hundred metres. Just as I reached the top of the steps to the building, two minutes late, my phone went again. 'You gonna pay?'

'Yes, I'll pay. But you'll have to give me time to get the cash.'

'I'll give you details later.'

Across the road, at the end of the park, loitering by a bench and doing nothing was a man of less than average height, in jeans, a denim jacket and a red baseball cap. Was he waiting for someone? Why was it suspicious to be doing nothing in an obscure place where there is nothing to do? Was I being super-sensitive?

'DCI Payne, please. He's looking for me, I believe.'

The officer picked up his phone without taking his eyes off me. 'Wait there, please, sir. DCI Payne will be down shortly.'

'Mr Duncan? Kirsten Pearman.'

I turned to look down on a disconcertingly young and small woman. Was this Mark's idea of a joke? She looked thirty at the most, which did not fill me with confidence. I wanted someone with experience if this thing went the wrong way. On the other hand, her red hair was stretched back over her head and tied in a bun, presenting her as strict, humour-less and uncompromising, which was probably a bonus in court. Black-rimmed glasses and sober business clothes enhanced her severity. It was purely her age that concerned me.

She shook my outstretched hand, her fingers cool and dry. With a gesture and no words she indicated a chair and I sat. Why did I feel as if I was back at school?

It was important for her to know my side before the police grilled me. 'Thank you for coming. Shall I tell you what all this is about?'

'There'll be an opportunity for that later. These interviews follow three stages. First I'll be briefed by the DCI as to the case and the reason for this interview, then we can have a chat in private before being questioned by the police.'

'Oh.'

Payne appeared. 'Ms Pearman.'

'Chief Inspector Payne.'

There did not appear to be any love lost between these two. Had she robbed him of convictions before?

They went somewhere else for fifteen minutes, while I sat and worried how it was all going to turn out. Kirsten returned with an unreadable expression on her face. I would have paid to know what she was thinking.

'You don't like DCI Payne,' I ventured as the door closed on the room allocated for our private discussion.

'We've crossed paths before. Tell me what happened from the beginning. Leave nothing out. I work best when clients are honest with me. If you are innocent and completely open with me, I will do my very best to keep you free. If you withhold information and I cannot get the full picture, then I cannot give any guarantees about your future. Is that clear?'

'Perfectly.' And I told her almost everything: about Ni-Petco, about my being drugged and abducted, that I escaped and walked home and about finding Alex and Lupus, but I didn't say why.

She had a small tape recorder and made a few notes as well. Unless her head was down in her notebook, her spectacled eyes were picking me apart, trying to ferret out my lies. Except there weren't any – only omissions.

'How did you escape?'

I was embarrassed to go into detail over that, so just told her I had overpowered Amy.

'And why did NiPetco abduct you?'

'That's not pertinent to the case.'

'Listen to me.' That look from a woman one third my age pinned me back in my chair. 'This question is going to come in court, and if you don't provide a credible answer, then neither judge nor jury is going to believe a word you say. If you're not telling me a pack of lies then NiPetco must have had a reason to do such a drastic thing.'

I was torn. I had taken extraordinary steps to hide my condition for decades. It was too difficult to break the habit now. 'Do you believe me?'

'Whether I believe you or not is irrelevant. I have taken your case and am duty bound to defend you, but I cannot do that properly if you're not open with me. And this is a key question that has to be answered.'

'Can you get me out of here today even if you don't know the answer?'

'Yes. The evidence they have is circumstantial, and there is as yet no proof that you had anything to do with the murder.'

'What about the witnesses?'

'That doesn't prove you killed Alex, only that you were there, or close, at the time.'

'Thank you. In that case, there is no need for you to know why I was abducted.'

A flicker of annoyance crossed her face. 'Final warning. If anything else comes up and you're arrested, you will have to tell me, or you may have no way to prove your innocence.'

The easiest response was simply to nod my assent. If a crusty and experienced old lawyer had pointed that out to me, I might have given in, but this girl? Would she have the experience or be clever enough to use the information without giving me away? Not likely.

'Lastly,' she said, 'the safest way to reply to any difficult questions or those which are going to lead you into trouble, is not to comment. If you're not sure of the direction the DCI is taking, look at me. I will probably advise you not to comment.'

'I am telling the truth, and I intend to continue telling the truth, as then I cannot be tripped up.'

'Yes, but when he asks you the same questions that I've asked to which you will not supply an answer, you must say "No comment".'

10

WE WERE SHOWN into a small, brightly lit room, sparsely
furnished with a table pushed up against the wall and two
chairs on either side. A recording machine sat against the
wall. A plain-clothes officer followed us in with a notepad in
his hand.

'You can sit this side,' he said, but it was too late because
Kirsten had already taken the seat he indicated.

DCI Payne entered with a file and a sheaf of papers. They
made a loud slap as he put them down on the desk. He
scraped his chair out. I expected him to give me a hostile
look, but he seemed perfectly amicable and, other than ignoring Kirsten, was well mannered. Was this a trap?

DS Edmonds, the other officer, read out the usual caution
and checked that I understood it. I gave my name for the
record.

Payne leant back. He asked me several questions that
were clearly designed to put me at ease: How was I holding
up? How long had I lived in my house? When did I meet

Alex? What was my occupation? All routine stuff. Then he got down to business.

'Before we get into it, did Ms de Villiers have a laptop?'

'Yes, but I don't know where it is. It didn't occur to me to look for it.'

He paged through his file. 'You said here in your original statement that you walked home from Reading – why was that? It's a long way.'

'I got into a heavy drinking session on Friday night. I woke in a strange room, not my hotel room, and without any clothes. I felt ill; I could barely stand. I think I had been drugged somehow. Anyway, I was so dizzy I fell back asleep again, and it was late when I woke and felt fit enough to get out of there. There were clothes in the cupboard. I put them on and left, but I had no idea where I was, not even which town I was in. I found that out from bus stop information. Without money, phone or a car, I was forced to walk home.' All the answers I gave him were truthful except one and those meriting 'No comment'.

'Hm. Were you harmed in any way, assaulted perhaps?'

'No, only drugged, and it must have been powerful.'

'Why do you think someone would drug you?'

'No comment.'

From the corner of my eye, I saw Kirsten give a brief nod of approval.

'Do you have any idea who that person was?'

'No.'

I told Payne about the pub where I'd tried to phone Alex. I did not tell him about the underpants and the tracking device, because that would have led in the uncomfortable direction I was trying to avoid.

'A witness has come forward to say that he saw you arriving home in your car at 22.45 hours on Saturday night. What do you say to that?'

'He must be mistaken. Who is this witness?'

Payne shook his head. 'If you did walk all the way from Reading, how come your car was in your driveway?'

'I don't know. I can only assume that someone from the conference delivered it for me.'

'Why would they do that? Why not give you a lift home at the same time?'

The water was getting deeper. 'I have no idea, except that maybe I wasn't there, but in the strange room, when they took the car.'

Payne's eyes narrowed briefly, but he conquered his frustration and went on. 'Forensics have confirmed that Ms de Villiers's blood was on your left shoe and a print of that was on the carpet on the landing. What can you say about that?'

He had jumped into painful territory. I heard my voice crack and cleared my throat. 'I could not avoid treading in her blood when I went to the upstairs phone.'

'The blood on your hands was not, as you claimed, only from the dog. Some of it was Ms de Villiers's.'

'Yes, that is true. I felt compelled to hold her hand when I discovered her and before I treated the dog.'

'Why didn't you mention this before?'

'I don't know. I was upset, I suppose. I'm not so stupid as to think you wouldn't find her blood on me. There was no point in lying about it.'

'Yours are the only fingerprints on the knife. What can you tell me about that?'

'I'm not surprised. It's my knife, as you well know.'

Payne studied his notes again. In the pause I asked, 'Chief Inspector, have you actually seen this witness who says he saw me, or did he just telephone you?'

He didn't answer.

'You haven't seen him, have you? And what's more, I guarantee you won't. How do you know that he's not the murderer and is trying to set me up?'

His head came up to study me. 'What do you mean, I won't see him?'

Edmonds spoke for the first time. 'He's coming in to give a written statement this afternoon.'

Kirsten put a restraining hand on my arm and interrupted. Her voice had a clarity and sharpness to it that forced us to listen and believe. From sitting quietly at the table, she was now commanding the meeting. 'No comment. Chief Inspector, are you going to charge my client? All the evidence you have mentioned so far is circumstantial. You have no motive. Other than his shoe, there is no evidence of the victim's blood on Mr Duncan's clothing, which there would be in a violent attack. Even if he did drive his car back at a quarter to eleven, that does not prove he killed Ms de Villiers. You have not mentioned what happened to the sample of cloth found in the dog's mouth, or the results of the blood trail up the stairs.'

'We are still waiting for the forensic results on those.'

Three loud raps on the door and it opened before anyone could reply. 'Sir, a moment please.'

Payne scraped his chair back and stalked to the door. He listened without comment, but his right fist clenched twice. As he returned to the table, Kirsten said, 'You have no proof that my client is not telling the truth. We will leave.'

The chief inspector was still standing. 'Ms Pearman, I agree, some of the evidence is circumstantial. But your client is not telling us the whole truth; there are far too many inconsistencies. If he's not prepared to clarify his improbable story, I have every right to be suspicious as to his motives for not doing that. Accordingly, he remains a primary suspect.' He turned to me. 'Apparently, the witness to your returning home at a quarter to eleven has withdrawn his statement. He was mistaken and was not in that road at all.'

Curbing the desire to say 'I told you so', I settled for, 'That's something. When will I be allowed back into my house?'

'When we've finished with it. I'll contact you. You do realise the cleaning of the place is up to you?'

I didn't know. Stupidly, I thought the police saw to that. 'Are there companies that do that sort of thing?'

'They're on the internet.'

WE WERE about to leave the building when Kirsten put her hand up for us to stop. 'What on earth was that all about, asking him if he's actually seen the witness? What are you not telling me?'

'Would you like a coffee? I need one. A two-minute stroll and I'll tell you.'

'I think my car is a better idea.' She pointed outside. A jostling group of maybe a dozen people crowded the entrance door. Almost all of them were brandishing a camera or a microphone or both – the weapons of their trade.

'Oh, God.'

Kirsten scanned the jostling band with a calmness born of experience. 'There's a couple of aggressive hacks there who I've sparred with in the past. Don't engage with them whatever you do. Ready?'

'Can't we go out the back?'

'No. Let's get it over with.'

The man in denim and a red cap was still doing nothing across the road. He looked up and walked away as Kirsten led us down the steps and into the scrum. A microphone was thrust in my face. Another on a pole held from further back wavered in front of my eyes. A strong whiff of BO mingled with a cheap perfume. Faces were too close. Someone's breath stank. Little Kirsten was pushed about as she fought her way through the mob, me too. An unceasing barrage of simultaneous questions from different quarters clashed in a cacophony of unintelligible sound. My temper was rising fast.

'How did your car get home, Andrew?'

'Why did you walk?'

'What time did you get home? We heard it was before ten.'

'Did you stab your own dog, Andrew?'

I couldn't hear the blip for the noise as Kirsten's car unlocked. A shrill male voice called out as I reached for the door handle, 'Andrew, tell us. Did you kill Alex de Villiers?'

No matter what Kirsten had advised, I couldn't resist. 'Who asked that?'

The mob hushed. A few heads turned back to see the speaker, but most were focused on me. A ceaseless clacking of cameras forecast the next day's headlines.

'Mike Green, *Northern Clarion*. Tell us, Andrew, our readers need to know.'

'No they don't need to know. That is a fallacy dreamt up by the press in order to sell more papers. And yours is a singularly stupid question. Please explain why I would admit something to you rather than to the police a few minutes ago. And if I had admitted it, would I be standing here now? Any half-intelligent child has the brains to know that. I suggest you find a career in something demanding less cognition.'

Kirsten snapped at me, 'Andrew, get in the car.'

I didn't care if any of the fingers clinging to the door were in the way. In fact, I hoped they were.

'Don't slam my doors, please.'

'Sorry. How the hell do they know to ask those questions? Only the police know those details. Sorry. I couldn't stop myself. That mob – they're a bunch of hyenas – it's insane.'

'True, but never, ever engage with them. One way or another they will get the better of you. If not that brainless young man, then one of the others will interpret your temper as murderous intent. And they reach thousands.'

It was stupid of me to react, and my loss of self-control was embarrassing. I resorted to silence.

Kirsten slowed with the traffic. She glanced across at me. 'Are you going to answer my question?'

'Yes, but I still want that coffee. There's a café on the left further down the road.'

'I'll get them,' she said as she parked the car. 'You stay inside in case any reporters have followed us.'

She walked quickly for a small person and in spite of a slight limp. She would no doubt react negatively to a personal question about why that was so, so I didn't ask. It was of no particular interest to me anyway. I had to admit, she certainly knew what she was doing at the police station and afterwards with the press. My initial judgement regarding her age and experience had been invalid. It's hard to reject first impressions, but I determined to keep an open mind.

'Well?' she asked as she fixed her drink in a cup holder and eased into her seat.

'I'm being blackmailed by the supposed witness. He originally wanted ten thousand pounds to not come forward after the police's request. I told him to get lost, because I knew it wasn't true. But he told them anyway. The reason I was a couple of minutes late this morning was because he called again, wanting fifteen thousand to withdraw his statement. He won't go physically to the police, because they'll identify him, and I'll bet he's the real killer.'

'Do you have any idea who he is?'

'Yes, but it's weak. NiPetco want me, because I'm a unique specimen. I suspect they were trying to frighten me into their loving arms by having me arrested. They always intended to withdraw the witness statement, because if I was found guilty of Alex's murder I'd be imprisoned and they would not get to study me for many years. I'm not convinced that's the answer, though, because it's a stretch to imagine such a company would kill Alex just to get at me.'

'What do you mean, you're a unique specimen?'

'That's what I don't want to tell you. I believe the implications of my secret getting out are enormous. No one else knows, except the person who told NiPetco what he suspects.'

Kirsten mellowed slightly – only slightly. 'All right, I can see it means a great deal to you, but the fact remains that it will have to come out in open court, should this go to trial. Your best course of action is to tell me, and I'll decide the way to handle it from a legal perspective. I promise you it will not go further than me. There is such a thing as client privilege, you know.'

I couldn't see how I could avoid telling her. 'All right, but you're not going to believe me, even though NiPetco do. I will have to get some documentation together to help prove my words, and that's all in my house, which I can't access. When should we meet again?'

11

1982: CHARLIE MAXWELL is sitting at a table by himself at the Thorn Tree café, New Stanley Hotel, Nairobi. He strokes the condensation down off his glass of Tusker to soak the beermat. It's an absent-minded act while he thinks on the traumatic events of two weeks ago. He's not concentrating on what's going on around him. He ignores the overlanders who are checking the messages pinned to the thorn tree itself, searching for friends who have come and gone or are waiting at some hostel for them. And he's blind to the other customers, even the couple of attractive women that every other man seems to be ogling.

When not providing helicopter support to the anti-poaching rangers, he has joined their patrols. With his military background, he's able to help and has been keen to do so. This, for him, is a worthy cause, exciting, and it allows him the freedom of a different identity. As Charlie, he's not the seemingly forever-young Andrew. He loves the elephants and their domain: the forests on the mountain and the savanna that stretches out on the slopes below.

The rangers are expert trackers and possess natural skills that Western people have lost. The poachers are experts too, but they lack discipline and don't appreciate the risks they are taking, nor do they care for their guns.

But Charlie was a soldier, he knows weapons and tactics, and he knows how to exert and use discipline to the patrols' benefit and safety. With his guidance and the rangers' natural skills, the patrols are more effective than the poachers. But the other week, for the first time, the poachers took the offensive. The rangers were ruining their way of life, destroying their hard-earned income, so they set an ambush.

Every step of that poacher-hunting sortie on the slopes of Mount Kenya is etched in his memory. The patrol left the trees and joined the jeep track to use Percival's Bridge across the ravine. A carved sign on the wooden structure brought a smile: "9000ft, Max Load 10 tons, Elephants are requested to cross in single file". Back into the trees on the other side and they ran into the ambush. The firefight was all over in a couple of minutes, but the aftermath was tragic. One ranger was killed and another injured. Four poachers were arrested.

The death of Felix Bulima had a profound effect on the others. He had been a cheerful man, fond of jokes – that Charlie didn't always understand – and one of those valuable people who have a natural capacity to bring others together into a team, including Charlie. Because they made him one of their team, Charlie felt the effects of Felix's loss more than if some other work colleague had died. Nevertheless, he's thinking now on how he failed to get into the same mindset as the others while they mourned their friend, unable as he was to reach the same level of grief as the Kenyans. He is, after all, an outsider, so it's not surprising, but it is disappointing. He's also worried that he failed them with his guidance; that walking into the ambush was somehow his fault, even though it was the trackers at the front who had missed the clues.

Charlie takes another gulp of beer and shakes off his gloom. Because his mind is elsewhere, he fails to notice the woman staring at him from two tables away. 'You're Andrew, aren't you?' she says, now standing over him.

Charlie jumps. He's been comfortable in his current identity for weeks now. To hear his real name comes as a shock. He knows this woman: she was an army wife twelve years ago. Right now she should be at home in England. No one he knows is supposed to be here. 'Andrew? No, sorry, my name's Charlie Maxwell.'

'No. You're Andrew Duncan.' She gives him a coquettish look. 'I'd know you anywhere. And you should remember me. God, but you've kept your age, though, Andrew. You're as young now as you were then. You and I had a very sexy dance once, much to poor Saffron's annoyance.' She gives a little giggle, lays a hand on his arm and sits next to him.

It hurts to hear Saffron's name used like this, but he has to keep up the pretence. 'Saffron? I don't know who you're talking about. Look, I'm sorry, but I don't recognise you, and I'm not Andrew Duncan.'

'I don't know why you want to deny it, but never mind. How long have you been here?'

Charlie is fidgeting, wondering how to make her go away. 'Six weeks, but most of that has been up country. You really are mistaking me for someone else.'

'Six weeks? You've learnt what they say about the Kenyan highlands, haven't you? It's known for the three A's: Altitude, Alcohol and Adultery.' She was grinning at him, her eyes wide and fixed on his, amused at her teasing. 'I saw you about a month ago with Mercia, and I thought, leopards don't change their spots. I didn't want to interrupt, so I left you alone.'

'Who do you think was the leopard?'

'Oh, Mercia, of course. I'm not sure if her husband has no control or is simply very tolerant. You need to be careful, though.'

Whooah! Treacherous territory. In fairness to himself, Mercia had told him she wasn't married. Now he knows, so that's the end of his Nairobi dallying for a while – until the next one, anyway.

A SUNLIT table in the pub garden beckoned me. It was far removed from a group of four men, who were at the loud, silly stage of drinking. Kirsten sat, and I fetched a bottle of Sancerre. As I left the bar three people followed me out – a couple and a bearded man whose long hair was held in place by a red baseball cap. He was noticeable because he was the only person there dressed in paint-splattered working clothes. He sat with his back to us at a table a few metres from ours.

I held my glass up and somehow managed to summon a short smile. 'Cheers.'

Kirsten merely nodded and gave me an inquiring look. She was grumpy and impatient, wanting to get on with business. This was not a social drink in her eyes. It wasn't in mine either. I'd only asked her there so we could discuss my condition in a relaxed atmosphere. I thought it would thaw her out a little and make the meeting less unpleasant. Not only was I in need of cheering up at the time, but I found her almost aggressive attitude towards me unnecessary, unwarranted and unsettling.

My documents were enclosed in a leather folder, which I put on the table. 'Payne let me collect this – suitably monitored, of course.' I pushed the folder towards her. 'I do not age. I stopped ageing at thirty-four.'

'That's ridiculous. It's impossible.'

'In your position, I would agree with you. It is impossible: everything dies, it's all part of the cycle of life, and yet I have not grown any older since I was thirty-four.'

She shook her head. 'How old do you think you are now?'

'I don't think, I know. Eighty-five.'

'That's ridiculous,' she said again. She stood, picked up her bag and gave me a look that would melt granite. Her hair was stretched back into her bun, and her thick-rimmed glasses amplified those piercing eyes – I wouldn't want her cross-examining me in court. 'I haven't got time to listen to this nonsense.'

Behind her, the single man's one hand was gripping the table top, supporting him as he leant back towards us. His head was slightly inclined in our direction. It was a ridiculous posture that could only have been adopted for one reason, given that there was no one else around us.

'Keep your voice down, please Kirsten.'

She melted a little, leant towards me and said more kindly, 'Have you seen anyone about this, Andrew?'

'If you mean a psychiatrist, no. I don't need to, I'm neither mad nor delusional.'

'Andrew, for heaven's sake, listen to me. I cannot represent you with a tale of impossibility.'

'Sit down, Kirsten. You haven't done me the courtesy of listening to everything I have to say. I've gathered these documents that prove my age: my birth certificate, my certificate of marriage to Saffron, Saffron's death certificate and my three pilot's licences.'

'Three? Surely you only need one.'

'Not necessarily, but in my case, my lack of ageing was being noticed by the specialist doctors who conduct aviation medical examinations every year – all pilots are subject to them. In order to avoid comment, I would switch doctors every four years or so. Eventually, it became necessary to change my name and get a new licence to hide my real age. I had to do that twice. I'm back to my real name now.'

Kirsten sat and reached across the table for the file. She turned the pages of each document with a delicate touch, as if they were papyrus. 'These look genuine.'

'They are. Although NiPetco have not seen these, the originals anyway, they do believe I have this condition, which is why they abducted me.'

'And how did they find out about you and believe the tale?'

'I'm not sure, but I think it was my GP. It's well known that Dr Smythe liked his alcohol and was a gambler. He was the person with whom I had the most contact over the longest period. He didn't do aviation medicals – that requires a special approval – but he did see me for general things over fifteen or twenty years. He would have noticed my lack of ageing, he had my personal details, and he needs to fund his gambling addiction through his retirement, so his selling the information to NiPetco is easy to imagine.'

'They could make a fortune out of you if they could replicate it.'

'They could, but there are greater issues at stake. The impact of the condition on the planet would be dire. Does that mean you believe me now?'

'I don't know, to be honest.' She waved one of the licences. 'These could be forgeries, but I don't see why you would want to do that. What about other people, friends – did they not notice this?'

'That has been a problem. People did notice how young I looked, and some commented. I found the best thing was to move on and cease contact. I've let a lot of friends go over the years. A chance encounter with a couple of people elicited a "You're the spitting image of a chap I used to know" type of comment. I've learned to rapidly scan a room or a group before I mingle to avoid that scenario. It can happen anywhere, even in Nairobi once.

'I feel isolated being so different to the rest of mankind. It gives me a different perspective, people are more remote, which has led to a lonely existence. Not that that worries me. Much of humanity is pretty despicable and not worth bonding with.'

'You formed a bond with Alex.'

'Saffron suffered terribly. It wounded me then and still has an effect on me now. After she died, I avoided serious relationships, making a few enemies in the process, I'm sorry to say. Then I met Alex, and I couldn't stop. I was going to tell her about myself soon. Let her know what I had got her into and what the future might look like for us.'

'I'm sorry.' She sounded as if she meant it.

'I have one other method of verification. Will you go and meet an old friend of mine? We've spoken on the phone and by email, but I haven't seen him in over forty years. Harry's a few years older than me – ninety-one, I think. Introduce yourself without mentioning me and carefully watch his reaction. Tell him you're trying to trace a relative and this is just one of a number of leads. I'll give you a background and some questions you can ask, amongst which will be what happened on the 18th of September in 1965 and who was with him when he heard the news. When you've left there, I'll tell you what he said.'

MY PHONE whined at me as we walked back to our cars. Kirsten looked puzzled.

'It's the sound of a turbine engine starting,' I explained as I checked the screen – unknown number. 'A personal quirk to make my ring different from everyone else's. Hello?'

It was Hymie Green. 'Andrew. How are you doing? I was really worried when I heard you were arrested.'

I beckoned Kirsten, and she leant in to hear. Whatever perfume she was wearing wasn't cheap.

'Terrible thing to happen,' Hymie said. 'So sorry, Andrew. I knew you couldn't have done it, you're just not the type. I said so to Nigel, and he agreed. In fact he said we should pull out all the stops, find those witnesses and convince them they were mistaken.'

'So it's you I should thank for my current freedom, is it?'

'No need for gratitude, Andrew. We just wanted to do the right thing and demonstrate our goodwill.'

'Well, I'm very grateful, even if it was entirely in your own interest to have me free.'

'No, Andrew—'

'How's Amy?'

'She's okay. She was a bit shaken to begin with, but she's fine now – understands. All's forgiven, I think. Anyway, Andrew, I wanted to speak and find out if you had given our very generous offer any further thought.'

'No, Hymie, I have neither thought about it, nor have any intention of changing my mind.'

'Such a pity, Andrew. Terrible waste of a golden opportunity, if I may say so.'

'Goodbye, Hymie.'

Kirsten retreated from my personal space. 'What's all that about?'

'That was NiPetco with a not-so-subtle attempt to get me back in their clutches.'

'Who's Amy?'

'The siren who suffered as a result of my escape.'

'Did you hurt her?' Aggression lay behind that question, as if Kirsten was ready to fly at me if I said yes.

'No, scared the daylights out of her, but no harm done. Shame at her failure to seduce me is most likely the worst. NiPetco are not going to give up. They've withdrawn their witness statements in order to capture me again. Surely you can see that if a massive pharmaceutical corporation accepts that my condition is real and is willing to resort to force in order to experiment on me to find out why, then you should accept that I'm telling the truth.'

She stared at me. I couldn't read her expression. Was she moving in my direction?

'I'll go and see your friend,' she said.

'Thank you. I'll arrange it. I'll tell Harry that my friend Kirsten is researching her family and believes he's the best person to give her information on one particular member she's not been able to trace. You're not sure if he was a relative, but you need to confirm it. I'll drive you there, but I won't come in. Much as I'd like to say hello, I don't want to influence things.'

Across the car park, at the pub's door, the painter who was at the next table was lighting a cigarette.

12

I TOOK KIRSTEN down to Devizes to meet Harry. No longer in the office, she undid her bun and shook her hair out. The act wiped the school principal off the board, and she instantly became an attractive young woman, smart as ever in her suit and a green blouse. Unfortunately, her attitude did not relax.

I was in the slow lane on the motorway with a brown Mini in the middle lane a few yards back. Rather than pull out to overtake a heavy lorry in front of us, I slowed behind it to let the Mini pass. But he didn't. Instead he slotted in behind me. Once there was a gap, I pulled out and accelerated past the truck, followed by the Mini. What was going through his mind?

The traffic slowed to first-gear speed because of an accident. The Mini was now two cars behind me.

The silence between Kirsten and me was not comfortable. 'Would you like the radio on?'

'No thank you. Have you any idea why your age froze at thirty-four? That would have been 1968. Something specific must have occurred for you to pin that figure down.'

'There's only one possible event at that time, and I've never been able to think of another explanation. I was an army helicopter pilot in '68 and we were based in the north of the Malay Peninsular up near the Thai border. It was just after the start of the second Malayan Emergency. I don't know how good your geography is, but that terrain is mountainous and covered in primary jungle as far as you can see. The trees reach over two hundred feet tall, with all the foliage concentrated in a dense canopy at the top. They all try to outstretch each other to reach the sun, I suppose.

'The day it happened, I had dropped my troops at a tiny remote helipad on a ridge line, which had been cut out of the forest so we could insert and resupply our patrols who were hunting the communists.'

As one does with vivid memories, I had relived the experience many times over the years, and I found I was telling Kirsten the story in the same voice I used for myself, ignoring my audience.

'To get out of this confined area, I climbed vertically until above the canopy, glancing either side for branches that could be sucked into the rotor, because if they could reach you they'd bring you down. Once clear, I eased into forward flight. For me, there was always a breath-again moment when the airspeed needle moves off the bottom stop, and the helicopter is leaving its extremely vulnerable position low over the forest with no airspeed. I remember clearly how my engine was giving its reassuring roar with no hint of trouble – until it stopped.'

I glanced across the car. Kirsten had ceased staring ahead and was studying me. Was she trying to judge whether I was living a fantasy?

'It may have been fifty years ago, but every detail of that event is still clear to me. There was a bang, a loud crack really, then a high-pitched screaming of components no longer functioning in harmony. The turbine wound down in a couple of seconds. A horn blared. Warning lights flashed on the panel. I won't bore you with the technicalities, but I stood the aircraft on its tail – that's what they taught us: put the tail into the trees first. There was no other choice anyway – I was too low over the treetops and too slow. I swear I saw individual veins in a million leaves. The top of the canopy loomed at me as the helicopter plunged into it, as if diving below the surface of a dark pool. The rotor was still turning, and it smashed into branches. The machine shook violently, twisting this way and that. I was a rag doll. My helmet smacked into bits of the cabin not normally within reach. Then I was through the canopy and falling clear, unhindered by vegetation. I suppose I landed tail down and that cushioned the impact. I don't know, because I was out – thank God.

'When I came to, someone was releasing my harness. A soldier's face, sweaty and dirty, was inches from mine. An excruciating pain stabbed at my chest, and my breath was short. They got me out and onto the ground, and cut away my flying suit. Another trooper was there. I heard odd words: puncture, lung, losing blood. One of them was on his radio and snatches of transmission came between the sounds of my own breaths: helicopter *now*, doctor, plasma. There was that odd iron taste of blood in my mouth, and something dribbled down my chin.'

Kirsten was silent, but she was still paying attention, so I continued. 'His words exactly: "You're all right, mate. There's another chopper coming, we'll have you out of here in a flash." And that was the last intelligible thing I can recall of that day.

'I have a hazy recollection of being carried up to the helipad to wait for the rescue machine, but nothing after that. I woke in hospital with a tube down my throat. It was bloody uncomfortable. I tried to reach to it, but my wrists were tied to the bed frame. I was pulling and tugging in panic. God, it's a horrible feeling being so weak. I gave up and tried to take stock, but my mind wandered and would not focus.'

I paused, thinking how that feeling of helplessness was one of the worst memories in this story.

'Go on,' Kirsten said. 'What happened next?'

'When I woke again, I felt clean sheets, saw white walls and heard machines that hummed and beeped. A face blocked my view. He had a white coat, a stethoscope round his neck and a clipboard in his hand.

'He was cheery and spoke in terse sentences. "You're a lucky fellow. Quick-thinking soldiers. Battle first aid. Another ten minutes and we couldn't have saved you. You almost died – exsanguination. Lost over four pints, old chap. You'll be weak as a kitten until you build it up again. You had internal injuries, broken ribs – one punctured your lung. We've got you intubated, but we should be able to take that tube out soon, now you're conscious and breathing on your own. Good job you're fit and are blood type AB negative. You can take any rhesus negative blood, and we had enough to fill you up again. Don't try to talk. Best go back to sleep. See you later."

'And he was gone. I drifted off again. I was thirty-four then and I'm thirty-four now, fifty-one years later. Of course it was years before I realised I wasn't ageing. Then it was time to think. Was it the massive blood transfusion? Was it the trauma itself – did the damage to my body change something within me? Or was I always programmed to stop ageing at thirty-four? So many questions, and more than a few impossible answers.'

'I'm also AB negative. It's quite rare,' Kirsten said.

The traffic moved again and I stopped talking. I took the next exit, checked the mirror, and sure enough, the brown Mini was behind us. Whoever this was, he was pretty useless at shadowing.

'Sorry about this,' I said, 'but I need to take a short detour.'

The next roundabout had five exits, the first one a dead end with a gate barring an entrance. The Mini was four cars behind us. I went round the circle once. The other cars peeled off, and two more joined the circus. I went round again.

'What on earth are you doing?'

'We're being followed by that brown Mini. I'm leading him a dance.'

Kirsten turned to look. The Mini stayed the course, but he must have realised that I'd spotted him. I went round a third time but stopped in front of the gate. The Mini shot past and I fell in behind him.

'For heaven's sake, Andrew! Stop mucking about.'

'A little patience, please, Kirsten. We'll lose him now.'

The Mini slowed, but went past the next road. I cut across the left lane and took the exit as he continued round for a fourth circuit.

'Sorry about that, but I'm not having the press or NiPetco or whoever finding out where Harry lives.'

'Really? Are you sure? Why would anyone do that?'

'This is not fantasy, Kirsten. When we met at the police station, there was a man across the road when I went in. He left when we were embroiled in that pack of hyenas outside. There was another man trying to hear what we were saying at the pub, and a moment ago we had a Mini holding position behind us.'

'Are you sure you're not getting a little carried away under this pressure?'

'I am not paranoid. I have to look at this with the perspective that if someone was prepared to commit murder, it's perfectly possible for them to follow me for some unknown reason. That assumes it's the same crowd involved. But what if someone else is keeping track of me? They could be from NiPetco or they could be whoever murdered Alex, if they aren't one and the same.'

Kirsten returned to her thoughts and I to mine. NiPetco wanted some answers. And another thing: that meeting back in June when Jakub Kowalski tried to convince me he was from UK Biobank, was that NiPetco's first attempt to snare me? If not, then at least two companies were after me. That was a bit worrying. Did they need me to be alive, or could they get what they needed from my corpse?

It was none of their business – great attitude, but not much use.

I PARKED opposite Harry's house, settled back for a long wait and closed my eyes while Kirsten went in to see him. To pass the time, I relived some of Dan Peabody's escapades. Things could have gone very differently if I'd had an accident there. I knew the dangers of being captured. Torture, imprisoned for life in some hell-hole, used as a political bargaining chip and conveniently forgotten by those who had needed me … I'd taken the bait with my eyes wide open. So why did I do it? The money would be worth nothing if I never returned. I did it because there was no future if the one person I wanted to share it with had gone.

I wonder sometimes if Dan's secret work made any difference to whatever the Americans were doing. Were the patrols effective? Are they still doing it with other pilots? Did the US government know what their secret organisation was up to? I'll wonder forever.

I'd never been shot down or had an accident, so it was good to do. It set my mind free and put me on a course that was both prosperous and exciting.

I was listening to Toby Keith's 'Don't Let the Old Man In' when Kirsten came out after an hour, having got on well with Harry by the look of things. She waved goodbye as she opened my car door. It was the first time I'd seen her smile.

She listened to the music as we left the residential area and turned onto the main road. 'Appropriate.'

'It's become my song. How did you get on?'

'What a lovely old man. But you should've warned me; he's sharp as a razor. It wasn't easy to question him about a fictitious situation and still be authentic. I felt quite uncomfortable when he began asking me about my family, although I think he was only trying to help make the link I was looking for.'

'What happened when you told him your name was Pearman?'

'He didn't say anything, but he did raise an eyebrow. I didn't have to mention the date, he did and made a face at the bad memory. "A good man shot in the back," he said. As we finished he asked me if he'd been any help, if I thought I was a relative of your friend. I evaded that by saying I still had other leads to follow. It's going to be awkward, I don't want to fabricate a story for the old boy, but he wants me to tell him how I get on, no matter how successful I am.'

'Are you a relative?'

'Not to my knowledge. What was he to you?'

'My company commander in the army, my mentor, an inspiration and a good friend. Did he confirm I was there when we heard the news?'

She nodded.

'Do you believe me now?

She didn't reply for a while, but continued staring out of her side window at the rolling downs of Wiltshire. 'Yes, I think so, but it's hard to accept that the impossible is possible. What do you think about it? Does it worry you? Will you want to die sometime?'

For decades I had contemplated my condition, but it had been an internal conversation. Faced with explaining it to someone else, I was tongue-tied. It was easier to tackle it in a roundabout way. 'I have an obsession. Answer me this – what is the root cause of almost all of mankind's problems?'

She gave a momentary frown. 'Abuse of our power over other creatures, destroying so much in our drive to progress, or a variation on that theme.'

'I suggest you've skipped the bottom rung of the ladder. To me, the root cause is overpopulation.'

'Go on.'

'There are now so many humans on the planet, we have upset the balance of nature. It was fine when a few hunters bagged animals, birds and fish for the pot. They did not deplete the populations beyond their capability to grow. But now we are dominant and abusing our power. We cut down forests, which destroys wildlife habitats, we overfish the oceans and pollute the water, we are forcing animals into extinction, all because there are too many of us demanding too much of nature.

'Global warming is a fact: the Arctic is melting, glaciers are retreating, sea levels are rising, deserts are expanding, food production has been lessened and fresh water is diminishing. Forests, our carbon sink, are being destroyed by the greed of humans. The urge to profit, admittedly on the part of a relatively small portion of the population, is one cause, but by far the greater reason is the sheer volume of people in this world who all want, or are told they need, the apparent benefits of civilisation: unlimited energy to support a consumer-driven lifestyle. But those benefits come at an extraordinary cost to our planet. We can't continue to rape the world of resources at the same time as allowing the population to increase and expect Earth to survive. It's not sustainable, and unless governments take drastic steps to control climate change, the ever expanding population will make it even more difficult to solve.'

Kirsten twisted round in her seat to observe me without straining her neck. Her expression changed subtly. I had become accustomed to her habitual glare by that time, so it was pleasing to see that her stern expression had melted. She seemed to be regarding me in a new light.

I forced my eyes back to the road. 'All these people need feeding, but our means to produce food is being whittled away by our own destructive behaviour. Food and particularly water are becoming even more scarce. We've already passed the point where some communities have been driven into starvation because the land they live on cannot support their numbers. In some places, Jakarta for instance, people are having to use ground water, because the city's supply is limited. This has caused the ground to sink, thereby stopping the run-off into the ocean, which allows flooding.'

'Yes, I read about that.'

Did I have an ally in her? I needed to bring her fully onside. 'Do you agree with me? What do you think results from overpopulation?'

'Well … it's not just too many people per se, it's the density of the populace as well. When you cram people together you get more crime and violence, relationships become increasingly difficult, and children suffer. It all leads to a breakdown in society. You can see it happening right here in Britain.'

'Yes, I know. Another aspect: new diseases are evolving all the time, and they're spreading faster than we can tackle them, because too many people are involved. It's too easy to find culprits: oil and energy companies, manufacturers – all chasing profits – but how harmful would that be if there weren't so many of us?'

'True.'

'I do not understand the drive to always be expanding. Countries become concerned when their populations are declining. To me, that's good. Surely the aim should be to have fewer humans, living more efficiently, than to have too many humans destroying the world. Quality over quantity.'

'Surely our quality of life is improving all the time. The big tech companies are constantly striving to make life easier for us.'

'They're smoothing their own path to extract more money from us with tailored ads – "just for you". I don't want their ads. If I want something, I'll look for it myself, not follow their biased suggestions. They have no concern for us as individuals whatsoever.'

Kirsten took a deep breath. 'That's a good rant, but what does it have to do with your condition?'

'For years I've worried what would happen if people couldn't die. We've agreed, I think, that the planet will not be able to support the vast number of humans. Ask yourself these questions:

'Let's say NiPetco develops a treatment that could halt ageing. Inevitably, they'll charge a lot of money for it, so only the wealthy of the world will be able to afford it. How is society going to develop with a rich elite living forever and a group of workers who are destined to die?

'Couples, forever young, will spend an unnatural length of time together, and disagreements will inevitably be amplified. How is that going to affect society?

'Those living forever will not need pensions, so they'll continue to work. What will happen when the young's access to the workplace is denied by those already there? The fabric of society as we know it will be destroyed.

'What will happen if the treatment is either inherited or given to a baby, so it requires mother's milk forever?'

'Oh come on, Andrew. It won't be as bad as all that. Aren't you exaggerating a bit?'

'The potential is there, so no, I don't think I'm exaggerating. Many factors could come into play that will mitigate the effects, but we can't rely on that happening. If someone replicated my condition, we'd probably find some way to manage it, but the world's population growth does need to be reduced to save our planet. Some very wise people think the same way, you know: Stephen Hawking, Einstein, Jacques-Yves Cousteau, Sir David Attenborough, Isaac Asimov, to name a few. I will take extreme steps to ensure I do not contribute in any way to what I believe to be an absolute disaster. I have to stop NiPetco and others like them from using me. The lack of their research will be a benefit to mankind, which is a sort of empty result. It will be a success, but it won't feel like a success.'

HERMIONE PHONED to say she had something for me.

You would be lucky to find a speck of dust in her home under normal circumstances. The pervading smell in the house was often the artificial fragrance of something that killed 99.9% of germs. Mark left stuff lying around and made a shambles out of everything he touched. He was simply one of those people who cannot work neatly. Hermione spent much of her time rushing after him, putting things away and polishing the surfaces he'd messed. Which is why I was surprised when I went into the kitchen and saw the splodge of last night's gravy that had dried on the counter and the pile of dirty cups and plates in the sink. Hermione immediately glanced away when I turned to her. More than being embarrassed, she was looking drawn and clearly finding it hard to cope. She was due very shortly, and Alex's death had hit her harder than she was letting on.

Mark was doing little to help. Had his attitude improved now I was closer to being exonerated? Not much. He was still miserable and kept his distance. Was it his cold that was causing his mood, or was he grieving for Alex? His concern for Hermione was also on his mind, so I gave him the benefit of the doubt.

'The witnesses retracted their story, Mark, so I'm no longer the prime suspect.' True or not, there was a chance the news would reduce his unease about me.

'There are still questions you haven't answered,' he grumbled. 'Why won't you do that?'

Hermione halted a potentially difficult conversation. 'Andrew, I'm sorry, with everything that's going on I forgot to mention it. I've some clothes that are – were hers. What do you want me to do with them? I could dispose of them if you want …'

Why won't these damn seemingly petty issues leave me alone? I hadn't even thought what to do with her personal stuff. All it did was force me to confront her loss, and I certainly didn't need more of it. I gave a useless shrug.

'She also gave me this to give to you if anything happened to her.'

The envelope was sealed and had my name on it. 'That's odd. Why didn't she give it to me herself?'

'She was worried you would open it too soon and stop her from doing what she was doing, or even do something silly before her investigation into child abuse was complete. I think she had a premonition something was going to happen, but she didn't want you, me or her friends to know.'

I tore open the envelope under the silent scrutiny of Hermione and Mark, the one worried and curious and the other ready to seize on my reaction as that of a cold-blooded killer.

There were two sheets, both sides covered in Alex's neat handwriting. Blue ink on cream paper, leaving broad margins on either side.

Darling Andrew, she began, and I swallowed hard. I skimmed the first few paragraphs and put the letter away.

Mark took a step forward. Such courage! 'What does it say?'

I almost responded with, 'It's none of your business,' but bottled the thought. His attitude was annoying me – Alex wasn't his wife. 'I need to study this. Thanks, Hermione. I must go and see if Lupus is ready to come home.'

My air of nonchalance was adopted to annoy Mark, which it did. He paced up and down on his side of the room, running his hand through his hair and glancing up at me in futile expectation of an answer.

Once in the vet's parking area, I opened the letter again and read it through – twice.

LUPUS WAS recovering well, but the vet wanted to keep him in for another twenty-four hours. The trouble was his tendons and muscles were so badly cut that, if he tried to walk, he could pull his stitches out. He was lying in his cage, groggy with painkillers, but he responded to me by trying to get up. He raised his head and gave me a look that said he'd rather be chasing something small and furry. Then his eyes closed again as his head fell back to the bed. When I catch the bastard that did this …

With a deep breath of clear air after the sick-animal smell in the surgery, I pulled out my phone. 'Kirsten, I have a letter here from Alex. I think you need to see it, it could have a direct bearing on my case.'

The receptionist showed me to Kirsten's office. Was it her small size that made the desk appear so large? Or maybe it was the great pile of files on one side that created that impression. A smell of perfume mingled with that of coffee. The room was devoid of any decoration. There were no pictures, no ornaments, nothing personal; the only writing instrument was an ordinary Bic ballpoint.

I said hello, put the envelope in front of her and sat down. She didn't reply but took the letter and pulled her chair closer to her desk. Other than during that trip to Devizes, she'd always been cold and professional, with her hair stretched back and her eyes fierce behind her distinctive glasses. Was there a lighter side to her, when she was not at work, for instance? She had shown signs of one during the drive and we talked of something other than the case. But now she was back in the office.

For her to adopt a professional image was understandable, but in doing so she made me feel I was constantly under suspicion. Did she do that with all her clients, or only those she thought were guilty?

'I see what you mean.' Kirsten raised her eyes from the letter. Her voice was steady, controlled, but the paper was quivering in her hand, even though her arm was resting on the desk. 'Your Alex was conducting what was probably a very dangerous investigation. She doesn't give enough detail, unfortunately.

'A white woman acquiring underage girls for sex trafficking and, with her help, a group of South Asian and British men grooming these kids. Alex has found a house where the girls are being held, and she's met one of two who escaped. We need the details. As a journalist, she must have kept a recording of her meeting with the girl, surely.'

Her stare somehow made me feel I needed to defend myself. 'She was getting too close to the gang, and I'm the ideal scapegoat. There's another aspect: in the Rotherham case in 2010, failure by the council and the police to investigate reports of abuse were attributed –amongst other things – to a fear of losing Labour votes amongst the ethnic minority and, in the case of the police, because they were scared of being branded as racists. It's possible a similar attitude today might mean they won't pursue this line of inquiry with her murder. This level of political correctness is stupid and sickening.'

The letter in Kirsten's hand had stilled. 'May I have a copy of this? She must have made detailed notes, the recording, maybe some photos to support her investigation, but she doesn't say where they might be. She had a laptop, but she says she left nothing on it as a precaution. She knew she was in danger.'

'Yes, but the laptop's been taken. She would go away for a few days armed only with a notebook. When she came back, she'd log all the information she'd gathered on the laptop and then back it up. But she hid the back-up somewhere.'

'Well, it says here that she has a secure box in a vault.' Kirsten stood and limped out of the room to the photocopier. She was back in a moment and handed me the original letter.

'I think the vault's in Reading. Should we give the letter to the police?' I said.

'Yes, we must, but they won't be able to do any better than us unless they can find Alex's back-up. I know that vault in Reading. Access is through personal identification, a biometric scanner, a unique customer code and digital photo recognition. No one but the owner can get in, although the police can access a box if they get a court order.'

'We'll have to leave it up to them, then.'

'Don't go to Payne on your own. I'll come with you to see fair play. Be very careful what you tell him.' She gave me a look I couldn't read. It wasn't aggressive, nor unfriendly for a change. There was something positive in it, something determined. 'These people …'

IT SEEMED to me that DCI Payne wanted to ask if I was going to confess, but he stopped short of so blatant an attack. All he said was, 'Well?'

He read the copy of Alex's letter, then went through it again before giving me his usual hostile stare. He only looked at Kirsten twice in the whole time we were there. 'This had better not be an attempt to deflect the course of this investigation.'

'Chief Inspector, the most likely killers are the gang whom she was researching.'

He shrugged and put the letter into a file. 'I'll look into it in due course. It's not the primary focus of our enquiries.'

'You need to get into that vault and find out what she knew.'

He bridled at my telling him what to do. In fairness, so would I have done in his position; but I couldn't help it, his antagonism was annoying me.

'You'll keep us informed, Chief Inspector?' said Kirsten.

Payne replied without taking his eyes off me, 'If I think it'll be appropriate – yes.'

13

THE NEXT DAY, I was again sitting in Kirsten's office, but this time nursing an excellent espresso. She was waiting to be put through to Payne and taking occasional sips from her mug. A thin line of frothed milk sat on her upper lip, but to point it out might embarrass her and invite anger.

'Chief Inspector,' she said eventually, 'I wondered if you had gained any value from the contents of Ms de Villiers's box in the vault. It's of great interest to my client to know. After all, his own life may be in danger.'

Kirsten frowned as she listened. 'And why is that? … Are you sure? … Thank you for being so informative, Chief Inspector.' The sarcasm in her final sentence was cutting.

'Well?' I asked.

'He merely said the information in Alex's vault did not merit any further enquires.'

'I don't believe that.'

'I've seen this before. When the police respond to something in so obviously negative a manner, it could be because they're already investigating that line of enquiry and do not wish to jeopardise it.'

'There's hope then?'

'I'd say there's room for cautious optimism. But I wouldn't hold your breath.'

KIRSTEN AND I had determined that Alex left a back-up of her information in an ultra-safe place. I'd seen her deleting all the evidence from her computer. She was paranoid about it being stolen, and it is much easier to keep a memory stick hidden and secure than a whole computer, which was indeed missing.

If she only went into Reading infrequently, then there had to be a more up-to-date back-up of her work than the one in the vault. The police, so they said, were not going to take any action using Alex's material. I was damned if I was going to sit on my backside and do nothing. That back-up had to be close to hand: in the house, in the garden, somewhere where she could reach it without leaving the property.

Once I'd checked out of the hotel, I went to collect Lupus from the vet. I needed my dog to be with me when I went home. It was impossible to guess what it was going to be like stepping back in there, the two of us together. I'd had the place professionally cleaned, but it wasn't the visual reminders that worried me so much, it was whether I could bring myself to get into the bed we'd shared.

Lupus was wearing a protective collar to stop him pulling at the dressing over his wound. He looked depressed, trapped as he was by the ridiculous cone. When I got him home and lifted him out of the car, he just stood there, as if mesmerised, staring at the wall. I led him into the house and settled him in his bed while I got the place organised.

What horrors awaited me in the fridge? A dish of Alex's pasta, a tub of the yoghurt she preferred, half a bottle of white wine – my preference was red. Most of the contents were hers or her choice. The tin of Lupus's meat I was looking for had gone furry, probably contaminated by the stink of inadequately smothered blue cheese. All this stuff would have to go. I got a fresh tin for my dog and blinked away the moisture misting my vision.

An insistent rapping hammered the front door. Half expecting the police, I opened it. A barrage of clicking shutters greeted me. There were four of them, and two were on the top step.

'Andrew, give us an exclusive. Well paid, mate.'

'Andrew, we need shots of where it happened, where you say you found her.'

'Andrew—'

I slammed the door in their faces. Intrusive bastards. I could not fathom how they had the nerve, the sheer lack of any semblance of decency, to invade people's lives the way they did. An idea of pouring boiling oil on them from the battlements above soothed my rising temper.

'Come on, bucket-head, let's take that thing off while I can watch you.'

Lupus's protective cone was tied to his regular collar with tapes. Rather than undo them, I took the whole assembly off. The collar felt as if there was a cut in the underside. Turning it over revealed a short incision across the inside of the leather. It had a slight bulge to it, and a short loop of string, just long enough to pinch, was sticking out.

'Oh, you clever, clever girl.'

With a bit of tugging and manoeuvring, the memory stick slid out from its cave between the two layers of leather that made up the collar. Even if Lupus let a stranger near him without tearing a chunk out of their arm, no one would think to look at this for a hiding place. I needed to get the thing into my computer, but I had to see to my dog first.

He had perked up and three-legged it into the garden when I opened the door. He hesitated, because he wanted to lift a leg to wee, but if he did that he'd fall over, so after a couple of ridiculous tries, he remembered his puppyhood and squatted instead. I had to keep an eye on him to ensure he didn't rip at the bandages, so I grabbed my computer and sat where I could see him lying on the grass in the sun.

The house next door was for sale and was empty. Its garden was hidden from mine by thick bushes except for a narrow gap where one had died. A head poked through, a camera was aimed. Lupus was on his feet, limping at speed towards the intruder. His barking almost drowned the man's words.

'Andrew, give us an exclusive, mate. Great money for your story. The public needs to know your side. We can put your slant on it, and that'll help your case.'

He ducked back as Lupus leapt at him. The thought of the dog straining his torn muscles made me wince. He had to be controlled; he would pull those stitches if he got excited.

ALEX WAS so organised. The material she left on the memory stick was gold dust. Much of her information came from one of the two girls who had managed to escape. Her description of Lou, what the child went through and her mental state set my emotions in turmoil: pity, anger, disgust – they were all there. Her words evoked feelings I thought I no longer possessed; feelings I'd only ever had for those close to me since Saffron died. But there I was applying them to a young girl I'd never met.

My love's murder was devastating, but it did not take long for anger to join my sadness. I was going to find the killer. And having seen her description of the horrors that Lou and others went through, and being surprised by my own reaction to her words, another dimension was added to my mission.

Alex's investigation had to continue. I would do it on her behalf. I would hunt down and expose this perverted gang to avenge the abused kids of this world. If I could do it so that other paedophiles were forced to sit up and take notice, even better. Perhaps I could instil a permanent fear in their heads, just as they saw fit to damage young minds for life. And in the process I would find Alex's killer, because I was more and more convinced they were one and the same.

There's great personal risk in this, isn't there, Alex? But I don't care; after all, something has to bring my life to an end somehow, at some time.

To be effective, though, I was going to have to suppress my memories of her and her dreadful end. If I dwelt on her, I'd lose focus and invite trouble.

She had neatly catalogued every piece of information: the address of the house where the children were held and abuse took place, the full names of two of the victims, four names that could be Pakistani, one that sounded Nigerian. Three British and a Frenchman were identified by their accents only. The abuse had been videoed. Alex noted that she didn't know if this involved third-party editing or whether the videos were processed in the same house. She guessed the clips were sold on the dark web, noting that it was something that needed to be researched and she'd have to find a person who could access the hidden part of the internet.

Kirsten had to be party to this.

'I'm sorry to ask this, but will you come round here to see this information? I've just collected my dog from the vet and I don't want to leave him alone. He's getting more lively and trying to get at his bandages.'

The silence that followed only magnified her resistance to the idea.

'Please.'

She sighed. 'Half an hour.'

Kirsten arrived a little after six. She looked prim and neat, and uncomfortable being there. In an attempt to have her relax, I offered her a glass of wine.

'No, thank you. This is not a social call.'

'I'm not making it a social occasion. I'm only being hospitable.'

She paced a small circle as if looking for something to do. 'I don't know how you can come back here so soon.'

'I have nowhere else to go, and I can't have Lupus in a hotel. He's certainly not being left in kennels while he recuperates. I'm going to have a glass; I feel I need it. Are you sure you won't join me?'

'Andrew, are you coming on to me? If so, it's inexcusable so soon, and in any case you're wasting your time.'

'*Bloody hell*.' My fuse was shorter than I realised. 'Where does that come from? I am certainly not coming on to you. Five days ago I lost the woman I loved dearly. I'm being hounded by the press, suspected by the police, stared at and avoided by neighbours, followed by someone, and more than likely hunted by a gang of child abusers for what I might know about them. I'm not the slightest bit interested in any other woman and probably won't be for a very long time. And I'm not interested in you, you're hardly my type. I'm merely trying to create a more congenial atmosphere, so it's easier to work together. But it's a bit difficult when you're so hostile.'

She glared at me and opened her mouth to make some retort when the uneven clicking of Lupus's claws on the wooden floor made her turn. 'Oh, Lupus, you poor, brave thing.' Kirsten crouched down to him and stroked his head under the bucket. Her face was transformed. Gone was the hardness, the set mouth and the steely eyes. She turned to look at me and Lupus licked her ear. She smiled and gave a chuckle. 'He's gorgeous.'

'I think so.'

She looked at the thin pile of bedding I'd left on the arm of the couch and appeared to recognise its significance. 'I'm sorry I spoke as I did. I have difficulty sometimes, in certain circumstances …' She limped over to the table, and Lupus limped with her. She laughed at him. 'You and me, Lupus.'

'Well, I apologise for shouting at you,' I said. 'I'm a bit raw at the moment.'

'Of course. May I change my mind?'

She pointed at Lupus. 'What is he? Not German shepherd, he doesn't have the dropped quarters. And why Lupus? It's a disease.'

I set my laptop on the table and opened the memory stick, left her to it and went to the fridge. 'Canis Lupus – wolf. He's half Malinois – Belgian shepherd. Neither he nor I knows what the other half was. Malinois are frequently used for police work. They can be ferocious, and are incredibly athletic and loyal. He may only be part Malinois, but in his mind he's pure bred, and that's what matters. He's a bit of a softy, really. In fact he failed police training for being too nice. What that actually means is that he lacked sufficient aggression – although the murderer might not agree with that.'

14

'THE HOUSE IS set back from the river off the road between Wallingford and Pangbourne,' Alex wrote. *'Its owner is a businessman who lives in Pakistan and seldom visits the UK. He renamed the house Shalamar Gardens in 2016. I have not yet been able to establish whether he is aware of the appalling things that go on in this evil place.'*

It was easy to identify the house on Google Maps. It lay between two other mansions with large gardens that stretched down to the Thames and must have been worth well over two million pounds apiece. The river ran more or less north-south. The division between Shalamar and the property to the south consisted of a hedge whose shadow indicated its significant height. The northern boundary was formed by a narrow channel that led off the river, ran past the house for eighty metres and ended in a small pool not far from the main road. A small boat was moored in the channel. Something about the image was unusual. Zooming in as much as I could, it was just possible to make out what appeared to be a pair of oars lying on the seat.

Seen from above, the building itself consisted of a central block, which was probably for the communal rooms, and two wings coming off it for bedrooms. It was double-storey, with dormer windows in the roof signifying a loft room. The centre section opened on the river side to a wide patio with sun umbrellas, folded at the time the satellite passed overhead. With the swimming pool at the patio's edge, it was easy to imagine lazy afternoons with bikinis, Pimm's, splashing and laughter. The obligatory tennis court lay alongside the southern hedge.

There was a detached double garage with a large parking area at the end of the driveway. It didn't appear that the house could be seen from the road, because of trees.

Across the river was pasture, through which ran the Thames Path, the footpath that travels for a hundred and eighty-four miles, mostly beside the river, from the Thames Barrier in London to Kemble in Gloucestershire.

The view from space revealed the contrast between Shalamar and its neighbours. The tennis court lacked a net, and the markings had faded to smudges. Next door's swimming pool had an automatic cleaner, its hose clearly visible. Shalamar's pool was a cloudy green. No bikini clad ladies soaked up the sun, and no cars stood in the driveway. The image was a snapshot; a state of affairs taken in a split second when nothing was happening. Whether it was a valid reflection of the place I'd have to find out, but it did not fit with Alex's description of the house.

LUPUS WAS curled up in his bed, He opened his top eye and regarded me with the expectation of an eternal optimist. Was I going allow him to run, truly run, again – to chase squirrels?

'Not until you're fully healed; I can't afford your vet's bills. Meanwhile, it's time for your antibiotic.'

My dog dealt with, I called Kirsten. 'If I can find the girl, Lou, who Alex mentions, will you interview her? I'm sure she won't want a man present.'

There was silence for a few seconds. 'Yes, I'll do that. Do you know where to find her?'

'No, only that Oxford springs to mind, because I think that's where Alex often went.'

'This firm employs a private investigator on occasion. He's good and discreet, but expensive. Do you have the means to employ him if you need to?'

'As long as it's not extravagant.' Did money matter if it kept me out of jail? 'I must do this. If I'm to prove my innocence, the guilty party has to be found. I also want to complete Alex's investigation for her. It's a good cause, a worthwhile cause.'

'Yes.' She put significant emphasis in that single word and gave me the PI's number. 'His name is Dick, but he prefers to be called Mitch. Please don't crack any infantile jokes.'

'I would have thought you were too young to know about Dick Tracy. Thanks, I'll get hold of him immediately.'

'It's not me that cares. Mitch does not appreciate being compared to a nineteen-thirties New York cop. He doesn't have much of a sense of humour.'

You should get on well, then … but I kept that thought to myself. Instead I dialled Mitch's number. He answered on about the tenth ring. 'Mitchell.'

I didn't tell him what it was about, but asked if we could meet, and that Kirsten had recommended him.

#

NEWBURY HAS a comfortable feel to it. With plenty of old buildings and alleys, it has the atmosphere and feel of a genuine country market town. Mitch's office was in a narrow Victorian house, squeezed between two larger dwellings in a cul-de-sac. An old green VW Beetle was parked outside. Pressing the top buzzer gave no clue as to whether it worked. No bell rang, no crackle came down the line and there was no weak, unintelligible voice. Waiting, I looked back the way I'd walked and saw the people on the main road as they took the five or six paces needed to cross the end of this street. On the far side, in front of an Indian takeaway, a man was standing, doing nothing. A moment later my curiosity was interrupted by a scratchy voice from the speaker telling me to push the door.

There was barely enough room to carry a briefcase up the creaking stairs, whose threadbare carpet did little to soften my steps. The office door, panelled and white, held a small brass plate in need of a polish. It read 'Mitchell Investigations'.

Mitch was a wiry man with a weaselly face. Stick a brightly coloured helmet on his head and he would have passed for a jockey. He was wearing what turned out to be his 'uniform' – blue jeans and a black leather jacket with a fresh shirt. He was about forty-five and sported a healthy tan.

Files and stacks of paperwork littered the office from the floor almost to the ceiling and gave off a musty smell that fought for dominance over that of a toasted sandwich. A plastic step-up stood in the corner to ensure the little man was able to reach the top of some piles. One chair had crumbs on the seat; I chose another and accepted an instant coffee. A closer look around while he was making it revealed that the only decorative item was a seven-branch, silver menorah with a little Star of David forming part of the main stem.

I told him the bare minimum of necessary information, although I did explain my situation with regard to the murder. 'Primarily, I need to prove it wasn't me that killed her, but I also want to expose this gang. What they're doing is appalling, and they must be stopped.'

Mitch picked at his teeth as he spoke. He hadn't taken any notes – perhaps he had a tape recorder running. He took a slurp of coffee. 'I'm old school,' he said. 'We don't have the death penalty in this country, more's the pity, so we should send those that don't belong back home for execution. It's the only solution for scum like this, and I'm including the "clients" as well as the gang. I played a small part in getting information on the previous Oxford gang of this type, as well as the Rotherham gang. You'd think they'd learn a lesson and stop, but I'm not surprised to hear there's another lot operating. Fucking depraved crowd.'

'So will you help?'

'Yeah, with pleasure.'

'Um … what do you charge?'

He looked at me intently, twisting his lips around, the toothpick waggling, making up his mind. 'Cost. Cost, plus a minimum rate so's I can pay the rent. I hate these bastards.'

The intensity of that last sentence was uncomfortable. I changed the subject. 'Is that your Beetle outside?'

'Yeah. It's a hobby. My Porsche's in for service.' He grinned at his tired joke, and I wasn't sure if he was having me on or not. Kirsten's opinion of his sense of humour had to be taken whence it came.

'Alex had a Beetle, yellow and with a little hole in the exhaust that made hissing pulses.'

'I know that sound. She was a lovely lady?'

'The best.'

He nodded his understanding, and a sense of empathy bound us for a moment. I left him with as much detail on the girl, Lou, as I had. My spirit had been lifted by Mitch's response; instinctively, I knew he was a man I could rely on. A team to solve this case had been formed – Mitch, me, and possibly Kirsten. She was on side all right, but how much she was prepared to get involved, I didn't know. She had a position as a barrister to uphold, so she would have limitations.

I DIDN'T hear from Mitch for two days, then: 'I've found her – Lou.'

'*Great*. How is she? Did you talk to her?'

'Nah. It wouldn't be right, and she'd be frightened of me. It's a woman's job. She's in foster care in Oxford. I've the details.'

'I'll give them to Kirsten, she said she would interview the girl. How did you do it?'

'I've contacts. I got nowhere with missing persons, it seems no one reported her.'

'Not her parents? That's despicable.'

'It happens – child's a burden to a single mum, so she ignores the kid's absence and hopes she doesn't come back, that sort of thing. No one knows who the girl's parents are. She's going to be fragile. Kirsten's going to have to be very careful with her.'

'Do the carers know what's happened to her?'

'I dunno. Depends what she's said, I suppose. She's likely to have clammed up over it all, trying to shut out the memory. I didn't talk to them, didn't want to arouse any suspicions.'

15

KIRSTEN, MITCH AND I reached the house at ten thirty. It took an extra twenty minutes to get there via back roads and narrow lanes to shake off any tails we might have had. For the press, or worse, the abusers, to learn where Lou was being held would be a nightmare and a betrayal.

Lupus was along for the ride and human company, and Kirsten had shed her dour professional image for the day. She had exchanged her glasses for contact lenses, and her long red hair cascaded down her back, allowing her features to relax instead of being stretched and severe. The change that the release of her hair made was amazing; the professional woman had been replaced by a pretty girl with a kindly expression that a traumatised teenager was much more likely to trust.

Mitch delved in his bag and brought out a tiny microphone. He faced Kirsten as she opened the top button of her blouse and looked up past his head into an overhanging beech tree. He reached inside and clipped the microphone to her bra strap, stepped back and examined her from different angles. The mic was not completely hidden, so he adjusted its position and checked again. Not a word was spoken, he merely nodded his satisfaction and handed her a little black box, a transmitter, which she put in her bag.

This was interesting. Kirsten was showing a side of herself that I had not seen before. My impression of her had been of a prim lawyer, one who would never have allowed any man to put his fingers inside her blouse. Of course I knew little about her, but it was surprising how she accepted Mitch's intruding hands without a twitch of a muscle. It was doubtful there was anything romantic in their relationship, but there was certainly a degree of trust and understanding. Something from their past bound these two.

With Mrs Fothergill, the lady of the house, we walked around the garden, which was about an acre.

There was a massive oak in one corner with a branch that stretched out over the lawn about five metres up. The double swing that hung from it conjured a childish desire to relive the excitement of that long, sweeping travel as the ground rushed up at you only to recede as you strained to peak higher and higher. There was also a kids' climbing frame for younger ones, a trampoline, bird feeders, a couple of bug hotels and a hedgehog house. It was a peaceful spot and clearly designed to settle and calm fragile children, to direct their minds away from their troubles.

As we walked, Mrs F. told us what she knew about Lou, which didn't amount to any more than we knew already – she was abused. Kirsten had already explained to her who we were and why we were there. She told the carer she needed Lou to tell us as much of what happened to her as she could. She said the conversation was confidential as parts might be used in court. Would Mrs Fothergill kindly wait out of earshot? Reluctantly she agreed, but insisted on being allowed to watch in case Lou broke down.

Mitch and I went and sat in the car to absent the scene of men. Consequently, we didn't see the child we were listening to. Lupus limped around, sniffing the flowerbeds and tree trunks before lying down in the middle of the driveway.

Kirsten spent a long time gaining Lou's confidence, chatting generally. Then there was silence.

'It's failed,' I said.

Mitch shook his head. 'Nah. Wait a bit, she'll come back.'

'Are you sure?' I asked after ten minutes.

He removed his toothpick. 'She's switched it off. She's got to gain the child's confidence and trust before she can ask questions. How she does that is her business, I reckon. Relax.'

We fell into a silence that was suddenly broken by Kirsten's voice. 'Did you have your own room?'

Lou had been crying, and she sniffed frequently. 'No, we was all in one room. It were in the loft, right under the roof and had a little window. Only two could look out at once, so we took turns. We could see across the river. It were pretty, like. The river made me feel better – sometimes. One time I were looking out and there were a family having a picnic on the far side. I waved and waved. I were hoping they would see me and come and rescue us.'

'Did they see you?'

'One of the kids did. She waved back, but the rest didn't see. I felt really alone then.'

'How many of you were there? All girls?'

'Yeah. Four. There was me and Kitty, Liz and Rache. It were Kitty what got out with me. I dunno where she is now.'

'And what used to happen every day? What did you do?'

'They gave us books, but they was for little kids, like. Too young for us. Sometimes we heard the stairs creak, and we knew they wanted one of us, or even all of us if they had a party.' Lou sniffed and sobbed quietly. 'When they'd finished what they did, we had to go back to the room. Everyone would come around and hug and try to help.'

'Do you know the names of any of these men?'

'There was white guys and brown guys. The whites didn't use real names. Like, there was Dick and Tony. If there was more than one man in the room, then we heard names. There was a French bloke. I dunno his name, they called him Frenchie and he sounded foreign, like. They cheered when they watched. They said things like: "Dick the Prick" and "Tony ride your pony". There was one they called, Yee-Haw, 'cause that were what he shouted when he were finished.'

A long period elapsed when neither Kirsten nor Lou said anything, but we could clearly hear Lou's muffled crying. It sounded as if her head was buried in Kirsten's shoulder, right up against the microphone.

'This is awful.' Lou's words and tears hooked something inside me and worried it. Long-buried emotions began to stir.

Mitch ignored me; he was staring straight ahead, tight-lipped. I had the sense of a piece of elastic about to snap.

'Go on if you can. You're doing really well, Lou. What about the non-whites, did they give any names?'

Lou blew her nose. 'Yeah, but I don't remember, 'cause they were foreign – but you hear them names anywhere. All of them lot treated us rubbish, like. They slapped us and pushed us around. We was just meat to them. Some I saw only once, some came lots. There was a black man, his name was Aruba, he liked to have me face him, so I could see him gob on me.'

'Do you feel like telling me what they did to you? You don't have to, but it would be a help.'

At that point Kirsten switched off her mic again, and Mitch and I sat in an uncomfortable silence. God knows what he was thinking, but he had chewed his toothpick into a fibrous mess.

'You poor thing.' Kirsten was back with us. 'No one should have to go through that. You're being such a great help, Lou. Is there anything else you think might be of use so we can catch these awful men?'

'No. I don't think so.'

'Well, if you do remember something, will you tell Mrs Fothergill so I can come and hear, please?'

Lou didn't answer. I imagined she'd signalled agreement some other way.

Kirsten said, 'Do you like dogs?'

'Yeah. I'd really like to have a dog.'

'Wait here. I'll be back in a minute, okay?'

Kirsten appeared at the car, her lips set in a firm line. In spite of her limp, she usually moved with fluidity, but now she was stiff and tense. She wouldn't meet my eyes, but she gave Mitch a brief glance. A consoling remark from me was not going to help. Instead, I slipped a lead on Lupus and gave it to her. The pair of them limped back to the garden.

'Did he help?' I asked Kirsten when they returned.

'Yes. Lou was very taken with him and seems to have shed her memories for the time being. She actually smiled.'

Lupus has worked his magic on you too, hasn't he?

Kirsten folded down one part of the back seat so Lupus could come forward from the boot and be next to her. She spent the whole journey home stroking the dog. We were nearly there when she said, 'Andrew, up to now my job has been to act as your barrister should you face a charge of murder. You may well be correct in thinking that the criminals who killed Alex have connections with, or were, this abusive gang. And I agree that one way to ensure you are not charged is to show that they are responsible. To that end I would normally do everything in my power to see this gang face justice. Everything that does not threaten my position at the bar, that is. If I were to do something that constitutes a conflict of interest or something unethical, it will not only damage our case but will ruin my career as well.'

'I understand perfectly. Thank you.'

'I haven't finished,' she snapped. 'From now on, I will take the necessary precautions to ensure our case remains on track, but when it comes to nailing them for their abuse, nothing is going to stop me, nothing. I'm going to get those bastards.'

'You mustn't jeopardise your future for my sake. Keep everything above board.'

'I'll do my job as your barrister. Don't worry about that. But my career is my business. There's no point in pussyfooting around with this.'

Mitch said nothing, but his head gave a single, sharp, emphasising nod.

16

ON THE TUESDAY night Mitch had skulked in the bushes by the pool just off the road. From there he had a clear view of the driveway, the garage and the parking area. Any vehicle and its occupants arriving at Shalamar Gardens would have ended up recorded on his camera. But there were no visitors.

For a few hours on Wednesday, I was parked in a lane that led off the road opposite the gates to Shalamar and had equally poor luck. All I saw was a supermarket delivery van and the postman. But at least that showed there was someone in the house to receive the shopping. The question was: was the house permanently occupied to monitor the girls?

Mitch had some other job on Wednesday night, so I crept into the position by the pool instead. It was twilight until around nine o'clock at that time of year, so I had to be extremely careful not to be seen. Just after seven, a car slowed down on the road behind me. It turned into the entrance and paused while the huge iron gates opened with a momentary creak.

The black BMW X7 glided to a stop. It was a big car, an expensive car, and it suited the house perfectly. The angle it was parked at did not allow me to see the number plate, and the windows were darkened, so the occupants weren't visible either.

Four men stepped out. One stretched. They were all cheerful and enthusiastic. The two on the far side of the car were facing me and I got good shots of them, but those closest were facing away. The group moved off towards the house. As they gathered at the front door, one made an obscene gesture, and they all laughed. I got one good photo before the door closed behind them, in spite of my normally steady hands quivering with disgust.

What had that proved? Nothing, except that in 2019 those four men visited a house on the Thames named after a Pakistani World Heritage Site. My suspicions presumed their guilt, when actually I knew very little. We were going to have to get more solid evidence than that, and we would need Lou to identify those men, first through the photos and then in the flesh, if she could bring herself to do that.

'How'd you get on?' Mitch asked me the following morning.

'I've good shots of four South Asians, but we know there are also Brits, a French and an African involved. We need to stick at it until we've identified them. Are you up for it?'

'I'm in this for the long haul, mate. I go to sleep at night thinking of ways we can take justice into our own hands and make these bastards suffer.'

'The sight of that lot joking and making obscene gestures before they went in … If I could have shot them, I would have done.'

#

MITCH CALLED me late on Friday night after a day of no activity at Shalamar. 'Got some of the bastards, Andrew,' he said. 'All four were whites. Three Brits for sure, and I think one was French.'

'It's time to let Lou see the pictures, don't you think?'

'Yeah, let's talk it over with Kirsten. She knows the girl.'

Kirsten agreed. 'But only if we take Lupus with us. Lou calmed dramatically when she met him. The tension drained out of her. She smiled for the first time and cooed and laughed when she stroked him.'

'There's no way I'm leaving Lupus behind,' I replied. 'He's got cabin fever, so he'll love the day out.'

Mitch and I were in my car in the driveway of Lou's foster home again on Saturday listening to Kirsten's hidden mic.

'I want to show you some pictures, Lou,' Kirsten said. 'They're photos of men. I would like you to tell me if you recognise any of them, and if you know their names. These men may have hurt you, so I'll understand if you don't want to see them.'

Lou was strong, her voice steady. 'It's okay.'

Silence followed. In my mind I could see the young girl looking through the photos, but I couldn't imagine what was going through her head as she saw the faces of her torturers again.

'No, Lupus, you silly dog. You can't have it.' Lou had a smile in her voice. 'Lupus stuck his wet nose on the photo.'

'Lupus, lie down,' said Kirsten. 'Do you recognise any of them?'

'The white guys wore scary masks in the room, the others didn't bother. But I saw some of them outside once. Him, and him … this one. I don't know this one, but I never saw none of the whites without a mask.'

'Were there any others that you don't see here?'

'There was another white guy, he was big – he's not in this lot. And there was that black guy I told you about.'

'So you can't put names to faces? That's a pity, but never mind. You're doing really well, Lou. You still okay?'

'Mmmh. No, Lupus, stop it, you silly dog.'

'Lupus, lie down – good boy. It was very brave of you to escape, Lou. How did you do that?'

'There was me and Kitty. They finished with us and went to get a drink, they said. They didn't close the door. Kitty was hurt and crying – and me. I said we had to go. Kitty said they'd kill us if we was caught. I said that would be better than doing this again. I grabbed her hand and we ran. I dunno how, but we found a way out through the kitchen. The cook saw us and shouted, but we was gone. Then we was at the river, and Kitty can't swim, and it's a long way, and I didn't know if I could swim that far. So we ran to the side and there was a little river, not very wide. I pulled Kitty, but she was scared of the water, but I pulled and we both went in. It were cold, but it were only a few strokes to reach the other side, and anyways we could touch the bottom. Kitty was spitting and coughing, but I pulled her out and we hid in the bushes. We was sore, I remember feeling so sore while we was hiding there – and cold from the water. The men was searching the garden with torches, but they gave up and we ran again. I said it were better not to go to the house next house along, better to go down the road a bit. Some cars passed us, but I was scared one of them might be the men, so we hid every time. We walked all night. I dunno where, we was lost. It were cold, and we was wet at first. Then we met a milkman with one of those electric cart things. He caught us trying to nick a bottle 'cause we were hungry. Told us not to worry and gave 'em to us. He said he know a nice lady who would help, and brought us here.'

'Did you tell the police everything you've told me?'

'I haven't seen the cops. I reckon they don't know about us. They don't care neither. Any case, my dad said you can't trust 'em. He hated 'em, said it's best never to tell 'em anything. That was the last thing he said to me before he buggered off.'

'And your mum – what did she say?'

'Nothing. She don't talk to me, except to tell me what to do. She'd kick me out the house when she got a man. That's why I left and ended up here.'

'Brave girls,' I said.

Mitch only nodded. He didn't want to talk.

Kirsten's voice again: 'Do you remember which of the men in the photos was in the room with you that night?'

'Yeah. It were him … and him. I saw those tattoos on their arms.'

'You've done so well, Lou – is there anything else you can remember?'

'I told that nice lady, Alex. I told her all this before.'

'I know, Lou. Unfortunately Alex can't help anymore and her records are lost, so if you can remember, it will be really good.'

I clenched my teeth. Ten days ago, Alex was murdered. Every day since she had been in my dreams and thoughts. I was beginning to accept that the memories were all that was left of her; but now two people, one of whom I'd never seen, were talking of her, with Kirsten reminding me that 'Alex can't help anymore'. Innocent words, but they revived my pain.

Lou's voice again: 'There's something I forgot. I didn't see him that night, but when they was looking for us in their garden with torches, I heard the voice of the one that isn't in the photo.'

'The black man?'

'No, the other one. The one they called Yee-Haw.'

HE COULD probably have jumped in and out of the car by that stage, but I had been lifting Lupus to make sure he didn't injure himself. I put him in the back, but he immediately crawled forward so he could be next to Kirsten in the seat beside him.

'Don't you dare steal my dog from me,' I warned her.

It was the first time I heard her laugh. 'I wish I could.'

A break in the fast lane gave me a chance to accelerate and move out to pass a military convoy, which was travelling at a disciplined 50 m.p.h. 'The abusers are not necessarily the people running this. Some of those we photographed might be organisers, but the others are just clients, I reckon. It's most likely not the cook or the cleaners, it might be the owner of the house, but if so, he's running it remotely and there has to be a front man here. We need to identify him – or her.'

Mitch twisted so he could see Kirsten in the back. 'It's worth finding out whether the servants, and there must be a few in that big house, are in the UK legally. If they're not, they might give us a little information under the threat of deportation.'

'And who do the abusers pay?' said Kirsten. 'If we knew who they were, you could peek at their bank accounts, couldn't you, Mitch?'

'I couldn't, but I could incur a heavy debt and persuade a friend to do it. But first we have to identify them. I'll take the photos to my mate and see if any are on the police system.'

I moved into the left lane ahead of the leading army truck. 'That the whites used masks could mean the events were videoed. Is there a way to link these men to the videos – provided we could find them, of course? They'll be on the dark web, I suppose.'

'How do we distinguish these videos from the thousands of others out there?' Mitch said.

'The easiest line of enquiry might be the woman that procured the girls for the gang. We need to ask Lou what she knows about her. There's a number of avenues available to us. Kirsten, if you'll work with Lou, Mitch and I will continue to watch the house and follow any clients to try to identify them. What do you think?'

17

'LOU ESCAPED THROUGH the kitchen, implying the door to the outside was open or at least unlocked,' Mitch said.

'It's worth a try. The front door is certain to be locked.'

We were parked in the lane opposite the gates to Shalamar Gardens, in Mitch's little Audi, not the Beetle, nor the fictitious Porsche, and keeping watch.

He had suggested using my car, but I didn't want to. 'I might be being followed. I've seen a man doing nothing in random locations. It would be NiPetco keeping tabs on me if I'm right.'

The sun had gone and the light was beginning to fade on Saturday, one week after I had first met and hired Mitch. I was eating a cheese and salad sandwich and Mitch had a cheeseburger – it smelt horrible, but it was his upholstery absorbing the molecules. There wasn't much traffic. Over the previous hour, the odd car had gone past but none slowed to turn in.

'This one's got its flicker on.'

'It's the Bee-Em I saw last time.' I swallowed my last mouthful, checked that my phone was in my pocket and that Mitch's voice-activated microphone was securely clipped inside my shirt. 'I'll try to keep in touch.'

The gates squeaked closed behind the BMW. I ran across the road and clambered over the garden wall, which was not high. Creeping through the bushes until the pool was in sight, I was just in time to see the front door close. Following the channel from the pool towards the river, the side of the house and the kitchen windows were in clear view. A cook, dressed in traditional *shalwar kameez* topped with a Western white chef's hat, was facing away from me and preparing something on a central table. The door to the outside, which we'd hoped would be unlocked, was actually open, releasing an aroma of spices and a reek of frying onions.

Access was easy, but the cook was a problem. The only thing to do was wait and hope he was drawn away. But even if I got through the kitchen undetected, what lay on the other side? Where did the abusers gather? Was there a bar, for example? Where did the appalling acts take place? There were scores of questions, and the likelihood of finding answers to all of them was slim.

In the grand scheme of things, getting out of there armed with enough evidence to destroy this gang and see its members and clients put away for years would be ideal. It would also be great to rescue the poor kids held there and save them from a further night of hurt and degradation. But that goal had to take second place to bringing the gang to its knees and saving countless other vulnerable children from a terrible fate.

The cook stopped what he was doing and crossed to the stove. Come on, get out, go to the loo or something. But no, he lifted a lid and peered into a pot, gave the mixture a stir and dropped the lid back with a clang. He walked towards a door. Was he going? No, it was a pantry. I seized the chance.

Stainless steel counters and cupboards, stacks of plates and rows of utensils, glasses on overhead racks and pots on hooks – the place was more professional than domestic, and capable of catering for a large number of guests. Through that lot and past the pantry, I was at the door into the main part of the house – the entrance hall, probably – and hidden from the cook.

The man was sorting through stuff in the depths of the store, knocking jars and tins together and around, but no noise came from the other side of the hall door. The handle turned without a squeak. A crash, glass on tile, made me jump and I let go. The cook exclaimed in Punjabi or Urdu or something – probably swearing. He was going to be busy clearing up his mess, so I waited until I heard muttering and the chink of broken glass from the pantry before trying the door handle again.

'Mitch I'm through the kitchen and into the hall. It's dead quiet and dimly lit – no one in here. Here's the geography: as you come in the front door to the hallway, the kitchen is on your left – the north side of the house – and the staircase is in front of you. It leads up to a landing. I can't see anything up there at the moment. Directly opposite the front door and beyond the stairs are glass doors to the garden.'

My earpiece gave a clear, 'Roger.' Mitch was recording my report, because the information might be invaluable in the future.

'Next to the kitchen and overlooking the garden must be the dining room.'

No sound came from that door. I opened it a crack and listened – nothing. I opened it wider and peered around – nothing.

'It's empty with no preparations made for dinner, yet we know some men arrived in the BMW. The chef is preparing food, so they must eat upstairs. Perhaps there's a bar up there. I can't see this lot going without a drink during their sessions.'

'Me neither.'

'There's another door opposite – on the south side – I'll check that next.'

I was exposed in the hallway with nowhere to hide. The ground floor was the only escape route, so I needed to clear that before going upstairs. Once again I struggled to hear anything through the door opposite the dining room because of my thumping heart. Could Mitch hear it? Stop it. Cease these stupid, distracting thoughts and focus.

'Mitch, it's a huge lounge. It mirrors the dining room on the other side of the hall. It's clear. It also has wide glass doors leading to the garden – the whole side of the house facing the river is glass. The place is as silent as the grave, too quiet. I'm going for the stairs.'

'Roger.'

The stairs were a dangerous place to be. They were totally exposed, and there was nowhere to run. I took them as quickly as silence would allow. If these men were going to eat on the first floor, either the cook had to carry the food up the stairs, or …

'Mitch, there's got to be a dumb waiter, which means they'll eat above the kitchen. I know the food is still being prepared, so that room should be empty. I'll check it first.'

'Roger.'

The first-floor dining room was above the ground-floor one, and a dumb waiter was set in the back wall. In front of it was a long counter with several *bains-marie*. Red power lights were on as they heated, ready to accept the cook's best offering – a buffet of some sort.

'I'm on the first-floor landing. The north side of the house above the kitchen is clear. The stairs go on up from the landing to the loft room where Lou said the girls are held. There's no sound from anywhere, it's eerie. I'm going to check the room above the lounge next. A passage runs south behind it, leading to bedrooms, I suppose. I'm dreading catching these guys in the act. I don't want to see it.'

'Take it easy, Andrew. Don't get caught.'

In eliminating the rooms one by one from being the centre of iniquity, the tension I was feeling was rising exponentially as the odds of discovering evil behind the next door went up. Another careful listen, and at last voices and laughter could be heard.

My stomach was churning at the mere thought of what I had to do. 'Mitch, they're all together in the room above the lounge, which sounds like a bar, but I heard no kids. I'll have to wait if I'm to catch these bloody perverts in the act. I'm going to find somewhere to hide. I wish I knew what they're going to do next – do they eat first, do you think?'

'Dunno, Andrew. I tell you what, I'll go down the side of the house like you did and see what the chef's doing. That'll give us some idea.'

The only place on the landing I could see to hide was under the top flight of stairs. It wasn't ideal, but I would hear any activity: if the men crossed it to go and eat, for example, or if the children were brought down the stairs. It wasn't comfortable squatting there, but at least I was out of sight.

'Andrew,' my earpiece squawked, 'another car's arrived. One occupant. He's coming up to the front door now.'

A voice down in the hall elicited an unintelligible reply. Heavy, ponderous steps thumped up the stairs. Heels clicked across the landing to the bar. The door opened, noise escaped, and a greeting was called out. 'Hey, Yee-Haw, we've been waiting for you. Tony, give the man a Jack Daniels – double.'

I had to see who these men were and hear what they were saying. With the door cracked open and no reaction from inside, I slid my phone – camera set, flash off – into the opening and studied the screen. The lighting was dim, but five men were in a close group. Two had their backs to me, one was bent over looking at something on his trousers, and two faced me. It was a scene like any other from a bar and provided no incriminating evidence at all.

The men facing the door had their eyes fixed on the man opposite them. The door would have been visible but out of focus to them. All it would take would be a tiny quick move-ment of my phone to catch one's attention, a split second for him to shift focus, and I would be in trouble. But the photos were essential.

I crept back to my hideaway and waited.

'Andrew, I'm in position. The chef's still working away. I can't see any final preparations going on. I can see the dumb waiter from where I am, and he hasn't put anything into it since I've been here. There's another man in there too, now. He looks like a live waiter.' Mitch sniggered at some private thought.

Ten minutes later Mitch called again. 'The live waiter's leaving.'

Footfall resonated on the stairs below. The man reached the landing and I squeezed back into my corner. He didn't stop: his steps continued on up the stairs above me. He must have been summoned – so there was an internal communication system.

'Mitch, he's going up to the loft. This is where it begins.'

A FLIP-FLOP slapped on the wooden steps above my hiding place – the man, accompanied by the soft landing of bare feet. Was it two kids or three? One of them was whimpering. I gritted my teeth again.

The man turned at the foot of the stairs, passed within a metre of me under the flight, and headed down the passage. He was holding each child by the wrist, pulling them along, his hands brushing against his baggy *shalwar* trousers. The kids were wearing simple shifts – easy to remove. The girl on my side of him, from her low viewpoint, saw me crouching in the dark. Her eyes widened, her mouth opened. I held a finger to my lips and she quickly turned away, her pale hair flipping across her face.

Five steps and she couldn't help but look back. It was only a brief glance, but I caught a glint of tears in the passage light. It was a plea for help that clawed into the darkest corners of my subconscious, unearthing emotions I'd entombed for decades. Her desperation was tearing me apart. If these kids had to endure another night of horror when I could have rescued them, how would I live with myself?

What do you want me to do, Alex? I can stop the denigration and abuse in store for these children. I can engage in this single battle and win, but to do that will be to lose the war with this gang. They killed you to stop your investigation. I owe it to you to continue your fight. But if I do, these kids will have to be sacrificed to face this night on their own.

Watching them being dragged to … I couldn't even say it to myself, I wanted to retch.

There were two doors on the left of the passage and two on the right. The first left-hand door would probably lead to the room adjacent to the bar. Did those bastards have access from there, or would they come out and down the passage? They would move soon, and the girls would be waiting.

I couldn't do this, I could not leave those children to their fate.

The only weapons I had were a pocketknife and experience. I went after the trio: the scrawny man between two girls, not even teenagers, dragging them to a lifetime of ghastly memories. Moving more quickly, I caught them up before they reached the first door on the left. The child who had seen me glanced back. I stabbed a pointing finger at her. Don't, girl, whatever you do, don't turn your head. She quickly looked away.

He was smaller and lighter than me. With an arm round his throat, my little knife slid easily through his skin. That shut him up. The sight of the blade with a smear of his blood on it set him quivering. By the smell of it, he had just wet himself. I had nothing to immobilise him. There was only one way … Running him head first into a door frame worked admirably. He was down.

One child was wide eyed and had both hands up to her mouth. The other, the blonde one, was calmer, waiting for instructions.

'Come on, girls.' I grabbed their hands. The blonde one caught on quickly. She knew I was their saviour. Her damp fingers clamped mine with unyielding strength. The other was a chubby child. She stood rigid, undecided, with an uncontrollable shiver running through her. She looked away, couldn't meet my eyes when I put my face down to hers.

'Trust me, I'll get you out of here, but we must run. Don't make a sound.'

She wouldn't budge. Those men could come out of the bar at any moment. We had to move, but this waif might panic and scream if I tried to force her. Blondie had no qualms, though; she grabbed the girl's wrist and pulled hard, jerking her out of her trance. 'Come on, Rache, we gotta go.'

Down the stairs as fast as I dared with these two in tow, we turned to the front door. The cook was there. He was bent over, checking the contents of some bags, and didn't see us; but he was blocking the way out.

A fight with the cook with the two girls close by was too risky, so it had to be the garden. The patio doors were open, thank God. We ran. A shout behind; the cook had seen us. Suddenly the house erupted into life. Chaotic yelling. The hall was lit, and floodlights turned the night into day.

I pulled the kids sideways to the little channel that Lou had crossed to escape, aiming to go up it to the road, but figures were darting about at the front of the house.

Mitch was there somewhere. 'Mitch, I've got two girls. I'm going to take Lou's route out of here across the stream to the house next door.'

No reply. I tried again – silence.

I wanted to check the mic, but Blondie was gripping my right hand and Rache was in my left. If I let go of her she'd fall behind. But then we stumbled on the boat. I'd forgotten that – it was perfect.

Rache was mentally numb. She couldn't think for herself. She was so scared, and she wouldn't move unless told what to do. I coaxed her into the boat, but she stood shivering in the middle.

'Sit down, Rache.' Blondie untied the rope holding us to the bank and jumped in. She was switched on and brave, this one.

In the glare of the floodlights, dark silhouettes were running down the lawn towards us. The channel was too narrow for the oars to be shipped. The quickest way was for me to use the mooring rope to tow the dinghy down the channel to the river. I couldn't go faster than a trot, because the boat was dragging on the bank. Blondie saw the problem and pushed again and again to keep the boat off the shore. The men were gaining on us.

Open water. I literally dived into the boat, and the force of it shot the dinghy out into the current. Yelling and swearing came from the lawn. I shipped one oar; Blondie was wielding the other. It was too heavy for her and almost fell overboard. I rescued it, shipped it and rowed. I hadn't done this for donkey's years, but it came back. Somehow we held a reasonably straight course to the opposite bank while being carried downstream by the slow-moving river. If my mic had failed, I'd have to use my phone to call Mitch, but until we reached land I had to keep rowing.

Where the hell was Mitch? We'd had no contact since the girls appeared. He would have been outside the kitchen door when we got out of the house and the chase began. Was he all right? What went through his mind, and what was he doing? The girls and I were going to need help on the far bank, so I needed to know.

I was facing backwards. In front of me Rache sat shivering with her arms crossed over her chest. Her hair was in straggles over her face. She was a picture of misery. I felt compelled to put my arms around her, warm and comfort her, but I had to keep rowing. Instead, Blondie's arms huddled her close. She was impressive, that one. She had seen more trauma in her ten or eleven years than most adults see in a lifetime, but still she kept her head. Her eyes were alive and eager. She had seen the chance to escape and had swung her whole being into making it work and carrying her friend along with her.

Behind the girls, the house lights were brilliant. The muffled sound of an outboard motor springing to life carried across the river. The engine noise increased in pitch. Another boat was leaving the bank. Damn, where did they get that from?

'I'm Andrew. What's your name?'

'I'm Liz, and she's Rache.'

'You've done brilliantly, you two. But we're not out of danger yet. When we reach the other side, we're going to run across the field and get into the woods. There's a road on the other side of the wood and my friend will pick us up there. The trouble is those men have found another boat and are chasing us, so we'll have to run really fast to the wood.'

Hell! These two had no shoes.

'There's two more of us in there.' The voice was high pitched and echoed her exhaustion from hours of little sleep, misery and hopelessness.

'What?'

'Them's new girls. April and Judy are still there.'

'*Shit*. Oh God. There's nothing I can do about it. I'm sorry. We can't go back.' *Christ*, that's depressing. What's going to happen to them now?

We bumped into the bank. Liz scrambled past me and onto land. 'C'mon, Rache, quick.'

Rache was slower, but she moved on her own at least. I didn't want to bully her, but she had to pull a finger out or that bastard was going to catch us. In the dim light, there appeared to be only one man in the other boat, but it was already in mid stream, the engine was screaming and the wake was a visible white streak in the water.

'Okay, you two, let's go. Run as fast as you can for the trees.'

At last I had my hands free and could call Mitch. We were probably out of radio range, so I didn't bother with it and used my mobile phone, panting out my words on the run. 'I've got two kids. We're on the other side of the river. Bring the car round to the road that parallels the river. I know the area. There's a dirt car park for walkers about the same distance up the road from the bridge.'

'*Christ!*' was his answer.

Good man, Mitch – he didn't argue. It hadn't been our plan, but he knew the situation was a fait accompli, so to avoid compromising what was going on, the best thing to do was to follow instructions.

I kept Liz and Rache ahead of me, within my sight. Liz went down with a cry of pain. Rache kept running. Grabbing Liz's hand, I pulled her up. 'You okay?'

'Yeah. I trod on something sharp.'

'Can you keep going? We'll look at it later.'

'Yeah.'

Thirty metres ahead Rache went down, and stayed there.

The man had reached the bank.

'What's up?'

Rache didn't answer. Liz was still beside me. She grabbed Rache and hauled her to her feet. Off they went again, hand in hand. It would have been a pretty scene in daylight: two young girls tripping carefree through the meadow. But it was dark, they had every care in the world, and they were running scared, very scared.

The trees were just ahead of us, looming as a dark wall ahead – cover at last. The man was a fast-moving shadow. It was hard to tell distance, but he had certainly gained ground.

I had to get these kids to safety. Twenty metres in, the forest enveloped us in its familiar embrace. But it wasn't my accident that came back to me, it was a different flash of memory – that anti-poaching patrol in Kenya. Deep forest protecting poachers who had killed one of our men, versus wildlife rangers who could die protecting their wards. And here I was again with a hunter after me and my charges. Was he a killer too? I shook off the feeling; this was not a time for losing focus. A massive oak loomed above us. 'Liz, you two are going to hide up in this tree. I'll lift you up, then you help Rache, okay?'

'Cool, yeah.'

'Once you're up there, climb as high and out of sight as you can, and keep absolutely quiet. No talking, no crying, no nothing. Got it?'

'Got it. Let's go.'

Liz was easy to lift, and she scrambled onto the lowest branch. Rache was heavier, but I got a good grip under her arms and lifted her onto my shoulders. She stood and caught Liz's hands, and she was up.

'Not a sound, unless you hear my voice when I come looking for you. I'm going to lead that man away.'

I ran again towards the road. There was no need for stealth, I wanted him to follow me. Where had Mitch got to? It was about a five-mile trip down to the bridge from the house, across the river and then back up this side of it. How long would it take him? Would he find the parking area I was thinking of?

Undergrowth crunched and twigs cracked beneath my feet; bushes parted with rustling leaves. I needed to catch my breath: I hadn't run that distance that fast for a long time. Trying to breathe quietly so I could listen was difficult. He was making the same noises I was. Keep going.

Lights from passing cars flickered between the trees ahead of me. Where was I in relation to the car park, though? Was it north or south of me? The traffic was light, and in a lull the sound of coarse laughter came from my right. The parking area was about forty metres long. At the far end two cars had reversed up to the fence, and a circle of figures were grouped around the space between them. I went to say hello. Whoever they were, there would be security in their numbers.

Except my way was blocked.

His left arm dangled beside his leg, extending into a long blade, a machete, which glinted briefly in the lights of a passing car. There was something odd about his right arm, though. It seemed unnaturally thick beneath his sleeve. It was a strange detail to remember; what mattered more was the machete.

More laughter and some female giggles came from the group behind him. What the hell was I going to do? I had led him away from the girls, but I was now in trouble, and if I couldn't get out of this he would go back to find them. Where was Mitch? How long had it been since he left? Would he find this place immediately? What about those people over there? They had a party going, and there were enough of them. I couldn't expect them to take on Machete Man, but they could distract him.

The sounds from the group changed. Rhythmic grunts and the odd gasp, and I realised I'd stumbled into a dogging session – a couple of women were pleasuring men in public. One of them was faking an orgasm. Her oohs of pleasure ended with a scream of ecstasy. It was too distracting, Machete Man couldn't ignore it. He turned to see.

It was my turn to scream, and I did, as loud and piercing as I could make it. '*Aagh! Help, help.*'

Behind him, men moved to see what was going on. One came from the rear of the estate car, buckling his belt and zipping up his fly. He was burley, and he wasn't happy at being interrupted. 'What yer want? *Piss off.* 'Ere, he's got a bloody knife. 'E's a fucking terrorist.' He adopted a half-crouch, his left foot and shoulder leading, his left hand was open and raised, edge on to Machete Man. His right hand was open, palm upwards by his chest. He was going to get carved up if he tried anything. Karate was not going to immobilise that blade; it was too long.

Two men ducked down behind the nearer car, but the other two came into the open. 'Put that thing down. Careful, Charlie.'

'I can't stand fucking terrorists,' Charlie answered, and stepped forward.

I had to stoke this fire. 'He's trying to kill me. He chased me from the river.'

Machete Man was holding his blade out in front of him, turning from the men behind him to me and back again. The doggers were shouting at him to drop the knife. 'Call the cops,' someone said.

A woman's voice: 'I'll do it.'

Cars passed by, their lights sweeping across the scene, but none stopped.

Machete Man's head was switching from side to side as Charlie moved towards his right and I took another step forward on his left. The other men completed a semicircle round him. The open side was towards the woods, but he was going to be boxed in if he didn't move. If he lashed out, someone was going to be hurt. He thrust his blade forward at Charlie. It was a threat; it couldn't reach. While he faced away, I took a step. He whirled on me, but he was still too distant. The other men were moving in on him, but weren't keen on getting too close.

Behind Charlie, four anxious heads were watching over the top of the nearest car: the two other men and the women. One of the women was on the phone. 'Police. Hurry this is a fucking emergency … Hello, yeah, there's a fucking terrorist in the woods with a knife … We're on the road …'

It was background; the reality was in front of me.

Machete Man knew his greatest threat was Charlie. He faced him more than he did me, even though I was his target. *Come on.* His nerve had to crack soon.

More headlights approached at speed. They dazzled me, and the other cars and the women vanished in the glare. The car braked sharply and pulled into the area, skidding the last metre, dust drifting up in the lights. Machete Man was staring. He too had to be dazzled. It was too much for him; he was outnumbered. He broke and ran, vaulted the fence and vanished into the darkness of the wood.

It was Mitch. 'What the fuck is going on? What are you doing? Where are the girls?' He spat his toothpick out onto the ground.

'Just in time, Mitch. Thanks.' Then, to the big man, 'Thank you for that. Sorry for the interruption.'

Charlie laughed. 'That's all right, mate. I can start again, but some of the others might have lost the urge after that. Who was that fucker, anyway? Would have carved you up proper with that bloody great knife. Glad to help.'

MITCH AND I crept through the wood towards the river, struggling to be silent as twigs snapped underfoot and branches brushed on noisy jackets. My attempts to recognise something that would lead us to the oak where the girls were hiding were fruitless. Not a tree nor a bush nor a pattern in the vegetation was familiar. To shout to them would be stupid, because I had no idea where Machete Man had gone – back to his boat, or was he skulking around the wood, knowing the girls must be there alone as they hadn't been in the car park? We could go and see if his boat was still there, but that would waste time. We needed to get the kids out of there and to a place of safety.

Eventually I gave in. How loud to shout, how soft? There was no way to tell what was effective. 'Liz, Rache.'

'We're here.' Close, only thirty metres away. That was more luck than judgement. 'Mitch, these girls have no shoes. Will you carry one, please.'

His reply was a grunt of assent. He wasn't talking to me.

With Liz on his shoulders and Rache on mine we made it back to the parking area with no sign of Machete Man. The doggers had given up and gone, thank goodness, or we'd have had to shield the girls from their fun.

The car's hazards flashed as Mitch unlocked it. For a second the amber glow picked out the girls' two frightened tear-stained faces. I ushered them into the car. Liz scrambled across to the far side. Rache was hesitant. Should I pick her up and shove her in? Should I lean across her to do up her seat belt – imposing close male contact after all she's been through? Luckily, Liz leaned over and grabbed her wrist. 'Come on, Rache. Fix your seat belt.'

The wheels spun on the gravel as Mitch stomped on the accelerator. He remained silent, while I waited for the explosion. He fished in his cup holder and found a fresh toothpick. 'What the hell have you done?' he said quietly before his anger raised the volume. 'We weren't going to do this. What the hell are we going to do with these two?'

'Take them to Mrs F.'

'She won't be happy with that.'

'She'll accept it. Two more girls have been saved. She'll be glad of that.'

'I doubt it. Andrew, you've just stuffed our entire operation. Those blokes will bugger off out of that house and we'll never see them again. If the police raid the place they'll find nothing unless they call in forensics. We're back to square one, back where Alex began. You've just flushed all her good work down the drain, and the gang will vanish without a trace. Sorry, but you're an idiot.'

If I looked at it with a cold heart, he was right. He was also furious, and I had a pretty good idea why catching this gang meant so much to him, why he was prepared to sacrifice two young girls to save scores of them. But it was not the time to ask him about it.

A quick glance to the back confirmed the girls were not hearing us. 'I shall never be able to put her look of desperation from my mind, Mitch. She knew the horror that was facing her. Her face … she was pleading with me. I could not ignore that, I'm sorry.'

Mitch didn't reply.

I turned to the back seat. 'You're safe now. We'll take you to a good lady who will look after you. Lou is already there.'

Liz was taking things surprisingly calmly. Poor Rache sniffed. She had been robbed of a childhood, raped, abused and subjected to the night's frightening escape with no vision of a better future. She was terrified.

'Okay, Liz and Rache, we'll have you safe and in a nice house in about half an hour. Are you warm enough? Are you hungry?'

There was no reply, so I presumed they were all right.

Mitch descended into a sullen silence, chewing away at his toothpick. I debated whether he was right and I should have focused on gathering evidence and not given in to a cry for help. I had taken a few photos round the door of the bar, but all the excitement had put it from my mind. As I picked up my phone, it rang. It was Kirsten. 'Andrew, where are you?'

'With Mitch, approaching Mrs F.'s.' I gave her a brief run-down on why.

She listened in silence and didn't comment, until: 'The police are looking for you for further questioning. There's new evidence, apparently.'

New evidence? Had another lie been conjured up to incriminate me? Would NiPetco ever give up and let me go? Am I going to have keep running for the rest of my life – forever?

IT WAS late, but Mrs Fothergill put some sausages and chips on to cook when she saw who we'd brought her. The smell of food had a visible and positive effect on Liz and Rache, who must have been starving. Mrs F. was clearly not happy about having more children, but she put her objections to the side and fussed over them. She called Lou into the kitchen. The young girl stopped at the door and looked warily at Mitch and me, ready to run. It was only a moment's hesitation, before she recognised the latest arrivals and rushed forward. The three broke down with little squeals and hugged each other in a tight group in the corner. Tears were streaming down their cheeks.

'You shouldn't do this,' Mrs F. said. 'What I do isn't strictly legal, but I do it because I care and the girls will live better with me than in some random foster home. I can't take any more, though. You're not going to bring any more are you?'

'No, I don't think so,' I said, knowing there were two more kids who needed help, although we had no idea where they were.

'So what she's doing isn't legal?' I asked when we were back in Mitch's car.

'No. She's supposed to report every child to the local authority so they can make sure standards are maintained. She probably didn't know she had to when she started, but she knows now, which is why she's nervous. We don't want her to report these kids, though, because that will put a spotlight on our activities.'

18

WE WERE STILL sitting in the expansive drive of Mrs Fothergill's house while Mitch fiddled with messages on his phone. What did her husband do? They obviously had pots of money to be able to afford this place and look after damaged children without official support.

I still had not looked at the photos from the Shalamar bar, but my phone rang before I could open the gallery. Mitch had started the engine. At the ring, he grumped something and switched off.

Out of the car, the gravel crunched under my feet. The birds had fallen silent long ago, but a subdued sound of traffic came from far away. A gentle breeze dropped the temperature and made gale-like noises into my microphone.

It was Hymie. 'Andrew, I hope you're well.' Oily little bugger. There was only one reason he wished me good health. 'We wanted to reach out to you with an improved offer.'

My eighty-five-year-old mind could not resist this opportunity to voice one of my pet hates. 'Hymie, why use a phrase like "reach out to you" when you could use a single, established word like "contact" or "make" me an improved offer? I cannot see the point in modern usage when it makes for longer speech. Never mind. You don't get it, do you? I'm not interested. I value my freedom, I don't wish to be a guinea pig, an object of experimentation, a research animal. I'm a free human and intend to stay that way. You can improve your offer any way you want, but money isn't going to change my mind.'

'Nigel says everyone has their price—'

'I bet he does.'

'This is not about money, Andrew; not much anyway. Please can we meet, just you and me alone somewhere, out of the public eye for your sake.'

'Why would that be? For my sake, I mean.'

'Because the police are looking for you. I suggest you meet me. There'll be no funny business, no Amy, no heavy-handed tactics. You have my word.'

Thanks for that reassurance, Hymie. A sudden warm and fuzzy feeling of confidence overwhelmed me. 'All right. You have somewhere in mind?'

Mitch dropped me off at the pub, a place which was new to me. I'd get a cab home. It was still drinking time when I arrived but the place was half empty. One glance was enough to see it needed a refurbishment and bar staff with more life and cheer than the current lot.

Maybe I was feeling self-conscious, but it seemed that, when I opened the door, what people there were all looked up and heads turned, not just to a new arrival, but to *me* specifically. I wished I had a hat to put on; having been on TV before, I didn't want the world to know I was there.

Hymie was sitting at a table in a secluded corner. I don't like having my back to the room, but on this occasion, facing the lawyer and the wall, I was less likely to be recognised. Hymie ordered a beer for me and a gin and tonic for himself.

'We – well, Nigel, actually, has upped his offer, Andrew – by fifty percent! That's now seven hundred and fifty thousand a year. I thought Don was going to have a fit when he heard.'

'I can believe that. I don't think Don has much of a sense of humour.'

Hymie sniggered. 'The Americans take money very seri-ously.' He leant over and tapped my arm. 'Unlike us Brits. In return you would need to sign a non-disclosure agreement. You must never tell anyone about the deal – ever.'

'Fair enough, but it still doesn't change my mind.'

Hymie took a deep breath and reached across the table again. I moved my hand out of the way. 'Andrew, you do know the police have a warrant for your arrest, don't you? You do know why that is?'

'*Arrest?* No. I know they want to speak to me, but that's no surprise, I've been waiting for it.'

'They've found a blue jacket of yours. It's covered in your partner's blood.'

Oh shit ... I stared at him, my brain frozen. 'Hymie this is a stitch-up and you know it. You know perfectly well I did not murder Alex.'

'I was coming to that. Nigel, Don, Paul and I can provide you with an alibi – we all met at our labs, you couldn't pos-sibly have done it. Of course, you would have to agree to Nigel's terms.'

'Of course.' You bloody shits. Alternatives refused to enter my mind. 'And if I don't, and take my chances?'

'Your own jacket, covered in her blood, no alibi for the time of death, and your car is there at your house. I predict a grim future, Andrew.'

'At least I won't have to be a human guinea pig.'

'You might be admitted to the prison hospital at some stage, where you would be in the hands of some excellent medical professionals. It's a possibility – just saying.'

'So you're telling me that whatever choice I make, I'm facing a life as an experimental animal. I can either do that while imprisoned in luxury, or I can serve twenty years or more in a prison being beaten up and hospitalised at your will?'

'I wouldn't put it as crudely as that, Andrew.'

'Is there any other way?'

'Well?'

There was nothing else to say to Hymie at that stage. They had me. There was a positive element to being their prisoner, though: if I succumbed, the press wouldn't be able to hound me as they had been doing. Their numbers had dropped in the previous few days as they'd found something more juicy on which to concoct a story, but some had been persistent, even sleeping in their cars outside my house and rushing to my door at the slightest sign of movement.

'So, effectively, you're going to jail me in that sterile, soulless room in your laboratory for what could be years.'

Hymie gave a confident scoff. 'No, not at all. We decided you'd be more comfortable, and therefore happier in the company house than in the lab in town. We don't know for how long you'll be a guest, and you could eventually see the room at the lab as a prison. That wouldn't be good for the cooperation we'd like to have with you.'

'Bloody right, it wouldn't.

I needed to speak to Kirsten and felt for my phone. It had gone. All my other pockets … no, no phone. *Damn*, I'd left it on the floor of Mitch's car. I'd put it there as I got back in after talking to this slimy creep beside me. Suddenly the need to contact Kirsten assumed an even greater importance, but even supposing that he lent me his phone, I couldn't do it with Hymie listening.

'I'll cooperate on one condition.'

The friendly half-smile that had been on Hymie's face throughout this meeting was switched off. He no longer needed to be nice to me. He'd won and was now in control. 'What?'

'My dog stays with me.'

NOW THAT I had agreed to NiPetco's terms, Hymie was not going to let me out of his sight. He drove me directly to the company 'safe house', as he termed the mansion at whose vast ornate iron gates we stopped. Hymie accelerated through as a guard waved from behind the gatehouse window.

Gravel crunched under the tyres. The car entered a dark tunnel of chestnut trees that loomed into being in the headlights, trunk after threatening trunk. A dark tunnel to match my frame of mind. A metaphor for my perception of being carried to my doom, of being imprisoned, of being under the control of another, strapped helpless to a lab table as white-coated beings sliced through skin and muscle to access my vital organs, paring off slivers of liver and kidney and spleen and heart and lung for examination under an electron microscope.

Ridiculous.

My black mood encompassed more than those fantasies, though. Alex's murder had provoked an anger that had been dominating my thoughts for days. My desire to hunt down the killer, to avenge her and so prove my own innocence, had pushed her actual loss into the wings of my mind. The grief was still real, though, even if suppressed.

For the time being, while I was powerless to resist Ni-Petco, my imprisonment would prevent any chance of finding out who killed her, so my thoughts were free to turn to the ghastly nature of her death and my future without her.

As the lights of the house came into view at the end of the long driveway, I pulled myself together. It was important to shed these depressing imaginings and focus on resistance. I would only endure this as long as the killer had not been identified.

'Who owns this place – Nigel?'

'NiPetco. All company execs stay here when they visit, as do guests, and the house is used as a conference centre as well. You'll see many different people while you're here.'

'I presume I don't need anything from home – you've provided a full wardrobe as you did before?'

'Of course.'

Smug bastard. 'Laptop? The contents of my office?'

'It's all here.'

'That's a bit presumptuous. Supposing I hadn't agreed?'

'In the highly unlikely scenario where you wouldn't agree, we would have returned it all.'

'What about my dog?'

'He proved to be a problem. None of our people could get near him. They had to lure him into the garden and shut him out, but they couldn't bring him here.'

'Of course not, he'll rip you to shreds. How are you going to get him here?'

'The first thing we'll do is have you sign the agreement. As soon as that's done, I'll contact the police and substantiate your whereabouts at the time of the murder. That will take the heat off, and we – you and I – will go and collect your dog and anything else you need. That okay with you, Andrew?'

Once again, I'd been violated – my house invaded, my property removed, secrets investigated. Nothing would have been stolen, but some git had the opportunity to see into the very core of my life – it was galling.

'Hymie, I need to make a call. I think I left my phone in a friend's car.'

'Of course.' Hymie showed his phone his face, and handed the instrument to me. 'Careful what you say.'

I have a good memory for numbers, and Mitch answered on the third ring. I asked him to post the phone through my letterbox and forestalled any questions by hanging up.

The interior of the mansion had probably not been altered, bar refurbishment, since it was built in early Georgian times. As soon as we passed through the front door, we turned right into the library. Sky-blue walls held paintings of important people, valuable horses and landscapes in every available space. A wide stone fireplace dominated the room. Tall, deep-set windows faced it, and bookshelves stretched to the high and ornate ceiling. My shoes squeaked on the wooden floor and padded silently over oriental carpets. A massive leather-inlaid desk, bare except for a thin document placed precisely halfway along the top and two inches back from the edge awaited me. A gold Meisterstück pen – the same one as before? – lay beside it, inviting me to sign immediately.

The room was heavy and depressing – it matched my mood, and I wasn't going to even lift the pen until I'd gone through the contract with a very suspicious eye. I was halfway down the first page when Nigel and Don came in.

There was no doubt in my mind that the child trafficking gang were responsible for Alex's murder, but NiPetco definitely had something to do with it, because my car was at home when I arrived, and they took its keys when they abducted me. Then there were the witnesses they could manipulate, their retracted statements and the alibi now offered to me. Did that mean that someone in the company – maybe even one of the unholy alliance who had just walked in – was involved in child abuse?

A close eye had to be kept on this pair to see if they showed any reaction to the commotion at Shalamar earlier. All the perverts had probably got the hell out of the place as soon as the girls and I had got away. If whoever it was didn't already know, he would eventually hear about Machete Man chasing and confronting me. Would he realise who it was that had ruined his night after he heard Machete Man's description of me?

'Hi there, Duncan. Glad to see you're aboard.'

Why did Nigel get up my nose so easily? There was nothing unusual in his manner, it was as obnoxious as ever. 'Hello, Nige. The name's Andrew.'

'Yeah. You just add your mark to that paper, and we can all relax tonight and get started tomorrow.'

I ignored him and Don, who hadn't done anything but issue a cold stare, and went back to studying the contract. Hymie and Nigel relaxed in some comfortable chairs that were clustered near the fireplace, while Don remained standing, leaning on the mantelpiece and glaring at me. I found it difficult to concentrate with Pettigrew and his cohorts in the room and had to read some passages twice to determine whether the meaning in plain sight was the full meaning. I picked up the pen and noticed Hymie looking over to see how

I was doing. I kept him on the hook and spent some time admiring the instrument, before aligning the paper to sign my life away.

LUPUS LEAPT on me at first sight, almost flattening me. I staggered backwards and bumped into Hymie. The dog slapped a tongue on my face before dropping to the floor.

'Wow,' said Hymie. 'That's some dog.' He put his hand out, but quickly retracted it at Lupus's snarl.

Mitch had been as good as his word in dropping my phone through the letterbox. Gathering Lupus's lead and harness, I was ready to return to the mansion. Hymie opened the tailgate of his Range Rover and Lupus jumped in without apparent effort in spite of his weak leg. We were off for a life in captivity. Not an inspiring thought.

As we left my gate and turned onto the lane, a figure stepped back off the pavement to merge with the bushes. It was a casual, natural movement, not a hurried I'm-about-to-be-discovered one. I had taken no notice the first time I saw him, but second time, late at night? It was not going to be the press at eleven o'clock, that was certain. Who, then?

'*Christ!*' Hymie, who was Jewish, lowered his window and a rush of cool fresh air drove out Lupus's noxious fart.

I struggled not to laugh. Lupus one, NiPetco nil. 'You've had him cooped up in the house too long.'

Once back in the mansion, I was directed to my room, which was as luxurious as the one at the laboratory. I was now free to come and go, however, and took Lupus out for the last time before we settled down for the night. He was moving with a pronounced limp, but did not appear to be in pain and had boundless enthusiasm.

The air in the garden was cool, and hinted of some flower or another. The only sounds were those of the gentle breeze through the trees and the subdued noise of distant traffic.

Under the agreement, I was allowed to live a normal life. In their warped terms, that meant staying on the property while they conducted their research, and then to be available at all times for the rest of my life, or until NiPetco had finished with me. To present a front of normality, I was allowed to talk to whomever I wanted, but the confidentiality of the project had to be maintained.

I was itching to talk to Kirsten in spite of the lateness. 'I'm sorry to call you at this time, but I don't know what other opportunity I'll have.'

'You woke me,' she grumbled.

I gave her a complete summary of what had happened. 'So I've traded my life for my freedom.'

'That's a pity, because it wasn't necessary.'

'What do you mean? The evidence against me is almost overwhelming.'

'Almost, Andrew, only almost. Look at this objectively. Lupus would never bite you—'

'He might, to protect Alex.'

'I can't say, but you're right; a jury could not discount that possibility. But – and it's a big but – you have no teeth marks, not even a bruise, which would certainly have shown had he got your arm. And the jacket sleeve has been torn off below the right elbow. We know Lupus tore the jacket, because the fragment found in his mouth matches it. So either he ripped the sleeve off, in which case the damage to someone's arm must be extensive, or it was done later by the culprit to get rid of his own blood.

'Unfortunately – and this does count against you – there is no sign of any third-party involvement whatsoever. The blood drops on the stairs were Alex's, perhaps dripping off the killer's hand.'

'Exactly. The case against me is too strong, only the NiPetco alibi is protecting me.'

'No, it isn't. There's enough uncertainty to protect you from a guilty verdict. You need to find that right sleeve, or a man with an injured right arm.'

'I'm not worried about a trial, I'm desperate to avoid arrest, because I won't be able to find this murderer or the gang of paedophiles if I'm stuck in a cell.'

'It won't come to that. I'm sorry, but NiPetco have conned you, Andrew.'

'*Shit.* The bastards.'

'What's going to happen to you now?'

'I don't know. They're going to take samples, and then I suppose I wait around until they've reached some conclusion before giving more samples. I have to admit that I'm very uncomfortable with it.'

'Good luck. Ring me every day so I know you're still okay. They can't do much to you for some time, as you must be available to the police until this case is closed. And that won't happen until they find the murderer.'

'Thanks. That's a positive thought.'

'Goodnight, Andrew.'

A supreme effort of will stopped me hurling my phone at the ground. Bloody Hymie, bloody Nigel, Don, the whole scheming lot of them. They had tricked me into that agreement with false information. They had conned me into signing my life away for no good reason. They can go to hell, I will *not* uphold my side of the deal.

As I put the phone away, I suddenly remembered I hadn't spoken to Hermione for a while and didn't know how she was. Had she had her baby?

Why did that concern me? After all, now that Alex had gone, any contact with Hermione was going to dwindle, especially with Mark's attitude towards me.

On one hand, it would be no bad thing. Hermione would be a constant reminder of what I had lost. She would unwittingly prolong my grief, so it would be best to sever the connection as soon as I decently could. Failing that, I would drift away from the couple as I had from so many other people in the last fifty years; sometimes it had been deliberate, sometimes life had simply moved on.

Alternatively, if I maintained a firm link with Hermione, would I not feel better? After all, she was grieving too, and Mark was being of no help to her whatsoever.

Again, why did this concern me? Did my rescue of Liz and Rache have something to do with it? Did the pitiful state of those children take me back to Saffron's struggle to stay alive? Did it rekindle the empathy I'd rejected after she'd gone?

I also had a need to convince Mark of my innocence. I didn't know why, really, because what he thought was of no importance, but I didn't want Hermione to always be suspicious of me. It was too late to call that night, though.

19

A NEW DAWN. Both Lupus and I needed exercise, so we headed outside at five thirty with the intention of walking round the perimeter of the estate, which was about three miles.

The property was defined by a brick and flint wall, capped with half-round bricks and two strands of electric fence. It was about two metres high, too tall to see over without jumping. With the exception of the main, trade and two other gates, it was unbroken.

A herd of roe deer watched with wary eyes as Lupus trotted comfortably beside me. He took more than a passing interest in them, but after a couple of strict words he smothered his killer instinct.

We came to an oak with a heavy branch reaching across the wall and over the adjacent land, whatever that was. Pretending my shoelace had come loose, I knelt to fix it and tighten the other, resisting the urge to wave hello at the CCTV camera that was fixed to the tree and pointing along the wall.

Half an hour later I was good for a shower and breakfast. Lupus's leg had stood up well. We would run the course on Monday if I wasn't on the operating table.

Breakfast was served in typical hotel style: a buffet of juices, fruit, yoghurts, cereals, breads and preserves, with the main course ordered from a menu. There was only one large table, and the sole occupant was Paul, NiPetco's biologist, the man who was eager to experiment on me.

'Good morning.'

My greeting sounded cold to me, but Paul gave no sign he was put out. Instead, he gave me a pleasant nod as his mouth was evidently full. He swallowed and sipped some coffee. 'Good morning. Settled in comfortably?'

It was the first time I'd heard him speak. He had a quiet voice that didn't match his sinister and clinical appearance. I wasn't sure what I expected, but a warm, plummy accent was not it. He was a biologist not an executive in finance or law or marketing. He was someone I was more likely to relate to. My bubble of anger had developed a slow puncture.

Once I'd armed myself with a coffee and a yoghurt, he swallowed, put his knife and fork down and smiled. It wasn't the sinister smirk I'd expected, either. My preconceptions were wrong, and I needed to stop making assumptions based on appearance.

'What do you have in store for me today?'

'The first thing we'll do is give you a thorough medical examination. As a professional pilot, you will have undergone similar procedures before. We'll also take a blood sample for an initial test of your DNA. That will be all for today. All over by lunchtime – a very relaxing start for you.'

'I imagine I'm going to get extremely bored in here.'

Paul raised his eyebrows and smiled. 'You deserve to know everything about your future while you're here, the protocols we follow, the samples we need from you and why we need them – everything. In that light, I'd like to add to Hymie's rather simplistic explanation of ageing, delivered when we last met. He only dwelt on the role of telomeres, which is easy to explain, but there is another, much more complex theory, than that. We think ageing is a result of unrepaired natural damage to DNA – damage meaning that the result is an abnormal structure. DNA suffers hundreds of thousands of lesions every day. Some are natural, some are the result of external influence from mutagens which change the DNA sequence. Many things can be mutagens, such as X-rays, UV light, oxidising agents, and so on. Natural damage to DNA comes from normal cellular activity, and most of it is repaired through normal processes. Some damage remains, however, and accumulates with age, resulting in the dysfunction of cells – a significant cause of ageing. Simply put, deficient DNA repair increases ageing, while increased repair reduces it.'

'I understand.'

Paul took another bite of bacon and made a face. 'Cold.' He pushed his plate to one side. 'You may be gifted with a perfect DNA repair mechanism, which would mean you have not accumulated any damage since you were thirty-four. But I think there's more to it than that. I want to see precisely what it takes to break down your DNA, then see if I can build it up again.'

'Invasive?'

He laughed. 'No, not at all. All done in the lab. The worst I'll do is take a tissue sample.'

Could I believe him? On the face of it, he seemed the most genuine of all those I'd met there.

PAUL WAS true to his word. The initial examination was carried out in a sterile room that smelt of disinfectant and gleamed with newness. In glass-fronted cabinets and on open shelves every drug (NiPetco's naturally) and item of medical equipment known to man was available for your modern doctor's use. Except that the practitioner was an ancient physician named Arthur. He must have been almost as old as I was.

Unfortunately for Arthur, he reminded me of the treacherous Dr Smythe, my doctor for so many years who, I believe, betrayed me to fund his gambling and alcohol consumption. It was unfair to take my anger out on Arthur, but he got no more than monosyllabic responses to his questions.

He doddered about, but he pushed and poked in all the right places, muttering to himself as he did so. I've undergone scores of aviation medicals, at least one every year over fifty years or so, so this was very much a non-event for me. In addition to the usual physical assessment, I had a lung function test, a chest X-ray, an ECG, a colour perception test, eyesight and hearing. A number of blood samples were taken for various things like cholesterol, liver function and so on. It took almost the whole morning, and I felt I deserved my lunch.

They were all there when I entered the dining room, grouped around the short bar counter. Nigel, the chief operating officer who threw his considerable weight around; Don, the chief financial officer who made no attempt to disguise his dislike of me; Hymie, NiPetco's slimy legal adviser; and lastly, Paul, the mild biologist. Nigel appeared to be the only one taking alcohol, the others had juice or water or, in Don's case, a Coke. At the sight of them, my appetite evaporated. The last thing I felt like was joining this lot for a meal.

A waiter was standing to one side by the window. 'Can I order lunch in my room?'

'Yessir. That's no problem at all. We have room service, or I can take your order now.'

'I'll ring down. Thank you.' Why was an American a waiter in an English country house? Was he a normal person working in the country, or had NiPetco imported him? I turned to go, but Nigel saw me.

'Hey there, Duncan. How did it go today?'

'It's Andrew, not Duncan.'

'Yeah. Don't know why I cain't get that right. You okay, though, buddy?' He put a big paw on my shoulder and squeezed. I dropped out of his grip and swept his hand away with my arm in what he could construe as a casual removal or a combative one. He was probably too thick-skinned to be offended anyway. His problem, not mine.

The interesting thing was, there had not been the slightest sign from Nigel that would indicate he knew about the girls' rescue on Saturday night. So if he was involved in the abuse, at least he didn't suspect me.

Don was watching me over the top of his Coke, but that was normal. I didn't see it when his attention was elsewhere, but a nervous tic developed below his left eye when he looked at me. I couldn't have cared less that he didn't like me, but I failed to understand why he was so hostile when we had barely exchanged ten words with each other. Surely my sarcasm on the first night was insufficient reason. It had to be something else.

Nigel raised his hand to my shoulder again, but stopped short of touching me. 'You wanna drink? Thirsty work, these medicals.'

'I was going to eat in my room.'

'Shit, no. You're part of the team here now. The burgers are tops. You wanna burger?'

'No, I'll just help myself to salad.'

'Salad? Jeez!'

I broke away to look at the buffet. Paul joined me. 'Just a spot of friendly advice, Andrew. Not a good idea to piss him off. He can be quite unpleasant at times.'

'So can I. But thanks.'

I turned back to the group.

As I walked over to them, a trigger was fingered in my mind. What was in front of me was a familiar scene, or at least one reminiscent of something I'd seen before. I couldn't assemble the entire picture sufficiently to remember what I was looking at, though. Maybe it was a case of déjà vu.

THE FOOD in the house was excellent, and the desire to eat too much was a personal battle that had to be fought. Reluctantly, I skipped the dessert.

I needed help from Mitch, but my phone was on charge in my room. With it in hand, I collected Lupus and walked round the garden out of range of any microphones. There was a statue of the goddess Diana with a sighthound in attendance. It stood above a fountain whose pool was about five metres across. I strolled around it counting the loose change in the water while waiting for him to answer the phone. This bunch were a tight-fisted lot: there were only about ten coins on the bottom, and most of those were coppers. The call went to voicemail.

I didn't want to leave a message so I tried Kirsten instead. 'Hello,' she answered. 'What's happening? Are you all right?'

'Physically, I'm fine, but I'm seriously annoyed about being conned into signing that agreement. As far as I'm concerned that makes it null and void, obtained under false pretences – you'll know the correct terms.'

'What concerns me is that with you in there, you're not working on this gang of paedophiles, and Mitch has other work that prevents him devoting any more time to it. He's away at the moment.'

'I'm very conscious of our lack of progress, and I need to get out of here. I didn't know Mitch was away. Will you help me if I ring at some ungodly hour?'

'Of course.'

Lupus was sniffing at something in the bushes, but followed when I walked back to the house. As we reached the edge of the driveway, a small white van pulled up about twenty metres away and a man stepped out. He didn't appear to have seen the dog and nodded a greeting to me.

Lupus snarled and started forward. The man froze. I couldn't see his face, because of the black baseball cap pulled low in the front, and his attention was entirely fixed on the dog. Slowly, he backed three paces towards the van door.

'Lupus, *down!*'

The dog stopped but was growling, his lip quivering and curled to show the yellow-white of his teeth. His urge to attack was dominating the interplay between us.

The man backed further away. His right hand was gripping the front of his overall at chest height; his left stabbed out towards Lupus for a second before he hastily withdrew it. 'Hey man, control that dog.'

CA Sole

I took a step forward. Lupus, menacing and growling, was with me. 'He's under control. Don't worry.'

'Why your dog want to bite me?'

'I've no idea. Maybe he knows you don't like dogs.'

'Hey there, buddy.' Nigel was standing on the top step and waving. 'I was looking for you.'

The man had reached his van. He wouldn't take his eyes off Lupus and felt around behind him for the door handle, which he opened with his left hand and then dived in. With the window down a little, he called through the gap, 'Control that dog, man. He bloody dangerous.' His clutch gripped with a jerk, and the wheels sprayed gravel.

Whatever it was he came for would have to wait for another time. 'You're a good boy, Lupus.'

He grumbled a bit and relaxed, but neither of us took our eyes off the departing van. I made a mental note of its number.

Nigel had gone back inside. He was in the entrance hall scrolling through messages on his phone when I found him and gave him a questioning look. His blue eyes were blank. 'Yeah?'

'You said you were looking for me.'

'I did? Goddam, I plain forgot. Straight out my head … Dunno, Duncan, dunno.' He laughed at his own stupidity.

'Less than a minute ago,' I said.

20

THEY DIDN'T NEED me the following day, so I spent it by going for my run, then took some time browsing the library and looking around the house. Keeping busy was important. With too much idle time on my hands, my thoughts would inevitably drift to Alex. Although natural, that route was a distraction, for the focus had to be kept on finding her killer. I transferred the photos from my phone to my computer to get bigger images, and studied them.

'*You bastard.* I knew it. It's not conclusive, but I've got you.'

Ever since I'd been there, I'd been trying to spot cameras in my room but I couldn't find any. It was a different matter in the public rooms: every one was covered comprehensively. What I couldn't work out was why they gave me so much freedom. I was allowed to roam the grounds and the house itself without restriction. There were cameras everywhere, so they knew what I was up to, but they didn't seem worried. It was all too innocent. Were they relying on my fear of arrest if I escaped and they retracted their alibi? Surely not.

MY ROOM was on the first floor, next to the one directly over the front porch. Below the window level, a narrow horizontal ridge of decorative brickwork ran around the house. It gave me an idea, but it wouldn't help Lupus.

Like any luxury hotel, there were an unnecessarily large number of pillows of various sizes for the bed. With my little pocketknife I cut five holes in the largest one. Lupus clearly thought I was daft. He let me fit him into the pillowcase with his legs through the little holes, his tail out of a hole in the closed end, and his head sticking out of the open end. Another slit over the middle of his back took the end of a sheet through it. My thirty-kilogram dog could be lifted off the floor in perfect balance, although he didn't look too happy about it.

At a little after three the next morning, I dressed Lupus in his makeshift harness and tied my two sheets together. He was completely trusting and fearless and hung over the drop outside the window as I let him down hand over hand. He didn't quite reach the ground, but even with his damaged shoulder he dropped the last few feet without hurt.

It's actually pathetic how reliant we've become on technology. Thirty years ago laptops had only just been invented, but I was going to be useless if I didn't have mine with me. Probably for their own convenience, NiPetco had brought my computer and office stuff in my laptop backpack, which made it easy for me to carry.

A quick glance to check that I had everything I needed, and I followed Lupus out of the window, which is where it got tricky. I could just get the ball of my foot on the ledge, which was better than a toehold, but there was a five-metre traverse to get above the porch roof. The plus of this hazard-ous route was that, unlike the interior of the house, there were no CCTV cameras.

Inch by inch, facing the wall, I crept left, keeping fingers on the brickwork round my window to aid my balance. In climbing, a vertical face is effectively an overhang, as one's body, by virtue of its bulk, is further over the void than the feet. The weight of the backpack increased my constant feeling of toppling backwards, with only my finger-hold giving reassurance – until the reach of my right arm ran out. There was a foot to go before I could grip the bricks of the next window with my left hand. Head sideways, cheek against the wall, I kept my breathing shallow. To expand my chest a micron too much would have tipped my balance.

The corner of the next window-surround appeared under my fingertips. Another few inches left and I had a better grip. I didn't know who was in that room, but they should have been asleep at that hour. The edge of the porch roof was below me. A little further and I was able to let myself down to its apex, where I took several deep breaths.

On the ground, I freed Lupus from his white jacket and bundled up the pillowcase. Tucking it in my belt, I left the sheets amongst the flowers and headed for the cover of the bushes. From there it was easy to get to the wall unobserved. The two CCTV cameras mounted on the overhanging oak branch faced along the wall in opposite directions. By ap-proaching the tree at ninety degrees to the wall, I was in the cameras' blind spot. It was easy enough to pull up on the branch and sit astride it so that the cameras were almost between my thighs. It was also easy to rip the wires from the back of one camera. Would it be noticed? That was anyone's guess, but I had to move quickly.

Ahead of the dead camera, I carefully wound the pillow-case round and round the electric fence wires, pulling it tight and hoping to create a thick enough barrier to insulate them. If they came into contact with the wall or with me or Lupus, they would earth through us, we would be shocked, and the alarm would go off and alert the guards.

Bright security lights came on up at the house, illuminating the entire area around it. Through the branches of my tree, figures were moving under those lights.

Now, my precious dog. I patted the top of the wall. 'Lupus. Come boy, come.'

He came close to the wall and looked up at me. 'Come on, you can do it, come. Lupus come.'

Shouts from the mansion. They knew which camera was out of action, and at least two silhouettes were running in our direction.

'Come on, Lupus, come on, boy.'

He whined his frustration and trotted around in a narrow circle.

'Come, Lupus, come.' I was getting desperate. I was not going to leave him, but he had to do this himself. He definitely could have before he was stabbed, but now …?

He turned and bounded at the wall. A massive leap, sheer momentum and a little scrabbling and he was over the pillow-case-wrapped wires and down the other side. What an incredible dog. He got a massive hug when I was down.

Orders called inside the wall were from a breathless man. A head appeared, peering over. A radio crackled. A guard was in the tree, and another behind him. The first one dropped into the grass; the other followed. They were about thirty metres away, and ten metres separated them. There was no point in running.

We were in a field. White shapeless bundles were scattered about, and the powerful smell of sheep tainted the air. Crouching down with Lupus, I wasn't sure if the men had seen us, but they would do soon enough, and they'd have back-up nearby. Torch beams swept left and right. One picked out a sheep. The light stayed on the animal while its owner tried to make out what he was looking at.

It has been said that the best form of defence is attack. Lupus was growling under his breath. It is the only way I could describe it: he sounded like a cat purring. He knew an enemy was there. I was holding his collar, but he wasn't trying to go, he was waiting for my command.

The man's torch was still on the sheep.

'Go, Lupus.'

The guard was watching the sheep clamber to its feet and run, not because of him but because it knew thirty kilograms of fury was tearing across the field at thirty miles an hour. The guard was still unaware when Lupus slammed into him. The man screamed in fright or terror or pain. His arm was being yanked back and forth, and flesh and muscle were ripping. The torch was lying in the grass, its beam fixed uselessly on a white mineral bucket. A baton, ready for a quick draw from a loop on his belt, came out easily. One blow and the clown was unconscious.

'Leave, Lupus.' I pointed to the other guard. 'Go, boy.'

Two legs were never as fast as four. The man was sprinting, but he didn't have a chance.

'Leave, Lupus.' He trotted back to me. Even in the dark, he showed he was pleased with himself, and it was certain the guard wouldn't be back.

The dark line of a hedgerow was not far. Under the protection of its shadow, we followed it along the edge of the field until we reached a gate leading onto a tarred lane. I was about to open it, when the noise of a high-revving engine disturbed the night and headlights flickered through the hedge.

A van skidded to a stop by the gate. The distinct sound of a sliding door. Subdued voices. Dark shapes, sinister against the early hint of a pastel-blue sky, didn't bother to open the gate – all four climbed or vaulted over it. The van moved on. Was it going to drop more guards further along? We had to get out of that field.

The guards would be betting on us running as far away from the estate as possible – wouldn't they? So, keeping close to the hedge for cover, we went back the way we'd come. The hedge was dense and high, and I couldn't see how we were both going to get through it. But just short of the wall the bushes were crushed as if a car had run off the road. The gap was bridged by a fence to keep the sheep in, but that was easy to get over.

There was no sign of the guards, who were probably running around on the far side of the field. The road was clear, and we were in the security cameras' blind spot. My phone gave our exact location, so I called Kirsten.

21

DAWN WAS NOT far away. Kirsten's skin tone was cool in the light of her instrument panel, enabling me to see the tension in her in spite of the cheerful front she was trying to put on. She was looking decidedly unprofessional, tousled and straight out of bed. From an early morning grump, her mood switched as soon as she saw Lupus, although she retreated into her own thoughts on the way back to her house for coffee and breakfast.

What is it with this woman? Why does she keep such a distance between us? It's not as if I'm trying to get her into bed – far from it. It's as if she's scared of me, when all I'm trying to do is bridge a gap so that ideas and conversation flow with ease and are not restricted by some barrier she's erected.

'Thank you for being so quick, thank you for even responding at all,' I said.

'I try to provide the best service I can for all my clients.'

'Beyond the call of duty. Thanks anyway.'

Leaving me to close her front door, Kirsten went directly to the kitchen and switched on her coffee machine. It sat in the corner on a counter that was notably free of clutter. In fact, the whole kitchen was utilitarian, neat and tidy, and, like Hermione's, smelt of household cleaner.

'It's too early for me to eat, but I'll put an egg on for you if you like,' she said as she filled a bowl with water for Lupus.

'No thanks, not just yet. I have to ask you something. It's important that I know. What's driving you? Why are you so determined to expose this gang of abusers?'

She was bending to put the bowl down. For a second she froze, the bowl just off the floor, then stood upright and glared at me. Her remoteness, her animosity were suddenly apparent for what they were: a defence mechanism, a barrier erected to keep unwanted men – me? – at bay. But her hurried rising to rescue me, her unkemptness had robbed her of her stern, professional façade. She could no longer hide behind her clothes of office. For the first time I was seeing a Kirsten who was pared back to reality.

'We've got to make up for what we've lost in letting the gang escape,' she said.

'So I screwed it up. I've said I'm sorry, but in retrospect I would do the same again.'

After a long pause, she shrugged and the aggression seemed to leave her. 'What they do is abhorrent. It must be stamped out.'

'No. With you it's more than that. It's personal, isn't it?'

She immediately dropped her eyes to watch Lupus at the water and said quickly, 'This is a professional relationship, Andrew. I'm here to defend you and that's all. You're asking personal questions, which is outside our remit.'

'You've been asking personal questions of me, some of which are not necessary for my defence.'

'I have to build a picture. Maybe I will never have to use the information, but it serves to increase my knowledge, so I can talk with more authority when I come to address the court.'

'You've been insistent on my being free and able to continue our investigation into the gang. Some of that drive is for the case, but your attitude and your actions say it's mainly because you want to bring them down.'

'I don't know what you're talking about.'

'You want background on me, and I understand that. I want to know your motivation as we conduct what could be a very dangerous investigation. I want to know how strong your commitment is, because my life may depend on it. Let me put it another way in the form of a personal question, and I'm sorry to ask it: were you abused as a child?'

Her whole body stiffened. It was subtle; I felt as much as saw it. Angry eyes flicked to me then looked away. Nothing was said for over five minutes.

She bent to stroke Lupus, her eyes on him, her talk directed at him. 'My mum had a tradition of going out with her friends once a month on a Thursday night, leaving me in the care of my stepfather. It was harmless enough to begin with, but he took greater and greater advantage of me and found many more opportunities …' Kirsten paused. Was that all she was going to say?

'I hated him, but I was too ashamed to tell my mum. Instead, I took refuge within myself and lived off my dreams of fighting him and tying him up and torturing him for what he was doing to me. One time he grabbed me at the top of the stairs. I fought him off, but I fell down the whole flight, breaking my leg in three places. That's why I limp. The left one is an inch shorter than the right.'

'Thank you. I'm sorry. I understand.'

She whipped her head round at me, tears welling in her eyes. 'How can you possibly understand? You've had a normal, protected life. You can never truly comprehend unless you've also been tied to the bed, beaten and raped. How can you? *How can you?*'

I couldn't look at her. 'I'm sorry. I didn't mean to upset you, to force bad memories on you.'

Another eternal period of time passed during which I acknowledged that she'd trusted me. I was probably the only person, other than Mitch, who knew her secret. It wasn't a matter of friendship, it was one of trust. She would back me up as I would her.

'It's all right,' she said. 'Maybe I needed to get it out, it's been bottled up for too long.'

It wasn't the right time, but I lacked a complete picture. I had to risk another explosion. 'You've had Mitch to talk to.'

'Why would I talk to Mitch? If you think he's hiding something, you'll have to ask him – and good luck with that. His business is not my business.'

'Something binds you two,' I said. 'It's unspoken, it's not romance, it's something else.'

Again she didn't answer for a while, but stood at the window with her back to me. Her words put mist on the glass. 'We were at the same school together, although I was a year ahead of him.'

'Ah. But that doesn't explain what I've observed. Was he also a victim?'

'No … but his sister was, and she was autistic.'

'Was?'

'She's dead now. You'll have to ask Mitch if you want to know more,' she said to her garden. 'What about you? What are your priorities? It seems to me that you're trying to accomplish two things at once, and I don't see how you can. I need to know which one takes preference.'

It was a valid question. 'I've been debating that very thing myself. I've always only had one goal – a lifetime need to keep my condition hidden from the world. That's long term. My current short-term goal is the destruction of this gang of paedophiles, thereby finding Alex's killer. I have to do this and still stay under the radar, because no matter what happens, my condition must never be made public. Does that answer your question?'

My phone sent out its high pitched cry, causing Kirsten to glance back into the room. 'Hymie – why am I not surprised to get your call, although it's a bit early for you, isn't it?'

He didn't greet me. 'Andrew, what you've done is extremely stupid. Unless you return here and fulfil the terms of your agreement with NiPetco, we'll annul the alibi and you will be arrested.'

'I think the police will get a bit fed up and suspicious with these false statements later withdrawn and rescinded alibis, don't you? I think you should review the evidence in this case very carefully, Hymie, and then see if you're still confident in your threat. From my point of view, I was asked to sign your agreement under false pretences, so therefore my signature carries no weight. Is Nigel there?'

He gave an exasperated sigh. His mind must have been scrambling to think why I wasn't worried about no alibi from NiPetco. 'No, of course not, it's five in the morning. Nigel is very, very angry. I've never seen him so furious. He's dangerous when he's like this. Why do you want to speak to him? Anything you want to say should be through me.'

'Ooh, I don't think you'd want to be involved, Hymie. Just tell Nigel that it's about Western boots.'

'What the hell are you talking about? I'll be calling the police shortly.'

'Good for you. Very public-spirited. Bye, Hymie.'

Kirsten turned away from the window. 'Dare I ask? Western boots?'

'Here – on my phone.'

She squinted at the images. 'Is this what you took in the house? I can't make out any recognisable faces.'

'I had to take them from a low camera angle with no flash, so the pictures are dim. The lighting is indirect and from below, not above – very sexy. See how everyone's feet are highlighted? Trainers, shiny leather shoes and this pair of hand-tooled engraved Western boots. I think their varying shades of brown reflect the subdued under-counter lighting very nicely. They belong to Nigel Pettigrew.'

'This is not evidence, Andrew, it could be anyone. The only way to implicate him is to obtain a video of the action or have him identified by a victim. Lou said all the white men wore masks, and she might not hold up in court as she could be intimidated by a defence lawyer. We'll have to do better, I'm afraid.'

'I thought you'd say that. It does reinforce my suspicions about him in my own mind, though.'

IT WAS Paul's turn to call. He did so not five minutes after Hymie, and probably under the lawyer's instruction, because I hadn't given Paul my number.

'Andrew, old chap,' he said, 'it's Paul. I'm sorry you've left, genuinely sorry. I thought we were becoming friends. Good people are in pretty short supply in present company.'

'Yes, I could see you have a problem with compatibility, Paul. Sorry about it, but I was taken advantage of, secured under false pretences, and I'm not going to sign my life away for someone else's profit.'

'I fully understand, Andrew, but it wouldn't be as bad as you're making out it will be. It's all harmless as far as you're concerned, and it will be a tremendous gift to mankind.'

'Now that's where we differ. Life on Earth is dependent on death, and the concept of increasing the world's population by never dying will kill the planet and mankind along with it. If we don't do something to curb population growth, nature will do it for us in some agonising manner: war, disease, hunger … It's fundamentally wrong, Paul.'

'But the achievement – it's Nobel Prize-winning stuff.'

'This isn't about personal achievement, it's well above that,' I replied.

'We could always keep it under wraps – never put it in production.'

Paul was either incredibly naïve, or incredibly stupid, to think he could convince me with such weak arguments. 'Do you seriously think NiPetco are going to spend all this money on years of research, keep me in luxury and then put your recipe in a safe?'

'I suppose not,' he said slowly. 'I wish you'd come back, though. It's not only about research, I'm starved of good company.'

'A herring in a shark tank. Keep in touch, Paul. I'd like to know what's going on behind the scenes there – if you can tell me. We should try to get together when it all blows over.'

'Herring? Good idea, though, good to talk, and I'll certainly keep in touch.'

I added him to my contacts list.

If I'd blinked I would have missed the flicker of a smile when Kirsten handed me a coffee. The hardness had drained from her face. Had her brief confession been cathartic and released some of her tension? 'Tell me, please.'

'I can't make Paul out,' I said after explaining what took place in the manor. 'If he's genuine, he's a good chap who doesn't see much harm in the world. If he's playing the good cop for this lot, then he's a damn fine actor. Of course, he has his own agenda. He wants to be the scientist that discovered the secret to eternal life. As he said himself: it's Nobel Prize material. So what is driving him, personal ambition, or his dodgy employer? Or is he just a nice guy looking for a friendly face when he looks like a serial killer?'

'Really?'

'He looks evil. I'm sure he's not, but he won't win friends on looks.'

22

THERE WAS A quiver in Nigel's voice that could only have derived from the rage that Hymie had warned me about. 'What the fuck do you think you're doing, Duncan—'

'Andrew.'

'Listen up, asshole. If I want to call you Duncan, it's Duncan you gonna be.'

'It's either Andrew or Mr Duncan. If you won't address me properly, you won't get a response.'

His voice dropped a couple of notes. 'What the fuck do you think you're doing? We have a signed agreement. Y'all cain't walk out like that.'

'I can do what I like. You obtained my agreement on false pretences. As I told your slimy little lawyer, he should take a very close look at the evidence again to ensure I actually do need an alibi.'

'What d'ya mean?'

CA Sole

'I can't be bothered to explain it all now, Nigel. Get Hymie to do his job properly. I wanted to speak to you about something else.'

'Yeah, what?'

'I have date-stamped photographic evidence showing you abusing underage girls at Shalamar Gardens.'

There was an almost inaudible gasp, followed by lengthy silence and the sound of uneven breathing. I waited.

'Crap. What are you on about? Where's this garden? Did you say abusing young girls? Horseshit. I'll sue. Y'all's gonna end up sleeping in the street by the time I'm finished.'

'So you want to challenge the evidence, do you? I want to be clear on this point. You categorically deny you have been to Shalamar Gardens and that you abused underage girls, mere children, there, in spite of photos to the contrary?'

'I want to see these photos. They cain't be me. It ain't possible.'

'Certainly, but only in the company of the police. I tell you what I'll do, I'll send you the most innocent one by email if you like. It puts you in the bar at Shalamar.'

There was another long silence.

His tone dropped, the excitement fell out of it. 'I ain't saying I was there or abused any girls. I did not, but I'm a high-profile guy that everybody likes. People like me, people respect me. I cain't afford to have that reputation destroyed, even by a lie. What d'ya want?'

'You and NiPetco to leave me alone. If you agree to this, I'll have my solicitor draw up an agreement for you person-ally to sign. I'm not having Hymie doing it.'

'That all?'

'For now. Do you agree?'

'You don't want money?'

'No, I want you to leave me alone, and that includes removing the man watching my house all the time.'

'We ain't watchin' your home. You're delusional.'

'Are you sure, Nige? No one is lurking in the bushes just down the road with his attention fixed on my front door?'

'Course I'm sure. NiPetco are not watching you.'

I believed him – sort of. But if it wasn't them, then who the hell was it?

KIRSTEN, MITCH and I were sitting round her kitchen table consuming a bottle of Merlot and thrashing out the best way forward. Lupus was chewing on a rawhide treat Kirsten had bought for him.

'I don't trust NiPetco one inch,' I said. 'Nigel Pettigrew is quite likely to have me abducted again before he signs that agreement, or even afterwards. They'll know where I am if I stay at home; I need to hide for a short while. I'm feeling hunted. I'm being followed and I don't think it's only NiPetco. I've seen a man loitering about, another was trying to listen to what Kirsten and I were saying to each other, and I've had to shake off two different cars when I've been out. I'm spending my driving time in the rear-view mirror. It could be the press, they're still an intrusion, but, I don't know why, I think it's someone else.'

'Well, you can't stay here, I'm afraid. I cannot be seen to be involved with some rather dodgy investigation on behalf of my client.'

'Exactly. I wasn't thinking of it, nor was I thinking of your place, Mitch.'

'It's way too small for two of us, and in any case, if you're being followed, we don't want them to know I'm involved either. It could hamper our efforts.'

Kirsten topped up her glass and pushed the bottle across the table to me. 'I have a tiny cottage not far from Uffington. It was left to me by my father. I think it started life as a simple cowshed and someone built on and made it habitable. It's empty at the moment and it's not too far away.'

'That'll be tremendous, thank you.'

'You may battle with the hot water and it's pretty basic; but it's remote, and has a good view of the Neolithic white horse which is cut into the hillside.'

'Kirsten, what's my position with the police? Am I liable to be arrested?'

'As it stands now, I don't think so,' she said. 'The evidence they have highlights you as a prime suspect, but there are too many doubts attached to it, and, in my opinion, several clues that show you could not have done it. But other things may come to light: NiPetco may introduce something else to incriminate you, and Payne can fix on an issue like a terrier and worry it to death, even if it's no good to him. He has to prove it's useless before he moves on.'

'Time is short. My fear is that Pettigrew will be on the next flight out to Houston, from where he'll have to be extradited. This will take time, and the police will have to build a case using my evidence, which is flimsy at best. At the moment I'm challenging him with a bluff. But most of all, if he goes home, I'll lose control over him. We need to find the van I saw at the house. That could lead us to the driver and who he's working for or with. Lupus didn't dislike him for no reason.'

'I'll do that.' His toothpick bobbed up and down between his lips as Mitch spoke. 'My mate says those men in our photos don't show up in the police system.'

'So the driver gains in importance. I'm going back to Shalamar.'

Mitch eyed me with suspicion, drained his glass and set it back on the table with a satisfied clunk. 'What for? Those buggers have gone. There'll be nothing there, no sign of what's happened. They'll have cleaned the place top to bottom – guaranteed, thanks to you.'

'Mitch, I said I'm sorry about that, but I'd like to know what you would have done if you'd seen Liz's face as she was dragged down the passage.'

'Stop it,' Kirsten snapped. 'I don't like what's happened any more than you do, Mitch, but Andrew's right. You didn't see the girl's face, and you didn't see Lou when she was telling me what happened to her. I did, and I can understand why Andrew acted the way he did. I can't condemn it as a mistake. It's something that's happened and it's set us back, but it hasn't stopped us.'

'Yeah, sorry. It's just that we have to make up so much ground now,' Mitch mumbled.

'All the more reason to go back there,' I said. 'They might have missed something. The girls might have left something behind that could give a clue as to their names or where they came from. It's also possible that the sleeve of my jacket was taken there to be burnt. There might be something, and I'm not going to sleep easily until I've scoured the place myself.'

23

MARGIE HOPE LIVED in a white, architecturally uninspiring, three-storey block of flats in Cowley near the edge of Oxford. The roar from the Eastern Bypass would not let up, and we had to raise our voices to be heard. Four teenagers surrounded Mitch's Audi as we walked away from the car.

Lupus was on the back seat and his growl could be heard through the partially open window. The youths decided the pathetic human trait of teasing a dangerous animal from the safety of their position was going to be fun. Mitch turned round and went back. He said something I couldn't hear, and the boys dispersed into a small group further from the car. Lupus settled.

Mitch ignored my question and rapped on Margie's door. I stood back and let his experience lead the charge.

'Yeah?' A cigarette projected from the corner of her mouth, and smoke billowed out with her single word. She had puffy, flushed features and an enormous cleavage. She must have been quite sexy when she was young. Since then, alcohol and nicotine and probably too many men had taken their toll.

'Are you the owner of a white Ford van, registration number—?'

'Who wants to know?'

Mitch pulled out a card I hadn't seen before, flashed it at her and tucked it away.

Thrusting her chin and breasts forward as if they would ward off attack, she said guardedly, 'What of it?'

'Can you tell me who was driving it last Sunday, please?'

'It's for hire, could be anyone.'

'Don't you keep a record?'

'Yeah. Suppose.' She stepped back inside and Mitch followed.

'Wait there,' Margie yelled. 'I don't want any bloody coppers in my house. I'll bring it out.'

Mitch raised his eyebrows and grinned at me. 'I'm not surprised. Bloody bomb hit this place last night. It reeks of booze.'

Margie came out with a file of papers, balanced it on her raised knee and pulled out a sheet. 'Here. Some bloke called Baqri, by the looks of it. Mohamed Baqri. What's this about?'

'His address please, Ms Hope.'

She passed the paper to Mitch, who took a photo of it. He tugged the file from her grasp and passed it to me to leaf through. She looked at me over the top of his head as she fielded his questions, a slight smile on her lips and a clear invitation in her eyes – purely for income.

I found several more records detailing Baqri as the hirer, and took photos of them. I'd almost reached the end of the file of white forms when a dark colour caught my eye. It was a page of photographs – all of young girls.

WHEN WE got back to the car, Mitch gave one of the kids a five-pound note. Before he started the engine, I showed him the photos on my phone. 'This was probably in the wrong file. Stroke of luck for us.'

'Right. They can't all be her daughters. Why didn't you say something?'

'If she's the woman acquiring the girls, she'd have gone on the defensive, clammed up and we'd get nowhere. As it is, she might still phone Mohamed Baqri and warn him.'

Mitch nodded. 'His address is not far, we'll be there in five.'

'It should be round the next bend on the right,' I said after fiddling with his GPS.

We turned the corner. A number of old or inexpensive cars were parked along the street. A small white van sat half on the kerb with the rear doors open.

I'd already released my seat belt. 'That's it, that's the one.'

A man was loading something at the back of the van. There was nothing leisurely in his movements. He was in a hurry and slammed the doors shut with an unmistakable tin-box sound that echoed down the street.

Mitch pulled in to a parking slot three cars back and opened his door.

I was already out. 'He's going.'

Mitch was ahead of me. The man was at his driver's door. He looked up in our direction, but his features were once again hidden from us by his cap. He hesitated, then panic struck, and he ducked inside and out of sight.

I wasn't going to get there, but Lupus would. The dog was three bounds away. The front door slammed, but the window was open. Lupus leapt and hit the van with a solid thump as the engine roared into life. His head was in through the window, his paws scrabbling for purchase. Screams came from inside. The van shot off, tyres squealing. Lupus fell back to the pavement.

'*Fuck*,' said Mitch. 'Don't set that creature on me, please.' But he knelt beside Lupus to see if he was all right. Which he was. 'Did you see his face?'

'No, but I'm sure I've seen him before. The same cap was on the man that Lupus took exception to at the NiPetco mansion.'

Mitch was silent for a while after we drove away, then he pulled into a parking spot and switched off the engine.

'What's up?'

'Andrew, it's time we took this to the police.'

'No.'

'Listen to me. I know for a fact that the cops are running several investigations across the country into gangs that groom vulnerable young people. They have a far better idea of how they operate than we have, and may even have some officers working undercover. They would benefit from our input and are in a much more advanced position than we are to do something about it. I mean, what can we do from here on? Suppose we find Baqri soon, what do you think we're going to get out of him? With their greater knowledge, the police are much more likely to get results from interrogating him than we are.'

'That man murdered Alex. I'm certain of it. And somehow he's connected to Nigel Pettigrew. I have got to prove Pettigrew's involvement in order to show I'm innocent and to get NiPetco off my back. And that has to be done without the police being involved.'

'You're probably right about Baqri, but what are you going to do about it? If you kill him in revenge, you won't have me on your side, and you won't have Kirsten either. If you turn him over to the police, you'll achieve what you could have achieved by talking to the police now, only it will be much later, with more damage being done in the interim.'

'I told you, I don't want to go to the police. I'll cooperate with them over Alex's murder, that's all.'

'Why not? I think it's time you let me in on what's going on. For all I know, I could be aiding and abetting a serial killer, with your insistence in avoiding the law.'

'It's nothing like that. I've done nothing wrong.'

'What then?'

It was becoming more and more difficult to avoid telling people what my problem was. First Kirsten, and now, if I gave in, Mitch. Who next – the police? My condition was going to be out in the open if I wasn't careful, and then what? Chaos. But could I stop it? I wasn't sure I could.

'Mitch, I want you to think very carefully on the con-sequences for mankind if we could live forever. Take a few minutes and think it through.'

'What the hell's that got to do with anything?'

'Humour me. Do it.'

I closed my eyes and let my head fall back while he con-templated this. How was it all going to end – would it ever end?

'Overpopulation,' Mitch said. 'Food running out, water, too, wars as we fight for resources, climate change would go out of control, which would mean the end of us all anyway. There must be loads more. Why?'

'Let's look at it another way. If someone developed a pill

or a treatment that could freeze your age, would you take it? Would you take it even though you know it could spell disaster? There's a natural human desire to preserve life, to not die at any cost. Would you fight that and reject the pill, accepting your own death as a certainty, when others around you have taken the pill and will live forever?'

'Would they put a warning label on the packet?' He sniggered. 'Sorry, not a joking matter.'

'No, in my position, it's not. You are going to have great difficulty believing me. If you do, I want you to talk to Kirsten. I managed to convince her by asking her to do something specific. I won't be able to ask that of you. Before I tell you what the problem is, you must promise me now, to never reveal it to anyone else. Not the police, not the press, not your brother or your lover.'

'I don't have either of those – more's the pity.' He held up his hand. 'My word.'

I told him, and it left me feeling uncomfortable: naked, exposed and emotionally flat. For decades I had held this secret so tight to my chest, and in telling Mitch, even more than after telling Kirsten, I had laid myself bare.

'That is hard to believe, for sure,' Mitch said when I was finished. 'But if you say Kirsten believes you, then I could be persuaded. After all, nothing's impossible. There's always a way, and I can understand your wanting to keep this quiet. Let's suppose I do believe you; I still think the cops have to be told.'

'No, I've got to solve this without their involvement. It's too risky.'

'*Bloody hell*, Andrew. Stop being so fucking selfish.' He turned towards me, his face flushed. 'There's a paedophile ring out there abusing youngsters. You succumbed to emotion and rescued those girls instead of getting evidence that would put the whole fucking gang away. You stuffed it up, and they've now dispersed to use another place and ruin the lives of more children. The police have the capability of shutting it down and putting those scum away, but you won't help.'

'It's not as simple as that. I tried to explain to you the danger to society, to humankind, of letting my secret out. It's a bigger picture than just me.'

His voice calmed to a more normal level. 'Then I'll do it. I'll give the cops everything we know about Baqri and Shalamar and let them have the photos. They'll find out who they are.'

I was torn. I wanted to help, I really did, but I had such a firm belief in the bigger picture that the thought of publicising my condition was beyond consideration. In complete contrast, I had taken the other route when I rescued the two girls. I could have ignored them and gathered evidence to bring the whole gang down. But emotions had intervened there.

'All right, Mitch, you do it. You give them the evidence. Just keep me out of it. Don't tell them of my visit to the house. We don't want them to take the girls away from Mrs F. either. And please don't tell them until I've been back to Shalamar.'

'Until *we've* been there. You're not going alone, it's too dangerous, and if you're going to search the place you'll need more than one pair of eyes. Tonight?'

24

SHALAMAR'S SUBDUED HALL lighting cast an amber glow over the parking area. Mitch and I crouched in the bushes, watching for signs of activity, but nothing moved behind the glass panels either side of the front door. Round the side of the house the grass glistened and the drizzle sparkled in the kitchen lights.

My shirt was damp, but despite the rain it was a warm night.

The cook didn't seem to have been spooked by my previous intrusion, because he had again left the outside door open. Who was he cooking for? Whatever he was preparing smelt delicious. Lupus sniffed the air; was he salivating at the memory of leftover curries? He loved them. Mitch too licked his lips and grinned at me. He came alive when action was in the offing: prowling around at night, chasing fugitives, lurking, spying – anything but the office. I could relate to that, and it was one reason we got on.

Mitch was carrying one of those big, heavy Maglite torches, the one that holds six D cells, clips into a belt loop and can be used as a baton. It was too cumbersome for me, so I opted for a head torch and a sheaf of cable ties. My only weapons were Lupus and my little pocketknife.

We had already agreed that searching the place meant we would have to immobilise the staff. The questions were: how many were there, and who were they? No one of any consequence was likely to be there after my break-in on Saturday.

A low whistle and a wave outside the door attracted the cook. He put his ladle down, came over and stuck his head out. Mitch whacked it with his Maglite. Simple, silent and clean.

Lupus went ahead into the kitchen; the smell was too much for him.

But I froze at a noise behind me. It sounded like half a gasp; one of surprise bitten off in mid intake. 'Mitch, lend me your torch a moment. I heard something.'

The Maglite was much more powerful than my tiny lamp and picked out every detail in the bushes beside the narrow inlet off the river. I couldn't see anything. Maybe my nerves were on edge.

The cook was groggy. Mitch secured him with cable ties and rolled him onto his back. He obviously couldn't understand English, so Mitch gestured and I pricked the skin below his right eye with my knife. Terrified, he barely flinched when Mitch rammed a large potato past his teeth, forcing his mouth to stay wide open and silent. Lupus came back outside and sniffed at the cook's stained jacket. Enticed by the aromas, the dog pushed his nose up to the potato that bulged from the poor man's mouth. His eyes grew to the size of fried eggs. We had to laugh, but I called Lupus away and we moved into the kitchen. The food tasted even better than it smelt.

Mitch grinned. 'Takeaway?'

We cleared the ground floor, room by room. Working as a pair, four eyes being better than two, we searched for anything, large or small, which might give a clue to who had been there. All the while, the threat that other staff members were somewhere in the building wouldn't leave me.

Under the stairs – what had escaped a sweeping broom? In the toilet cubicles – what had fallen from a pocket? We moved upstairs. First the dining room, then the bar where I'd seen those men. That they had definitely been in there helped to intensify our inspection. But there was nothing. Next door was one of the bedrooms. Was this the one where Liz and Rache were being taken when I first saw them? My jaw tightened as we entered. We stripped the bedding, searched under the beds, in the cupboards, in the drawers –nothing. It looked as if they'd done a thorough job of sanitising the place. We completed that floor and climbed to the loft.

The smell in there was different. It was hard to explain. It was more an odour of kids' bodies than of adults', or was that my imagination? Lupus was excited; he was sniffing everywhere and wagging his tail. Had he picked up Lou's scent?

Dust lay all around. Didn't they bother to clean this room? Were the children not worth it? Were they just dross to be used and tossed aside? There must be little fingerprints all over the room.

'Psst!' Mitch held up a small teddy bear he'd found under a cupboard. It wasn't proof of anything, but it was something. He pulled a ziplock bag from his pocket and popped the bear inside. And that was all we got.

'Where the hell are the rest of the staff, Mitch, and where do they sleep? The cook was making dinner for more than just himself. I don't like not knowing what we're up against.'

'I don't like being up here with only one way out. I feel trapped.'

'I know. Let's go outside. There must be separate servants' quarters on the other side of the house. Also, if we follow my escape route to where the dinghy was moored, we might find something they dropped when chasing me.'

'We'll check the cook on the way.'

The kitchen was empty. The food was bubbling and, judging by the smell, had caught. The cook had vanished.

Mitch swore. '*Shit.* How the hell did he get free?'

'He had help. Come on, let's get out into the garden.'

If anything, the rain had intensified. I wasn't damp any more, I was soaked. We traced my route from the hallway doors out onto the lawn and down to the mouth of the inlet. What had happened to the cook, and where were he and the person who freed him?

It was Mohamed Baqri we'd seen that morning, and Lupus had recognised him. Had it been Baqri with the machete? Did he live at Shalamar, because that's where Machete Man came from? And was Baqri there as we were both nose down to the ground searching for something unknown? Thank God my dog was with us.

We were at the stake to which the dinghy had been moored. 'We were chased along the bank before I jumped into the boat, but I don't know how much further the men ran.'

'Let's go on a bit, then,' Mitch answered, his torch sweeping across the wet grass.

Lupus growled.

Three men were between us and the house, silhouettes. On the left was a scrawny one – was he the cook? In the middle was a short man; and the one on the right was tall and broad shouldered. He carried a machete. As they came closer, we could make out more detail. The weapon was held in the man's left hand and his right arm was bandaged. Lupus was almost certainly slashed by a right-handed blow, and the right sleeve of my jacket was missing. If it was this man who stabbed my dog and killed my love, then he was ambidextrous – and that, in a man with a knife, is not funny.

'The river, Mitch. Can you swim?'

'Yeah.'

'Shoes off.' Eyes fixed on the trio. Toe of left shoe on heel of right, lever it off. Right toes down behind the left. Pain stabbed my foot. I recoiled, but could not afford to take my eyes off Baqri. Standing on my left foot, I pulled something metallic out of my right heel and slipped it in my pocket.

'It's all over, Andrew. You can't get away. Give yourself up.'

'Mark?' Surely not; I didn't know what to think, Mark wouldn't be that brave or that stupid – but it was him. I'd recognise his voice anywhere. 'What the hell are you doing here?'

'Yes, it's me. I've been following you. I knew you'd eventually do something to incriminate yourself. And now I've caught you burgling this house. Why? Are you a criminal? Is this what you do? I was hiding in the bushes and I saw you assault this poor man. As soon as you'd gone inside, I released him. When he recovered, he fetched the big man and we came after you. I know you killed Alex. Give yourself up.'

The men stopped five metres away. Lupus was snarling. I couldn't afford to take my eyes off Baqri, even though I had to talk to Mark. 'You stupid idiot. You're meddling in something that's way over your head. I didn't kill Alex, I'm not burgling the house and I didn't hit the cook – my friend here did, admittedly with my full support, although it looks like he should have done it harder.'

'Stop lying, Andrew. Just stop it. You need to give yourself up and face justice.'

'*Mark*, stop whining and listen to me very carefully. You are in great danger standing where you are. Move away from those men for your own safety. Get out of reach. The real killer is the man on your left. His name is Mohamed Baqri.'

'For God's sake stop trying to lie your way out of it, Andrew.' He was almost squeaking he was so agitated. 'You killed Alex. I know it, the police know it, and I'm going to phone them now.' He fished his phone out of his pocket and tapped in his PIN.

Baqri stepped back. The machete glinted at the top of the stroke, and the instrument shattered in Mark's hand. He screamed, and carried on screaming.

'No police.'

Lupus was itching to attack. His snarling was a constant low-pitched backdrop to Mark's wailing. I kept my hand on the dog to calm him. This had to be solved without committing Lupus to another knife wound, or worse.

'My fingers. My fingers have gone!'

'You'll live. Wrap your jacket round your hand and stop the bleeding.'

'And stop crying, for God's sake,' said Mitch. He turned to me. 'You want to go for a swim now?'

'I can't leave Mark here with him.'

'I'll call the police. This guy's a psycho.'

Mitch tapped at his phone.

'No,' Baqri shouted, and took a step forward.

Lupus was louder. He reared onto his hind legs against my grip, his body quivering with rage. He was beyond listening to my voice commands.

Baqri hesitated. An age passed. Man and dog glared at each other. Lupus was straining and hard to hold. Baqri turned and ran, glanced back, and ran. I held onto Lupus's harness until the killer was out of sight, because the running man may have been too much temptation for him. The cook was hopping from one leg to the other. He made up his mind, gestured negative signs at Lupus and tore after Baqri.

'Mitch, let me have one of your plastic bags, please. How come you carry them anyway?'

'In another life I was a real detective,' he said as he shone his torch onto the grass where I was searching.

I put Mark's finger and tip in the bag, zipped it closed and wiped my hand on the wet grass. 'We'll grab some ice from the kitchen for these, then I'll take Mark's car to drop him at the hospital.'

'Fancy a curry before we go?' Mitch wasn't going to give up on this one.

'Really tempting, but it's burnt.'

'I'M SORRY.' Mark was crying. He nursed his hand, which was smothered in his jacket. Blood oozed out from the wrapping onto the passenger seat. 'So sorry. I was convinced it was you.' His fingers, buried in ice in their bag, lay on the floor at his feet.

I drove his car and took him to the Accident and Emergency department, intending to go home and then drop the vehicle back with Hermione. 'Forget it. I never suspected you were in love with her.'

His response was silent tears.

A degree of empathy had crept back into my soul during the rescue of the girls. After decades, I was looking at people with more interest in how they felt, what they wanted – but Mark did not summon such feelings. Although, any change in me wouldn't happen all at once, would it? There would have to be relapses. Or was I becoming more polarised? Kinder when something touched me and less tolerant of fools? Mark was being pathetic and therefore fell into the latter category.

I tried, but failed, to hide my irritation with him. 'So you've been following me.'

He nodded and sniffed.

'What car have you been using?'

'God this hurts. Will I get my fingers back, Andrew?'

'Maybe. What car have you been using to follow me?'

'A brown Mini. It's my brother's.'

'That was to Devizes, but you also checked that I went to the police station, didn't you?'

'I had to. If you hadn't, I'd have reported you then and there. I was also listening to what you told Kirsten when you went to the pub – but that's all.'

'I thought so.' If that was all, as he said, who else was following me? NiPetco, the press, the abusers, who? 'How much did you hear?'

He grunted with pain. 'Nothing, really. I couldn't make it out. But I wanted to know if you confessed to her, and why you did it.'

'And the disguises, the beard and the clothes, which I'm pretty sure you don't own?'

'From the dramatic society wardrobe, of course.'

'I bet you enjoyed the dressing up and acting the furtive spy.'

He sniffed. 'I haven't enjoyed anything since she died.'

'How the hell do you think I feel, Mark? Have you thought how Hermione feels? Have you given any thought to that? I'm still sleeping on the couch because I can't bring myself to use our bed. With everything I do in trying to pin down the real killers and continue her investigation, I have to force my memories into the background in order to focus. You seem to think you're the only one who misses her. You're a selfish little twat who has no right to claim the greatest grief. All you've done is muddy the waters.'

He burst into a fresh set of tears.

25

MY EMPTY HALL felt cold. It was not the temperature, it was a perception brought about by the lack of Alex's warmth. Every time I'd returned home since … I had missed her welcoming hug. There was no longer anything to look forward to in that house, and I determined that as soon as this saga was over and I had time, I would once again reinvent my life: change my identity, sell the house, sell most of my possessions and move to somewhere remote. I had done it before to escape detection, and I would do it again, even if it was a chore.

Lupus had fresh water, but his food bowl required a top-up. After giving Baqri the fright of his life, he deserved it. He downed a biscuit, but immediately raised his head, listening. He trotted through to the hall. I followed. In so many ways this dog was my leader. He would hear things, smell things and know things long before I was aware of them. What was it now: the press again, NiPetco, or something more sinister?

A heavy knocking shook the door. A dark outline was visible through the stained glass. Lupus growled. DCI Payne stood with his fist raised, about to knock again. Payne eyed the dog and took a step back when I opened the door. 'He's mended well,' he said.

'Yes. He's tough, thank goodness. What can I do for you, Chief Inspector?'

'I was passing and thought I'd take the opportunity. May I come in?'

I stepped back and Payne entered, keeping me between himself and Lupus.

'It's all right, he won't hurt you unless you're a threat to me. Turn right for the lounge.'

'It seems you have not been truthful with me, Mr Duncan.' He chose an upright chair near the window and lifted it a bit closer to the centre.

'Oh?'

'Our lads have been examining the contents of Miss de Villiers's vault. There were two memory sticks in there. One contained information pertaining to the subject of her investigations, the other was more personal in that it records a recent copy of her will. You failed to mention that you're her sole beneficiary. With the exception of a few charities and a friend, she left you her entire estate, which is substantial.'

'Rubbish. When I met her she was scraping pennies together and was absolutely desperate to sell her articles, but no publications were interested in the field she was working in.'

The DCI shrugged. 'We need to have another chat down at the station, Mr Duncan. I'll be in touch.'

'One moment, Chief Inspector, please. I haven't had a chance to tell you, but on Sunday I believe this dog identified the murderer …'

Payne flushed with anger. 'I'm not warning you again, Mr Duncan. If you think you can divert this investigation with idiotic stories based on your dog's evidence, I'll charge you with wasting police time in addition to anything else.'

'Listen to me. Lupus has two normal reactions to people. If he likes them, he'll be friendly and approach them; if he sees them as neutral, he ignores them as he did with you. I have never seen him be aggressive to anyone without cause. He took one look at this man and I had to restrain him. It was the man who stabbed him and who killed Alex.'

I scribbled on a scrap of paper pad and gave it to him. 'That's the registration of the van he was driving. I've told you about it. You can't ignore it.'

What I did not do was let him know we saw Baqri again on Wednesday, because when he questioned Margie Hope, the van's owner, he would realise we'd been interfering again.

Payne's eyes narrowed. He tried to stare me down, failed then turned and left.

So, Payne had found me a motive for the murder. That was worrying. Being a beneficiary to a 'substantial sum', whatever that meant, was another piece of evidence to add to everything else the police believed: the presence of my car at the time, Alex's blood on my hand, and, worst of all, my failure to answer all their questions. If Payne didn't trace the van and Baqri, or if the suspect went underground, I was no closer to getting off his hook and pinning Alex's murder on Nigel.

Mark's car keys were in my pocket. When I pulled them out something fell to the floor. It was an orange outline of a bull's head with great sweeping horns – a lapel pin, the thing that had embedded itself in my foot at Shalamar. That motif rang a bell. Where had I seen it before?

Returning the car could wait. Hermione wasn't going anywhere in her state at the moment. Two minutes on Google revealed the image to be the symbol of the Texas Longhorns, the athletic teams of the University of Texas. How did it get to be on the lawn at Shalamar Gardens? Who lost it? The answer was obvious, and by adding the tenuous evidence of the boots, the picture came more into focus.

Nigel Pettigrew, according to Wikipedia, was born in Austin, Texas in November 1970. That made him almost forty-nine. He gave the impression of being much older, but that was probably just his arrogance. Pettigrew was the chief operating officer of NiPetco, the giant pharmaceutical company which is headquartered in Houston, Texas, blah, blah, blah; he graduated from the University of Texas in 2002, blah, blah; he supports the Texas Longhorns football team; he has stated publicly that he might run for Governor of Texas at some point in the future …

That pretty much clinched it.

THE LAST thing I wanted was to be reminded of Alex's mutilated corpse dripping blood down the stairs. Yet every time I saw Hermione, her mere presence brought back that previous phase of my life; a phase that had ended in tragedy.

Hermione answered the door after a long wait. She had been induced on Monday, so I supposed she'd been doing baby things.

'How are you?' I asked. 'How's the newcomer? You're looking well.' She wasn't.

'Michelle's such a good little mite. I wish the others had been so easy. She's sleeping right now. I'm okay, Andrew. It gets easier each time – for me, anyway. How are you? What's happening? Do you know where Mark is? I haven't seen him since this morning.'

'I've come to tell you about him. Mixed fortunes, I'm afraid. The good news is that he no longer believes I did it.'

She sank into a deep armchair, looking worn out and shaking her head as she grappled with the unlikely activities her mild and grey husband had been up to. Hermione had become very much the housewife since she married Mark. She was so family-orientated that little existed for her outside her home. Alex had told me how, before that, the two of them got up to all sorts of tricks. Circumstances change people.

'Will he be all right?'

'Oh yes. He's lost the tip of his middle finger and the index finger is down to the first joint. I put the bits on ice, and they might be able to stick them back on again. They perform miracles these days.'

Hermione passed a hand over her forehead and sat up. 'I hope he'll now snap out of his miserable mood. Silly man. He's been so wrapped up in himself and the lives he acts out that he hasn't been able to see reality. He thought the world of Alex—'

'You knew? I guessed.'

'Of course I knew. Alex knew as well. He went doe-eyed whenever she was around or we talked about her. He's been living a double life, an imaginary one with her and a real one with me. But I've kept quiet. He's a good man really, and he's never let me down or betrayed me, except in his mind.'

'His acting personality?'

Hermione nodded. 'He'll be back with his tail between his legs. We won't mention it, and it will all blow over and be forgotten in a month or so. Silly man. He was convinced you were the culprit, and he couldn't stop worrying about how you seemed to be getting away with it. From what you've told me, he actually found the courage to go charging about in the middle of the night to prove it was you.'

'It's over now. Time to move on. Hermione, what are you not telling me about Alex? Who was she, really? To me she was an independent girl, happy forging her own career in a difficult profession and not being paid enough for some dangerous activities.'

Hermione sighed. 'She made me promise not to tell any-one who she was, but I suppose it doesn't matter now. She wanted to make her own way in life, not rely on her father's wealth. He, of course, wanted to give her everything, have her live a life of luxury shielded from the dangers of a vicious world.'

'I had no idea. I thought she was living hand to mouth when I met her.'

'That's what she wanted you to think. She knew she was privileged, but she wanted to start her adult life on equal terms with everyone else, not have the advantage of wealth behind her. She wanted people to take her for the person she was, not anything special because of her heritage.'

'Which was?'

'The de Villiers family date back to William the Conquer-or. Alex's ancestor was a loyal friend to William and was granted huge estates in England. To a great extent those have been sold off. I think all that's left is the house, which is large but manageable, and the farm of about a thousand acres. Money from the sale of properties has been invested. There's a management company to handle it all. Alex used to add her signature where it was required and tried to ensure no one was cheating her. She did little else other than make sure the employees and tenants were fairly treated. She hated it.'

'Apparently she left most of it to me. You too, I'm sure. It's insane; what am I going to do with it? All it's done so far is give me a very strong motive for killing her.'

I waved goodbye to Hermione from her front step and walked towards my car. As I reached the pavement, a man further down the street was getting into a little blue Vauxhall. He drove past me and disappeared round the corner.

Usually when I left Hermione, I felt down because of the memories she evoked, but on this occasion I sat in my car trying to absorb the news, which had pushed Alex's murder to one side for the moment. The idea of so much wealth and a country house of enormous proportions did not excite me. If I thought anything of it, it was about its upkeep. I didn't need it, and I had more immediate problems to consider.

The street led to a T-junction where I turned right. In my rear mirror, I saw a small blue car pull out from the kerb and follow me. I saw it, yes, but with my mind on other things, it was of no concern. On the motorway it was still there. That made me suspicious. The traffic became heavier, and I did something I hate others doing – switching lanes whenever there's a gap. The Vauxhall slipped back and, as I kept manoeuvring through the jumble of cars, disappeared altogether.

LUPUS APPEARED to be asking me when our next adventure would start when he greeted me. The poor dog bored easily when left at home.

'Not long,' I said. 'I'm going to pack a bag, get you some food and then we'll go and look for Kirsten's cottage. Somewhere new for you to sniff.'

Google Maps said the drive to Uffington would take forty minutes as the traffic was normal. As I'd told the others, I was spending my driving time in my rear-view mirror, because of the number of times I'd been followed. This trip turned out to be no exception. A white Honda had been keeping a steady distance behind me ever since I got on the motorway. It wasn't Mark, that was certain; he was still crying over his fingertips. Was it NiPetco, or the press? There was a danger of becoming paranoid, but no harm would come from being careful. I left the main road and took a three-mile detour that involved several crossroads with random decisions at each. By the time I was back on the planned route the Honda was nowhere in sight.

The cottage was about two miles from Uffington as the crow flies, and set on the edge of another hamlet of a dozen houses. Kirsten had warned me, but the narrow lane was so disguised by vegetation I missed it at the first pass. It was more of a track than a lane, with a bank and a stone wall on the left side and a thick laurel hedge on the right. The entrance to her cottage consisted of two stone pillars and a very tight turn to get my car between them. Once in, there was no room for another vehicle, and visitors would have to park on the main road.

The building itself looked a bit run down and was surrounded on all sides by bushes only two metres from the walls. It was a bit confining for me. Lupus rushed inside to investigate the smells that had built up over the last three or four centuries. Ten minutes later and he was outside looking for wildlife.

The interior was spartan. There was originally only one room, a living room, but it had been sub-divided from the kitchen by a counter at one end. Somebody in recent times had added a minute bathroom to the outside wall. Hot water was supplied by pipes that ran through a small range cooker, which needed to be permanently alight. The living room was tiny with a bed, two chairs and a smallish fireplace with some wood stacked at its side. The thought of a fire made me conscious of the damp cold in there. A narrow window looked out, just as Kirsten said, to the white horse itself.

A firm knock on the door gave me a jolt. No one was supposed to know I was there.

'Hello. Saw you drive in here. Thought I'd come and say hello. I live on the other side of the main road. Name's Ivan, but I'm not Russian.' A man of average height and shoulders that pushed the limits of his tweed jacket laughed at his own joke. He was trying to look past me into the room.

'George.' I held out my hand, which he pumped enthusiastically with his own, which was hard and calloused.

'Welcome to our little community, George,' he said. 'You'll soon get to know everyone. We're a friendly lot. This is not a permanent place for you, is it? Will you be staying long?'

'I don't know. I'm hoping for peace and quiet to write for a while.'

'Oh, a writer, eh? Novelist? Non-fiction? How very interesting. Perhaps you could give a talk. I know that almost everyone would be fascinated to meet and hear a real author. What do you write?'

I was tempted to say erotic, dinosaur romance, but thought better of it. 'Horror.'

'Oh, goodness.' He gave a silly titter. 'I can think of a few here who will love you for that. Is your partner joining you?'

'No.'

He peered round me again. 'It is a bit small for a couple, I suppose. Can I help with anything?'

Lupus had come up behind him and was sniffing at his baggy corduroy trousers. They had turn-ups, which showed how outdated they and he were.

Ivan started suddenly and shrieked. 'Oh, God! Hello doggie, you gave me such a fright.' He bent down to look Lupus in the eye.

I put a hand under his shoulder to pull him up. 'Don't do that. Stand up. He doesn't know you, and I won't be quick enough to control him. Lupus, inside.'

'What a beautiful doggie. Is he vicious?'

'He can be – with the wrong person. And I don't think he likes the diminutive "doggie". He's bigger and more adult than that.'

'Yes, of course. Silly me. Anyway, George, I must fly. So good to come face to face with a real author. I'll set something up for you to meet our lot soon.'

Please don't. This was unfortunate. I hadn't bargained on being discovered so soon and had an image of that busybody rushing back to his cluster of houses and telling everyone of the famous author who has graced their community: and he's got a lovely dog called Lupus, but Lupus might bite, so do be careful; and he hasn't got a partner, as they call a girlfriend these days; and he doesn't have many possessions with him, as there was only a holdall and a box of food and the dog's blanket …

Except that neither his manner nor his clothes suited a man of Ivan's age and physicality.

26

ABOUT TWO HOURS later, after I'd settled in with my limited possessions, built up the stock of wood beside the stove and lit it, there was another tap on the door, more timid this time.

Not Ivan again, surely. It wasn't surprising to be visited by a busybody in such a tiny community, but it was remarkable that it happened so soon after I'd arrived; almost as if I'd been expected.

Lupus, who had decided that the warm patch in front of the stove was his, raised his head and got to his feet. There was no sense of urgency to his movements, though, and my initial suspicions died. He went to the door and waited.

'Hello, Paul. What on earth are you doing here?'

How the hell had those bastards at NiPetco traced me? I had shaken off the only tail on the way there, and only Kirsten and Mitch knew where I was. A tracking device on my car? Maybe, but Ivan had appeared so soon after I'd got there, they had to have known where I was going ahead of my arrival.

Of course! I had pinpointed the cottage on Google Maps using my laptop, and NiPetco had twice had the computer to themselves. I'd been worried they'd plant a bug in it, but so much had been going on, I'd forgotten about cleaning it – idiot.

Lupus sniffed at the biologist, found nothing of interest and wandered back to his chosen warmth.

'Andrew, good to see you again. My being here is pure coincidence. Incredible actually. I live in the village, down the far end – end house, in fact. I'm taking a few days' leave, since I couldn't experiment on you.' He laughed. 'That dreadful gossip Ivan has told everyone about you. He's been to every house. Terrible, like an old woman, cannot keep things to himself. Must be the first bearer of news, and all news is important if it affects our tiny hamlet.'

'Come in. Would you like a drink?'

Paul agreed to a small Scotch, so I gave him a hefty double. His tongue needed to loosen.

We chatted. Two people, neither of whom had many friends, had latched onto each other in a search for companionship. What was it like living in such a tiny community? How often do you come home, Paul? Are you married, and is your wife comfortable with your working arrangements?

Paul was settling in nicely. Little truths were starting to emerge. After first telling me how his wife was comfortable with his spending so much time at the NiPetco estate, the whisky eventually broke down his barriers and he almost resorted to tears, admitting she had left him. He was alone and there was no one at work he could relate to.

'Paul, do you really live in the village?'

He stared at me, his eyes bulging behind the thick round lenses. That shocked him. It wasn't only the tone of my voice: the truth of what he'd told me had been questioned, and just when we were getting along so well. It was a long wait before he replied. Did I not trust him?

'No, not any more. I'm sorry. Paul, I think you need to come clean with me. I want to believe the best things about you, but some of your intentions do not gel with a good future for me. What do you really want? To be the first scientist who discovers the secret to freezing your age? Do you want that no matter who or what is destroyed on your path to success?'

'Yes – I mean no. No, I don't wish anyone harm, of course I don't. And yes, to be known as the man who made such a discovery would put me on a par with Louis Pasteur and Alexander Fleming – remembered long after I'm gone.'

'Do you realise the implications of not growing older, Paul? The world's population will grow even faster than it does now and become a permanent threat to peace, democracy and personal liberty as people fight over food, water and land. Overpopulation and freedom are incompatible.'

'It will only affect the small number of people who can afford it. We will restrict it.'

'You're going to play God? Do you realise what my future will be if NiPetco get their hands on me?'

'Well, as I've told you several times, I just want to examine you in a non-invasive way. You'll stay with us in luxury and participate in harmless experiments. I can't go into detail, because it will depend on my findings as we go along.'

'Yes, I know what I've been told, but what do you think my future is going to be when the experiments are over? Don't bother answering. If you've even thought about it, you probably believe I'll be put back into society unharmed. That will not be the case, I promise you. NiPetco is doing this for massive profits in the long term. If I'm released back into the wild, I'll be snatched up by some other big pharmaceutical corporation and have to go through it all again. Decades of my life taken away from me so others can make a whopping profit, and you will be remembered in posterity.'

'Oh God no, Andrew. It's nothing like that. You're being paranoid, truly. No, I want to persuade you to undergo harmless examination, that's all. Why are you being so aggressive all of a sudden? I thought we were friends.'

'So you support my abduction, by force if necessary, in order to achieve your ambition? You support my captivity: unable to interact with society, unable to have a relationship or get married, have children or live a normal life for decades. And, when the experiments are over, I'll be killed to prevent any other company following suit. Is that your measure of friendship?'

'Andrew, that's insane. No one's going to do things like that – it's criminal.'

'Who is Ivan, Paul?'

'I told you, he's the village gossip, that's all.'

'But you don't live in the village, so how would you know that?'

I almost felt sorry for Paul. He was not cut out for the role he was being asked to play. He was leaning forward and rubbing his hands against one another, as if washing them.

'I used to live here, and I just met him in the street.'

'Let's put it another way. What's the connection between Ivan and NiPetco?'

'Nothing … not as far as I know. That's the truth, Andrew. Why are you questioning me like this?'

'Are you here on NiPetco's orders? Did Nigel himself ask you to do this?'

Paul swallowed and dropped his eyes. He mumbled something. I had to restore his confidence. 'What role does Don play, Paul? Why is he so antagonistic towards me?'

Paul sat back looking relieved. The questions had moved into safer territory. 'As far as I know, he's just the financial director for the UK – honestly. His attitude is weird to everyone. I wouldn't worry about it, I doubt it's personal.'

'Lastly, Paul, do you know Mohamed Baqri?'

'Who?'

'At a guess, I'd say he's of Pakistani origin. Big chap, strong, athletic. Have you seen him at the estate at all?'

'I have seen a couple of men who may be from that part of the world. I can't say I noticed anything about them, though. Why, what has he done?'

'What did these men do at the house? Who did they see?'

'I don't remember seeing them doing anything. I saw Nigel talking to the driver once. I remember that.'

'What does Nigel want you to do, Paul? Where is he now?'

'Why are you being like this, Andrew? I bumped into Ivan and he told me you were here, so I came to say hello. There's nothing more to it than that.'

'I need to know who else is out there. Is Nigel there, Baqri, Don, anybody else?'

Silence.

'Paul, I believe you're a good man at heart. Whatever you've been asked to do is not in your nature, so I think Nigel has got something over you. I don't want to know what it is, but please think of my future. My life is at stake here. Tell me what's going on. Were you sent here to recce the place? Are you going to report back to them?'

'I don't know what you're talking about. There's nothing going on, it's just an extraordinary coincidence.'

'Paul, I told Ivan my name was George.'

It took a whisky pause for that to sink in.

27

PAUL'S MOUTH FLAPPED open and closed, but no words came. Clearly embarrassed at being caught in such a lie, he stared at me. Another knock on the door, and his head flicked round, alarm and fear in his face.

The cottage had probably never seen so many visitors before – hostile visitors, that was. Lupus was my weathervane. His reaction was to vacate his warm spot and head quickly to the door. Before he got there his tail was wagging.

Kirsten, typically, cuddled Lupus before she greeted me. She was looking the most informal I had seen her: red hair down, no glasses, and dressed in black jeans and a leather jacket like Mitch, except that his jeans were his usual blue. The little man grinned, dropped a holdall to the floor and gripped my hand, but his eyes were on Paul. He raised a questioning eyebrow.

'This is Paul. He's the chief biologist for NiPetco. He heard I was here and popped in to say hello.'

'Popped in?' Mitch muttered. Then, audibly: 'We wanted to see how you're getting on, and give Kirsten the opportunity to check on her cottage. We brought sleeping bags.'

Paul had risen to his feet out of good manners. Embarrassment, guilt, shame and a host of other miserable expressions crossed his face. He'd been caught spying on me for the enemy, and his task wasn't over. Sweat glistened on his forehead. Fidgeting and shifting his feet, he was clearly anxious to be out of there. His genuine attempts to form a friendship with me had been destroyed by his own deceit, which must have added to his distress.

Would his guilt make him susceptible if I called in a debt? And if I piled on the pressure, would he crack? 'Paul is leaving to tell the boss of NiPetco that you two have just arrived, so his plans may have to change.'

'Oh,' said Kirsten, 'that's a pity. It would be nice to talk to someone in your position.'

'No, no, I … I'm not going to report anything. I … I don't even know where Nigel is.'

'Paul, really, you should go and tell Nigel what's happened. He won't have counted on having two extra people to deal with. At least phone him.'

'No. H-he's not here, as far as I know, and there's no reason he should be. It's n-no good phoning, he doesn't answer this late.'

'Why? Is that because he's abusing children at this hour?'

'What? I don't know what you're talking about.'

'I hope not. Paul, get over your embarrassment at deceiving me. I've put it behind me. I really think your loyalty to your company should take precedence. So go and tell them to be prepared for a surprise.'

He was saved from another stuttering reply by a friendly rhythmic knock on the door. Crunch time. But it was only Ivan.

'George, old man. Good news.' He was standing on the threshold, trying again to peer around me. 'I've managed to put together an evening tomorrow for the village to meet an eminent author.' After a silly giggle, he added, 'I say, you haven't seen Paul, have you? I told him you were here, and he was going to come and see you again, but he's been an awfully long time. I hope he's all right.' He tried to see round the other side of me.

'You'd better come in, Ivan.' I tugged at his arm. He resisted, which was natural, but with greater strength than I would have imagined. He stepped round me, and as he did so I caught a fleeting glimpse of movement in the dark behind him. Lupus growled.

'Oh, silly doggie. I'm your friend, no need to be cross with me. Here, have a biccie.' Ivan pulled a dog treat from his pocket.

'He doesn't eat those things. Don't feed him please, Ivan, he's not allowed them.'

The biscuit fell to the floor anyway. Lupus sniffed it and left it. That attempt at poisoning him and getting him out of the way had failed.

If it came to a physical confrontation, the odds were unknown. Our side consisted of Mitch and me and Lupus, with limited help from Kirsten. NiPetco had Ivan and an unknown army, possibly including a machete-wielding killer. Paul might help us, but he was more likely to hide in a corner. The danger was that if NiPetco got the better of us, they might well dispose of Kirsten and Mitch, because they would be witnesses. They wanted me alive, so I would be safe enough for some time to come.

'Who else is out there, Ivan?' I closed the door and latched it.

'No one. Why?'

I introduced everyone and in doing so moved close to Mitch and Kirsten. 'This guy has to be immobilised. Get some rope or cord, even string will do. Oh, and the biggest kitchen knife.'

'Gotcha.' The beauty of working with Mitch was that he didn't ask stupid time-wasting get-in-the-way questions, he followed instructions and discussed the merits, or lack of them, later.

Kirsten said, 'There's some rope in the shed. Do you want me to get it?'

'*No*. Do not go outside under any circumstance. It's far too dangerous.'

She went to a cupboard, fished around and put a ball of string on the counter.

Ivan, in his busybody style, was telling the room how he kept the local community together with news and views. It brought them all into a really close community, he said.

With a simultaneous pull on his shoulder and a hard push to the back of his knee, he dropped. But he was fast, turning and half onto his feet when he saw the dog's teeth inches from his face. He froze as Lupus breathed on him. Ivan was not what he pretended to be. Any normal person would have been shocked into immobility for a few seconds.

'On your stomach, Ivan. Lupus won't touch you unless you attack me or I tell him to. So be a good chap and do what I say.'

Ivan rolled onto his front and put his hands behind his back without my having to tell him to. He knew the drill, so what was his profession? Paul's hand was up to his mouth, his expression frozen in shock. I had a feeling that Paul might switch his allegiance if he understood the evil he was supporting. It was therefore important not to let him see us, but his current side, as the violent ones.

With Ivan's thumbs tied tightly together with multiple rounds of string, he was out of the action, at least until he got the opportunity to stretch his arms over his feet and round to his front – if he was that supple.

'What's your background, Ivan, or whatever your name is? You're not the village busybody at all, are you?'

Ivan said nothing. He was sitting on the floor with Lupus at his feet, facing him, so he wasn't going to move.

From behind, I went through his pockets and retrieved his phone. Tapped it, showed it his face and it opened. His expression remained blank when I said, 'Recent calls?'

Nigel answered almost immediately. 'Yeah, what the fuck you guys doin', Ivan? Where we at? You got him yet?'

'No, they haven't got me yet, Nigel. I suggest you get your fat arse over here to the cottage and we can talk about this as civilised human beings.'

Angry breathing greeted that introduction. 'You alone, Duncan?'

I couldn't be bothered to correct him again. 'Paul and Ivan are here with me. Do join us. We can have a party.'

I put Ivan's phone in my pocket. 'Is there another knife for me please, Mitch?'

He was holding a kitchen knife with a foot-long blade. He handed me another slightly smaller one over Ivan's head. 'You've got a longer reach than I have.'

Paul was fidgeting, his eyes flicking back and forth from one of us to the other. 'What are you going to do, Andrew? Are … are you going to kill us?'

I crossed the room to him. He retreated a step, but I put a reassuring hand on his arm and whispered in his ear, 'Relax, Paul, my friend. I've no intention of hurting anyone unless they try to attack us. Ivan there is not what he seems. I think he's a dangerous man, a professional. The knives are for protection.'

Lupus was on his feet. He trotted to the front door and gave a little growl. Ivan twisted round to see if he was the subject. Someone tried the handle. A heavy knocking rattled the door within its frame. The dog's snarl became more intense. Keeping the knife behind my back, I unlatched the lock and stood back. 'Come in.'

Nigel filled the frame. He ducked under its low, eighteenth-century lintel and stomped into the room, his boot heels clacking on the wooden floor. He glared at everyone whose eyes he met. Paul, a nervous kitten by the kitchen counter, looked away; Kirsten, beside him, stared back with her courtroom severity; Mitch's face was expressionless, though the long blade he cradled was an adequate substitute; Ivan, immobile on the floor, was looking elsewhere. Lupus was staring up at Nigel, inches from his right hand. Nigel slowly raised it out of the way.

I kicked the door shut and latched it. 'Where's Baqri, Nigel?'

'What the fuck's going on here? Who are these guys?'

'Where's Mohamed Baqri, Nigel?'

'What the hell are you talking about? What's goin' on?'

Nigel was standing in his wide-legged stance. That was fine: with one leg out he would be more out of balance. I used the same trick that worked with Ivan: a strong kick to the back of his left knee, a simultaneous pull back on his left shoulder, and he went down with Lupus breathing in his face. I could never be this effective without my canine friend. Nigel's thumbs were thicker and fleshier than Ivan's, but it made no difference; the string cut a bit deeper, that was all.

'Nigel, now I have your full attention: Baqri, the assassin you hired to kill Alexandra de Villiers, where is he?' I was taking a chance, I didn't know anything of the sort, but it was worth a try.

'What the fuck …?'

'Don't claim you don't know Baqri. You've been seen talking to him. He was the driver of that van when you called me away from any discussion with him, remember? And Baqri has an injured right arm where Lupus here savaged him in my house when he killed her.'

'You're talking a load of crap. I dunno what your game is, Duncan, but you're making a big mistake. I'm going to sue the fucking shirt off your back.'

'After you've experimented on me, no doubt.'

Mitch was grinning at me. He was enjoying this.

'What exactly are your plans for me, Nigel? You're going to take samples, work out what's going on, try a few things and see if you can concoct a pill or something. Then what? Are you going to kill me so you don't have to pay me millions of pounds and so your competitors can't get hold of me and try the same thing?'

Paul was staring intently at Nigel. His reaction to the answer was important. Had I cast enough doubt in his mind for him to at least question NiPetco's motives?

'Don't be so goddam stupid. I'm a guy that everyone looks up to, everyone respects. I'm well regarded. I'll be running for Governor next year. Why would I destroy that for some little jerk like you?'

'People can make mistakes. They'll change their mind as soon as you're convicted of child abuse and murder.'

'Bullshit,' Nigel muttered.

'I told you I have photographs that prove you abused underage girls at Shalamar Gardens. I have your lapel pin, the Longhorns one. Guess where I found it – in the garden at Shalamar. I can prove you know the man who killed Miss de Villiers. He reports to you for orders, doesn't he? And he's outside somewhere, isn't he? It suited you to have her killed, because she knew you're a paedophile, and she was getting close to exposing the gang, including Baqri and some clients. It also suited you to have her killed because it could result in my arrest. NiPetco could then give me an alibi, thereby bringing me over to your side.' I paused, waiting for him to respond, but he didn't. 'Anyway, that's plenty for the police to chew on.

'*Oh*. My sincere apologies, Nigel, I forgot to introduce you. Terrible manners. The chap over there with the grin and a large knife is Mitch. He's my professional assistant. The lady is Kirsten Pearman, my barrister. She's taking all this in, including your reactions.'

It was quite enjoyable to watch this. Nigel was squirming. He'd lost his bluster, and I could picture his mind racing through his options. He must have realised the police would be there soon, so he had to stick to some semblance of normality.

Paul was shocked, that was clear. To hear that his boss was a paedophile and possibly a murderer, a charge Nigel hadn't defended, must have made Paul question his loyalty. What was it going to take to swing the biologist solidly onto our side to get better odds? It wasn't that he would be much use. Maybe he could run errands or make a phone call, but better that than have him undermining us somehow. He started to say something, but had to clear his throat. 'Is this true, Nigel? Did you have his wife killed? Did you abuse children? That's horrible. How could you do that?'

Nigel didn't answer. He merely shook his head.

Ivan hadn't moved from his position on the floor. He was suspiciously quiet. I checked his thumbs; they were going blue but were still secure.

Kirsten radiated tension. The image I had come to recognise as her pretty, feminine, cheerful side was absent now. The prosecutor's unwavering glare was there, just not amplified by spectacles. This wasn't an act for the court. This was the real thing – fury bottled up for more than three decades and about to blow. I should have recognised it, because she hadn't taken her eyes off Nigel since he came in.

No matter what contortions a leopard undertakes to get into position to strike, its eyes never leave its prey. With slow and purposeful movements, Kirsten pulled her sleeves up to her elbows. From somewhere a knife appeared in her right hand. She must have found it when she was looking for string. The blade was only the length of her middle finger, but long enough to cause damage. I could see it, but Mitch was not able to, which is why he did nothing. It was five paces down the length of the room to Nigel. She took the first three at a measured speed.

'*No*, Kirsten. Mitch, grab her.'

He leapt, wrapped his arms round her, pinning hers to her side. She fought. Mitch's hold broke. I went for the knife, missed and was slashed across my forearm. In her rage she couldn't see us: Mitch and Andrew. We were just two obstacles in her path. Mitch clamped her arms again. She kicked backwards at him, her eyes still on Nigel. I caught her hand and managed to prise her fingers open. The little knife dropped to the floor. I stood on it.

My body blocked her view of Nigel, breaking her tie to him. Her hard eyes turned on me. 'Give me the knife.'

'What happened to innocent until proven guilty in a court of law, Miss Barrister? You want to ruin your career? You almost did it.'

She held my gaze a little longer before her head dropped. I stared at the top of it, half expecting her to erupt again, but she muttered, 'Sorry.'

My imagination heard a gasp of relief from the room. Paul's hand was up to his mouth. Kirsten stepped back to be beside Mitch, who had a gentle hold on her upper arm in a gesture of support.

Kirsten regained control of herself. As if nothing had happened, she said, 'Andrew, you must call the police. You must do it before the situation deteriorates and you do some-thing that could be construed as a wrongful act.'

'That's rich, coming from you. I'm not doing it yet. I need to find Baqri.'

'She's right,' Mitch said. 'We won't be able to control this lot forever, and if this Baqri is a professional, they'll need a firearms team.' He pulled out his phone and tapped it three times. From the far corner of the room he watched the rest of us as he spoke.

'I'm not waiting till they get here, he could be long gone.' I said. 'Nigel, does Baqri have a gun?'

'How the fuck would I know?'

Ivan shifted to a more comfortable position. His voice was still recognisable, but he dropped his village gossip style for a hard, no-nonsense tone in a West Country accent that came more naturally to him. 'He won't. He follows some tradition of his. Silent methods only: garrotte, knife and so on. You'd better be careful, he's an evil bastard.'

'Why would you offer me that advice, Ivan?'

A few seconds passed before he replied. 'You have more urgent things to worry about than my mental processes. I'll tell you when there's more time, but for now let's say that some things have been going on in the NiPetco management that I can't agree with. The time has come to right some wrongs. Plus, I have no desire to see anyone killed – except Baqri. He's pure evil.'

'Did you try to save me for Nigel's experiments?'

Ivan shrugged. 'Actually, no, but think what you want. I'd better tell you about Baqri. You probably don't know that he's a graduate of a school for professional assassins.'

Paul gave a little gasp.

'For two hundred years from the eleventh century the Nizari Ismaili sect had a select band of warriors neutralise their enemies by killing prominent figures. They focused mainly on Islamic leaders, but later on Christian ones, including the Crusaders. Promising young men were trained in stealth, disguise, strategy, languages and killing – almost exclusively with a knife or sword. They never used distance weapons such as arrows. Getting up close was a matter of pride. When you think about it, if you can prevent a war in which hundreds of lives will be lost, the use of an assassin to take out a leader and force submission is a pretty good idea.

'They were eliminated by the Mongols, but a few assassin schools still exist. Of particular interest to you is that there are at least two in the tribal areas of Pakistan. Baqri went to one of these. The end product is a professional killer who can be hired. Their motives may be ideological or religious or political. They may have no motive other than to be paid well. The trouble with Baqri is that he's a psychopath who has found a profession he truly loves.'

Ivan paused. Everyone was staring at him, waiting for some answer to the ghastly scenario he was painting. He didn't give it. 'I don't think he would shy away from coming in here and slashing all of us in one frenzied sortie. A blood-bath is his idea of paradise.'

'How do you know this?' I said.

'He takes something, maybe several things. It has the effect of cancelling all emotion and feeling, but it also makes him talk. He was rambling on one night, telling me all this stuff. He's lost count of how many victims there are. It was not a night I want to repeat. I kept a distance between us as much as I could and got out of there when he fell asleep.'

'He's scared of dogs,' I said.

Ivan nodded. 'Common trait across the region.'

'Mitch, how long before the cops get here?'

'I don't know. We're a long way from a firearms unit or even from a station of any size. Could be half an hour, perhaps more.'

'They'll need a helicopter with an infrared camera.'

'I told 'em that.'

Nigel was still on his stomach. I tapped him with my foot. 'It's time to stop playing silly-buggers, Nigel. You can't escape prosecution on a host of charges, and you know it. Do us all a favour and help. Why is Baqri here? He's a killer. Why have you brought him here, when you want me alive?'

He grunted. He was uncomfortable, and his bulk hindered his attempts to sit up. 'I didn't bring him. He came hidden in the car's trunk. I told him to stay out of it, but he wants you, because you know it was him who killed your girl. You'd better not go out there, Duncan, he'll carve you up.'

'It might have been him that did it, but it was you that ordered it.' I could hear the bitterness in my voice.

Ivan said, 'I'd appreciate it if you untied me. I don't fancy being helpless if Baqri gets in here. He'll kill you, you're his target, and he'll kill everyone else because we'll be witnesses or because he simply likes to round things off.'

'Why should I trust you? You tried to poison my dog a short while ago. After which you'd have been able to over-power me.'

He shrugged. 'No reason, other than what I told you I suppose, but the more able bodied men there are, the safer we'll all be. I didn't tell you how that evening ended. He has an ornate silver hip flask with typical motifs from that part of the world. He took a sip, and I said I didn't think he drank. He replied that it wasn't alcohol, offered me some, and when I declined he laughed, opened his mouth and stuck out his tongue. Red dribble ran down his chin.'

A light tapping came from the door. Kirsten and Mitch looked up. For the first time, Kirsten appeared worried. As far as we knew, there was only one person out there.

28

THE COTTAGE HAD one door and two windows, one at each end. At the kitchen end, the window was above my car, which was parked so close to the house that the passenger door could not be opened wide enough to get in. The window in the living area opened to the garden, where it was dark and thick with laurel and prickly holly bushes – excellent places for Baqri to hide before sprinting a few steps across the grass to attack.

The assassin would be waiting for someone to emerge from the secure environment inside. Would he watch the door or one of the windows? And while he waited, was he also working out how to get inside to satisfy his blood lust?

Every choice I faced could end in disaster. If I opened the door, I'd be back-lit and he could charge at me unseen, knife me and get inside. If I chose a window, I'd be vulnerable as I climbed out, but he would not be able to get inside without serious opposition from Mitch and Ivan, if I freed him. Paul might help, too – he might. With the kitchen window, my car was in the way, blocking any attempt by him to attack me at the worst time. If I chose the garden window, I'd be jumping out into the dark unknown. Whichever I chose, the most sensible thing was to let Lupus go first – he'd flush the killer from hiding before I had one leg out. But the thought that Lupus had been cut before wouldn't leave my mind. I clipped his lead on him.

The tapping on the door had stopped, but was the man still there, waiting?

I pulled Kirsten and Mitch back from the others and spoke quietly. 'I'm going out the kitchen window.'

'Don't be silly, Andrew,' Kirsten said. 'Wait till the police get here, let them deal with him.'

'They could be ages, and he could escape and go into hiding. No, I want this finished tonight.'

Mitch put a hand down to Lupus. 'Let your mate here go out first. He'll find Baqri long before you do and might even take him down before you get there. I'll be right behind you.'

'No on both counts. This is not your fight, Mitch. I won't have you exposed to danger in my personal battle, and this bunch need watching. Ivan there is a pro of some sort, he could be dangerous. See if you can get Paul to help you if you need him. I think he's at last seen Nigel for what he is. And finally, I'm not taking Lupus. I won't have him exposed to another stabbing.'

'Now you're being stupid, Andrew. Lupus is a dog, a wonderful dog, but he's still a dog and will probably save your life out there.'

'Rather this man escapes than you or Lupus get killed,' said Kirsten, taking both points of view into account. She certainly didn't want Lupus to be harmed.

'If I were normal, I'd be approaching the end of my life anyway. I should die in a few years or sooner. What difference does it make whether it's now or later? We're wasting time. Hold onto him now, will you, Kirsten. And that applies to the long term if it things go wrong … please.'

Surprise and a flash of alarm crossed her face for a moment. With pursed lips she nodded her agreement, but her guard was down just long enough to show her concern.

Mitch took the dog. I crossed to the kitchen window and pulled the curtain to one side. A sliver of moon had risen, its light casting a dim silvery glow over the driveway and reflecting off the roof of my car.

The window was jammed – probably paint. When opened it was going make a noise that would be heard outside. It was still the best option, though. One push, two, three times, and the window gave with the predicted cracks. The whole room was watching. Paul had his hand to his mouth, Nigel was gently shaking his head, Kirsten looked worried, Mitch clearly thought I was crazy and was hanging onto a straining Lupus, while Ivan appeared completely dispassionate. When he saw me looking, he shrugged and said, 'He claims to have much better night vision than most.'

I slithered down into the gap between the wall and my car – trapped if Baqri came. Inching my way to the front, desperate to break free, I ducked as a hairy monster launched itself out of the window and across the bonnet. Lupus landed on the far side, but was immediately beside me as I got clear of the car. His lead was still attached. Had Mitch released him on purpose? I could have let him go and he'd have searched the property in a couple of minutes, but I wanted him close, for his protection, not mine.

It was best to clear the lane first. We walked slowly down the hill with the stone wall on our left. It was built on a bank and loomed well above head height, its individual rocks barely visible beneath dense moss. An assassin could jump off there and flatten me to the road before wielding his knife. To our right the bushes were thick and dark, an ideal place for someone to hide and leap out and attack. But why would he wait there? He would have had no idea that I was going to start my search in the lane. But was there a gap; could he get from where he was skulking in the garden to the lane?

As cars passed on the main road a hundred yards uphill, reflected light flashed down the track, but it didn't help. Lupus was showing no signs that another person was anywhere near.

We reached the end of Kirsten's property and were beside a field. It was time to retrace our steps and search the garden, which was going to be much more dangerous.

Between the sandstone gateposts, we paused to listen – nothing.

The only way to get to the garden from the front gate was past the front door and on to the end of the cottage. Dark and forbidding, the bushes leant over almost to the roof. Baqri had probably left the area by the door already, but still this needed extreme caution. Lupus was my scout, my advance warning. I wasn't sure, but if he were working in a true police role, he would probably have been loose and searching for the killer well ahead of his handler. But Lupus was my friend not a working dog, however much he thought he was.

At the end of the building the garden opened in front of us. Thin clouds scudded across the moon, subduing its meagre light. It was hard to make out detail. Nothing moved, and Lupus gave no sign of trouble. Ahead was a forty-metre stretch of lawn, with its dense laurel borders. In the far corner beneath a massive tree – an oak, maybe – was an old wooden shed. My eye was drawn to it as it stood in stark contrast to the vegetation; it was a human construction, and it was where a human would hide. It was easy to assume that Baqri was skulking in or behind the shed. Of course, he might have wanted me to think that.

The sensible thing to do was to set Lupus free to find the bastard, but that was too dangerous. Not that he had any qualms.

Someone was there. Lupus knew it, and he wanted him. He was pulling me directly towards the bushes beside the shed. Baqri's thinking was plainly that, hidden there, he was within striking distance of the shed door. I would go to it, open it, look inside and he would stab me in the back. Well, that wasn't going to happen.

I tightened my grip on the knife more for the comfort of it than the protection it offered. I didn't want to use it. He was worth more alive than dead with so much information on the gang of abusers. In any case, I wasn't a killer; but I needed a weapon. How was he armed? I'd only seen him with a machete, but he'd used my kitchen knife on Alex. A machete is not easy to hide, especially if you're travelling. I had to assume he had one.

Who the hell was I kidding? Baqri was a trained assassin with, maybe, scores of corpses to his credit. I had never even been in a knife fight, and there I was heading into an uneven and deadly contest.

These thoughts were bringing me closer to the confrontation and highlighting my fear. Yes, I was scared, I didn't mind admitting it to myself, but fear has to be overcome, and this man had to be caught.

Lupus kept pulling me to the bushes beside the hut, but he wasn't looking in there, he was looking up.

LUPUS WAS going to have to be freed at some point. With his lead in one hand, I would not be able to fully protect myself. Human expressions, emotions and feelings should not be transposed to dogs. They don't necessarily think what we're thinking, and false assumptions lead to trouble. I knew this, and while Lupus was a weapon in my armoury to avenge Alex, I believe his own revenge was what drove him that night.

A heavy branch projected out over the hut roof. Baqri could be on the roof, or in the tree above it. The only way up for Lupus was via the roof, but that overhung the side of the hut, meaning the dog could not climb it as he had Nigel's estate wall. Not without me, that was. Unclipping his lead, I positioned myself about two feet away from the hut's side and bent over, hands on knees for support.

Lupus knew what to do, he'd been trained by the best. His dark shape hurtled towards me and leapt. Thirty kilos landed on my back. I staggered. His claws scraped for purchase. But it was only a step up. He didn't stop, he sprang up off me and onto the roof. I swore he'd taken chunks out of my skin.

The low, guttural sound of an angry dog viciously shaking its victim, screeches, scraping and thumping resonated through the hut from the wooden roof. Nothing could be seen from where I was. Then a crash and a scream of agony came from the far side.

Baqri was on the ground crying something in his own language – a plea for help most likely, which fell on my deaf ears. Lupus was savaging one arm. The other was feebly trying to fight the dog off one moment and then scrabbling on the ground for his knife. It was out of his reach, and I kicked it further away. With my face inches from his, I passed my long kitchen knife slowly across his line of sight and down to prick his rasping throat. His eyes bulged, and a low moan escaped his quivering lips.

A thirty-kilo dog had flattened a ninety-kilo man and was busy crushing his ulna and radius bones. It struck me that there was merit in some things the Romans did in the Colosseum. I should settle back in a nice comfortable armchair with a glass of malt and watch this killer's agony for half an hour. Maybe the others would like to join me.

But I was weak. 'Leave, Lupus, leave. Good boy, good dog.'

I took time to stroke his ears and he sat back, panting, but his intense stare never left the man who killed his mistress. At that moment, at least, Lupus had the same train of thought that I did.

Baqri started jabbering, in Urdu I suppose. I couldn't understand and certainly didn't care what his problem was. He was in pain, half burbling and half crying. He was going nowhere, not with his right leg twisted at an impossible angle. Which gave me an idea.

There was no sign of anyone from the cottage. Putting my phone onto record, I said, 'Do you speak English?'

Tears of pain glinted on his cheeks. He nodded.

'Do you know Nigel Pettigrew?'

He shook his head gently, as if anything vigorous would bring on more pain. I took hold of his right foot, but didn't move it.

'Do you know Nigel Pettigrew? American. Big man. You went to see him at his house. I saw you there.'

Another shake of the head. His eyes were closed, his teeth gripping his lower lip. Sweat glistened in the moonlight.

I gave his foot a little tweak. His back arched, his eyes opened, and he stifled a cry. 'Yes, sir. I know big American man. I not knowing name.'

There was one answer I wanted above all others, but first some easy questions. 'Have you seen him at Shalamar Gardens?'

'Yes, sir.'

'Have you seen him with young girls?'

'No, sir. But I taking girls to him and other men. I not knowing what they do. They closing door.'

'That's very good, Mohamed. Well done. Would you like to go to hospital so they can fix your leg?'

'Yes – no. I much pain, sir.'

'Did Nigel tell you to kill that lady where this dog attacked you?' I gave his foot another little shake.

'I no killing lady.' He was gasping. This man had found inflicting pain much easier than taking it.

Alex's mutilated corpse blocked my vision, and once again my hand clutched her cold, sticky, bloodied fingers. Baqri, Pettigrew's instrument, was responsible, yet he had the gall to beg me for mercy. Since experiencing Liz and Rache's trauma I had succeeded in taking a more compassionate view of humanity. Mark had elicited no sympathy from me, but I did him no harm. Baqri, on the other hand, took me down to a place well below anywhere I'd been before. I would never treat an insect or a snake the way I wanted to deal with this monster. 'Shall I put the dog on you again?'

'No, sir. No. Please sir. *Aagh!*'

'Let's try again. Did the American tell you to kill the lady?' Tweak.

His head came off the ground. '*Aagh!* Yes, sir. He telling me, "Go finish that bitch." That what he say, sir.'

Nigel Pettigrew's hired psychopath had killed in frenzied blood lust while the big man sat in the comfort of his mansion issuing orders and plotting how to use other people's lives for his profit. I found it difficult to summon words.

'All right, Mohamed. You stay here. My dog will look after you. I advise you not to move. I'll be back shortly, and we'll see about getting you to hospital.'

'No, sir. No hospital.'

'Why, do you want to go through your life with one foot facing backwards?' I switched off my recording and left him under Lupus's unwavering stare.

29

I HADN'T EVEN closed the cottage door when Kirsten asked, 'Where's Lupus?'

'He's happy. He's standing guard over Baqri, who doesn't dare move a muscle.'

Mitch laughed. Ivan raised his eyebrows and gave a nod of satisfaction. Nigel didn't react, he was focused on the floor in front of him. I guessed he was worried about what Baqri would say under questioning. Bit late, Nige.

'So, Nige, I have all the answers I need to have you leave me alone. Your instrument Baqri has told me just what he did for you, and what he did to supply you with underage girls.'

The fact that he gave me that information while I twisted his broken leg did not bother me one iota. Baqri slaughtered Alex, and Pettigrew was a paedophile and a murderer. He surrendered any rights he had the instant he embarked on his trail of abuse.

Nigel continued to stare at the floor in front of him. Most likely, he was thinking his future as Governor of Texas was over. Pale-faced, he muttered, 'It's all lies.'

Nudging Ivan's foot with my own, I bent down to look him in the eye. His face was expressionless, almost innocent. He was used to this stuff. 'You're a contractor aren't you? Who are you working for – Nigel?'

'In part, I was.'

Nigel gave him a sharp look. 'Whatd'ya mean? I hired you, you work for me.'

'Not entirely. I was asked to do some things I didn't agree with, so I made choices and tried to retain an ethical path in your unethical company.'

Nigel didn't even try to reply to that and returned to studying the floor.

A shot rang out. The sharp crack of a handgun – crisp and loud and close. The noise stunned the room. For a second everyone was rigid with alarm.

Nigel's head whipped up. Mitch flicked his attention to the garden window. Paul's eyes were wide, his hand over his open mouth. Kirsten looked at me as if I could tell her what had happened. Ivan raised an eyebrow as he studied my reaction. He was far too calm for my liking.

I started for the door in a stupid gut response. '*Lupus*. Has Lupus been shot?'

'No, Andrew. Stay inside,' Kirsten and Mitch chorused.

'That won't be your dog,' Ivan said from the floor.

'What do you mean? You know who's out there?'

'Yes. Untie me, and I'll come with you. We'll sort this out.'

Could I trust him? If he was working for someone other than Nigel, and he obviously wouldn't defend a paedophile, then he was better than some. I took a chance.

I couldn't waste time untying the knots at Ivan's back and used the knife, nicking him. 'Sorry, not intentional.'

He shrugged and rubbed his thumbs. 'You ready?'

I nodded and looked down at the knife in my hand. It wouldn't be much use against a gun, but … 'Let's go.'

IN SPITE of the drama it had witnessed a few minutes earlier, the garden appeared peaceful and undisturbed. The oppressive nature of the bushes had not changed, nor had the distinct outline of the shed in the far corner. I had left Baqri on the other side of the building with Lupus watching him, even though he was in no fit state to move. There was no sign of them from where we were. Ivan moved cautiously but with confidence. As we approached the hut, dark and angular amongst the vegetation, the immobile outline of a man became apparent. The shapeless lump on the ground was Baqri. He was no longer moaning in pain; he was out of his misery.

Another form bounded towards me. I put my hand down and held Lupus's head to my thigh for a few seconds, but my eyes were on the man. He turned to face us and raised his right hand, pointing at me.

I stopped, but Ivan continued the last few steps to the shed door. 'Put the gun down, it's not necessary,' he said.

'So you say. I don't trust this guy.'

He was American, but I didn't recognise his voice – it was hoarse – and I couldn't see who he was. 'Ivan, you want to explain now?'

He took a deep breath. 'Sure. About nine months ago, I was contacted by Hymie Green to join NiPetco security. I was appointed as the head of a particular section of the team, which operated in the background. We were not seen by the public. I don't suppose I have to tell you how secretive pharmaceutical companies are. The scope for industrial espionage is huge, and preventing that is a primary function of security.

'I'd been in the job for a couple of months when I was approached by another of the executives. For some reason he trusted me and felt I was his kind of person. He said he was fed up with NiPetco; he disliked Nigel intensely and wanted to go his own way. He said there was another position he was hunting and he felt that the two of us could come as a package to our mutual benefit. Well, I wasn't happy in the company either, and with Nigel in particular, so I thought I'd play along with his suggestion and see how it developed. Without committing myself, you understand. When Nigel had you abducted, that was the final straw for me. I've done a few bad things in my life, but using people like that is not one of them.

'This director and I were getting along and I was looking forward to some progress towards this new job he'd promised. Then one day he asked me to drive him to a house after work. He was going to drink with friends and would not be able to drive afterwards. These trips became regular, usually on the same day every week.'

My questions were building up, but to interrupt him while he was in the groove might result in lost detail.

'There were usually up to four or five other men that visited at the same time, and he'd be in the house a couple of hours. They drank a lot those nights. I sat in the car, or went into the kitchen and scrounged a bite off the cook while I waited. I don't know why, really, but I assumed the place was an expensive brothel. I never saw any girls, though. Then one night, it was hot, and I reckon a window was open, because I heard the kids. Sounds of crying and pleading ...' Ivan stopped talking for a moment. It was too dark to see his face, but I imagined he was collecting himself.

He went on, 'Male voices, too. I couldn't hear exactly what was said, but there was cheering and laughing. That didn't fit with the cries the kids made, and I understood what was going on.'

'What did you do?'

'To my shame – nothing. Not at first, anyway. I was under contract to NiPetco, still am, so all I did was refuse to take this out-of-hours duty. Time passed, and you learn a lot just by listening. I heard talk of a journalist investigating a child trafficking gang, and this one director mentioned her. I guess her talking to one or two of the wrong people was how they found out about her.'

My neck was going into spasm. I couldn't wait for the next detail, I had to know everything that happened to her: why it was done, how it was planned, who was involved, every detail, all included in one great big chunk of information. 'Go on.'

'I was asked, in an indirect manner, to shut her up. As soon as I demanded clarification on what that meant, the subject was dropped. Then Mohamed Baqri appeared on the scene. I know a killer when I see one, and this guy was a psychopath, no doubt about it. Pure evil. Killing an investigator was unnecessary and dangerous. When your lady was killed, I knew what had happened, and I knew who ordered it.'

'Who?'

'He's standing right here. He shot Baqri to stop him talking, but what are you going to do now, Don?'

'Y'all broke our agreement. You're a rat, Ivan, a stinkin' rat.'

'Killing innocent women was never in any agreement I made, Don. Neither is helping paedophiles. You've dug yourself a deep hole in the shit now. Are you going to kill Andrew and me? Let me tell you, if you shoot Andrew, his dog will kill you. If you shoot the dog first, Andrew and I will be on you so fast you won't know what hit you, so think very carefully.'

Don. Of course; how could I have been so stupid? I didn't even think of him. He had Alex killed because she was about to expose the paedophiles and destroy their gang. He didn't like me because I probably had access to all the evidence she'd collected. Nigel, however, went straight up my nose, mainly because he was so bullish and prominent. Consequently, he slipped neatly into the role of paedophile and murderer. Nigel had the boots, too, and it was the boots in the photo I took at Shalamar that singled him out. I had forgotten that Don, the man of few words and overshadowed by Nigel, also wore Western boots.

Ivan was still speaking. 'If I were you, Don, I'd run. Killing more people isn't going to solve your problem. In any case, the police are already on their way, and they've got a firearms unit with them. They should be here shortly. If you go now, you at least have a chance of getting away. If you hang around, they'll have you in a flash. There'll be no chance of escape then.'

Don gave a slow, understanding nod, then raised his arm and pointed his gun at me. 'Right, but y'all's comin' with me.'

30

HIS GUN PRODDING me in the back, Don pushed me towards the hedge that ran by the lane. Behind me, Lupus, who was being restrained by Ivan, for certain with difficulty, was whining to follow. A cool breeze had risen, carrying with it the sound of sirens from beyond the village. How long would it be before they got here? How was this going to play out?

Don shoved me again. 'On your left there's a gap in the hedge. Get your ass through there.'

I saw what he meant, and wondered why I hadn't seen it when I was in the lane with my dog. It was a squeeze, with branches scratching at my face and clinging to my clothes.

Don was right behind me. 'Go right.'

I set a deliberate leisurely pace down the hill and away from the main road, but he prodded me with the gun again. 'C'mon. Git movin'.'

With a longer stride I was almost jogging. 'You want me to run?' If we ran he would not be able to hold the gun in my back.

He knew that. 'This'll do.'

Cloud crept over and it became too dark to see the surface clearly, and too dark to avoid the odd branch that hung over the track. I heard a distinctive sound, or I recognised it, long before Don did – an approaching helicopter. It was going to be over our position, guided by its GPS, in a minute.

Aside from the pilot, the normal aircraft crew consisted of two Tactical Flight Officers. One of them operated a Forward-Looking InfraRed camera that produced a negative image on his monitor. The warmer the object under surveillance, the paler the image, so in our case he would see a white human shape holding a white canine by the hut. And it would show two humans as white figures close together, hurrying down the lane away from the cottage. There was no escaping this camera, for it did not rely on light, but on heat. Even if we hid in the bushes, the warmth of our bodies would be visible to it through the vegetation.

'That's the police, Don. They'll have us pinned down very shortly.'

He didn't answer, but kept pushing me on. Did he know where he was taking us? The sirens had stopped. The cars must have been close, if they weren't already there.

'I don't know about the States, Don, but this is what's going to happen here tonight. That helicopter is watching us with a thermal-imaging camera. He can see everything, and he'll be telling the guys on the ground exactly where we are. They'll have dogs and a firearms team as part of the ground force. If you don't surrender when told to, they could let the dogs do the work and bring us down. I don't fancy that, as the dogs won't know that I'm an innocent person. Or, Don, they could tell the firearms boys to use their night scopes and pick us off. I don't think they'll do that, because they won't want to deal with the flak if they shoot a hostage – me. Whatever, there's no chance you're going to escape. Please, Don, I really don't fancy being brought down by an angry dog. I've got one, I know what they can do.'

'*Shuttup*. I don't need your cheap advice. I'm gonna get outta here, and y'all's comin' with me. I need you.'

'You need me to ensure you escape, and you need me for experimentation later, right? That means I'm safe. You're not going to shoot me. I can just tell you to bugger off and walk away, and you'll do nothing about it because you won't kill me.'

'No, old fella. It ain't like that at all. Y'all's my getaway card, but if things ain't looking good, you're history.'

A voice called out from behind us. He was using a loudhailer, although he probably didn't need one. It was so quiet, anything above a whisper would carry to the bottom of the valley. 'Don …'

The negotiation began. A chief inspector identified himself. He told Don how futile his attempts to run away were: he was completely surrounded. Nobody wanted innocent lives lost, it would go much easier on him if he put the gun down and gave himself up immediately.

Don yelled back at him, '*Fuck off.*'

We had descended some way down the lane from the cottage. The high bank and wall to our left were still there, but the hedge on our right was low enough to see over into the field beyond.

The policeman continued his argument in a calm but authoritative tone. I caught a fleeting glimpse of movement above the wall, a dark head snatching a glimpse of our progress. Another shadow was in the field, moving faster than we were, getting ahead of us. I didn't think Don had seen those men. He took long strides behind me, his gun knocking into my back. He appeared to be focused on the path ahead, but occasionally trod on my heel, causing me to stumble.

'Don,' the officer called in the same steady tone. 'Please be aware you're surrounded. The helicopter is watching you. We have two dogs that will track you, and two firearms officers have you in their sights. They are equipped with night-vision equipment and a rifle. Each of them is a crack shot. Please give yourself up now to avoid unnecessary injury to yourself and Mr Duncan. Put the gun down, raise your hands, and you'll come to no harm.'

Don didn't answer, but pressed himself hard against me. The heat of his body was immediately apparent, as was the stench of stale cigarette smoke. He was much taller than me, so his cheek rested on my head above my left ear. His gun was rammed into the right of my neck. To an amateur, we were one target.

Were those marksmen able to separate individuals in the dark? Wouldn't the dogs be a better bet? But would Don's reaction to a dog be an accidental pull on the trigger? Ivan – with Lupus in check – would realise that danger, wouldn't he?

Two intense, blinding beams of light stabbed at us from the darkness ahead. What was behind us? How close were the police? With the gun in my neck, I couldn't turn to see.

'Put them flashlights out or I'll kill him right now. *Put 'em out.*'

The torches died and the world went black in front of me. You can't hurry the return of night vision. Don had to be struggling, too.

A familiar sound: a soft pounding, a rapid scratching at a hard surface – paws and claws. Lupus hit us like a locomotive. Together, Don and I were floored. He recovered, but dropped the gun from my neck as long teeth punctured his wrist. He fought the dog, leaving me free. I was on him and pinned his other arm down to the road. He was strong, though. He bucked and heaved, and I battled to hold on. Lupus was locked on with his teeth, being thrown around but going nowhere.

In the background the DCI was furious. 'Who let that dog go? Piggot, was that you? Hardcastle? I expressly said no dogs. Which one of you let that animal go?'

'Not me, sir.' Twice.

Their denials were lost as other officers joined us. One took over Don's left arm from me. The other hesitated, as Lupus had the right one in his jaws.

'Lupus, leave. Good boy.'

'Thank you, sir. I've got 'im now. Bloody hell, that's quite a dog you got there.'

The peak of the crisis had passed and the tension had evaporated. My laugh was of relief. 'He was once one of yours.'

TORCHES FLASHED here and there, describing random arcs of light about the scene. When they picked up the hand-cuffed man on the ground, they held steady before moving on. The chief inspector joined the group, backed up by other officers and two dog handlers. The marksmen walked up the track towards us, their sniper rifles held muzzle down across their bodies.

The DCI pointed at Lupus, who, I had just noticed, still had his lead attached. 'What the hell's going on? Whose dog is that?'

'He's mine.'

'Oh.'

One of the handlers passed his own lead to his partner, so he could hold both police dogs. He came closer. 'Lupus?'

Lupus leapt towards him, wagging his tail. The handler looked up at me as he held my dog close to him. 'I trained him, but he failed because he was too friendly.'

'He is, most of the time, but he's fiercely protective of me and anyone he likes. You did a good job. He's saved my bacon a few times recently.'

Kirsten, Mitch and Ivan joined the group.

'Ivan, did you let Lupus go?'

'It's my fault,' said Kirsten. 'I knew he'd help you out. I persuaded Ivan to release him.'

The situation had been resolved without any orders from the chief inspector. His face was grim. 'That was not wise. Do you realise that this man could have pulled the trigger out of fright or unthinking reaction and shot Mr Duncan when the dog attacked? That's precisely why I ordered that dogs not be used.'

He didn't get the last word, though. 'Yes, well … I didn't know the situation, and your orders wouldn't apply to me, anyway. It worked, though, didn't it?'

31

KIRSTEN APPROACHED THE restaurant from the north. Without dark glasses she was squinting and shielding her eyes from the sun. She'd come from the office and was therefore armed with her charcoal suit and forbidding façade. Standing outside the demarcated café area, she scanned the tables against the light. She didn't see me at first, and I didn't wave. An odd, some would say unpleasant, side of me found amusement in watching her search. At last she saw me and took her first step forward.

I stood to greet her, but my mood took a dive. What the hell are those two doing here? Jakub Kowalski and his sidekick, Sonia, the two incompetents who lied about representing UK Biobank back in June, appeared behind her. He spotted me, switched direction and waved. Jakub led, Sonia was in his wake, and he was three steps behind Kirsten.

I stood and pulled out a chair for her. Jakub thought I was grinning at him and responded with a genuinely happy expression. Lupus leapt to his feet from under the table and nuzzled up to Kirsten. She made a fuss of him, stroking behind his ears and rubbing his head against her leg. 'Good boy. Lie down now.'

Jakub's disappointment was clear. He hesitated, perhaps he was undecided whether to approach me or not with Kirsten there. But he had already announced his presence so he could hardly back out; and he had Sonia there in support.

'Andrew,' he said, extending his hand over Kirsten's head and effectively stopping her from standing. 'Good to see you again. What a coincidence.'

Coincidence? Not likely. I didn't respond to his sweaty paw. He dropped it.

Sonia was beaming. Kirsten was clearly, and rightly, annoyed about being ignored and subjugated. She stood to look at whatever ill-mannered oaf was behind her. He gave her a salesman's smile, but it faded under her withering look.

'Jakub, Sonia. How can I help? As you can see, we were just about to have lunch.'

'Yes, sorry for the intrusion.' He had the skin of a rhino, and was not put off by the hostility.

'Sorry,' said Sonia.

'Well? Who are you representing this time? UK Biobank had never heard of you, so that was a lie.'

'Ah, yes. Sorry about that. Sometimes it's necessary to tell little untruths in order to achieve your goals. As you so rightly guessed, we represent a major pharmaceutical corporation. They have come up with an amazing offer that I can't imagine you refusing. We'd like the opportunity to discuss it with you.' Jakub's eyes flickered briefly at Kirsten. 'In private, of course.'

'Oh, don't worry on that score. There are no secrets between Kirsten and me. You can speak freely in front of her – she's my barrister.'

Jakub took a figurative step backwards. 'Oh. I didn't realise. So sorry, we won't interrupt you now. I'll be in contact later to arrange a better time. You'll be amazed at the offer, you really will.'

'Don't bother, Jakub. I don't like your approach, I don't like your manners, I don't like your lies and deceit, so my answer will be the same.'

Jakub allowed brief disappointment to cross his face, but quickly recovered his sales attitude. 'This is a once in a life-time offer, Andrew, really. You can't afford to miss out on this. It's awesome.'

'How do you know what I can or cannot afford?' I turned away from him and waved at a waiter to bring some menus. 'Now go away and don't bother me again.'

Lupus recognised my tone of voice and came out from under the table.

'Well, we'll be on our way,' Jakub said, eyeing the dog. 'Enjoy your lunch.'

'Enjoy.' Sonia smiled brightly. 'Byeee.'

We watched them thread their way between the tables to reach the open pavement, Jakub striding ahead, with Sonia's high heels clicking rapidly behind him.

'Mitch called and said he couldn't make it,' Kirsten said. 'He's looking for a man who has stolen a chihuahua. Apparently it has a ruby and sapphire studded collar. Why would anyone steal a tiny dog when all they want is the collar? … Andrew, what the hell was that scene about just now?'

The waiter took our order. When he'd left, I explained, then said, 'Kirsten, why don't you let your hair down? This is a social occasion, and you look as if you're about to get someone hanged.'

She looked so pretty when she laughed. The stern school ma'am vanished in an instant. 'I have to go back to the office, and this do needs a mirror to avoid a mess.'

'How are you? I haven't heard what progress the police have made in investigating the gang.'

'I'm feeling good, actually, the best I've felt in a long time. We thought Don was going to be a tough nut to crack, but apparently he crumbled and has been telling the police everything he knows. With other leads they had, they've pieced together a solid case against the gang. I feel … liberated, I suppose. Thank you so much for doing everything you did.'

'It's been rewarding. I've helped do some good: four young girls have a renewed opportunity to live as normal a life as they can, both you and Mitch have received some satisfaction, and a bunch of perverted monsters will be put away, although probably not for long enough. There were some tense moments at times, though. You risked Lupus's life to save me. I never thought you would have done that. Don could have shot him.'

'It was a tough decision, you or Lupus.' Kirsten gave a little smile and leant back in her chair. 'Andrew, what happens now? What's next in your life?'

'One advantage to this condition is that there's no time pressure to get things done before I die. The disadvantage is that without a foreseeable end there's a danger of drifting along instead of getting on and doing something.

'We brought down one gang of abusers, but I'm no further forward in my personal crusade on overpopulation. Somehow I have to convince the world, every government, of the disastrous effects of too many humans. And to do that I need to find a figurehead or two. People who are not afraid to stand up and be counted, serious people, scientists who know what they're talking about and can inspire and lead. I'm not that person, I'm too much of an introvert, and in any case I must never draw attention to myself. If the world comes to know about my condition, I'll become a celebrity and be hunted a hundred times more intensely than over the past few weeks. That's the last thing I want.'

'If you think we're fighting a losing battle trying to convince governments to do something about climate change, what do you think it's going to be like telling the world's population to reject a basic human physiological need – procreation.'

'I know. It'll be tough going, which is why we need some heavyweights on our side. On a positive note, Alex left me, quote, "a substantial sum". I don't know how much that is, but the description of her estate, holdings, house and so on has me believe it's in the millions. If so, I could use that to fund the start of a campaign. She'd be one hundred percent on side with that.'

'Forget about solving the impossible, you haven't answered my question.'

I returned her gaze for a while before responding. 'I'm not sure yet,' I answered finally. 'That attempt to talk to me just now shows that NiPetco was not the only company aware of my condition, and that was not the last attempt these people will make to snare me. Whatever I do has to take this threat into account. One thing's for sure, I have to change identity again, but to which of my characters depends on where I go and what I want to do.

'My favourite is Charlie Maxwell. I feel I'm really doing some good in Kenya. I love the life and there's satisfaction in protecting the animals, not to mention getting poachers arrested. The trouble with Charlie is the risk I run with the false ID that I did myself. Dan Peabody, however, was a professional job and is very unlikely to be cracked. His original work will not occur again, but that doesn't stop me from using the alias. Not in Kenya, though, as I'm already known there as Charlie. I think I'll ditch the other two and just use Dan's passport for any other work.'

'Are you going to carry on flying forever, or doing other things that normal thirty-four-year-olds do?'

'I could do. I've had periods, short periods, when the whole situation has depressed me. I've even wondered if the best thing would be for me to take my own life and die when I should die. All the things I worry about with respect to overpopulation and the consequences for mankind would then fall away. I could not be held responsible for exacerbating the problem.'

She reached across the table, but stopped short of touching me. 'How can you talk like that? You're not suicidal.'

'No, I don't have any mental health issues to my knowledge – which is a subjective view, I suppose. I have used my limited talents in doing things of value under different guises. I did consider getting involved in conflicts that are unfair, such as helping the Kurds after Trump deserted his allies. Maybe then, if I were killed, at least my problem would be solved while I was doing something worthy.'

'You shouldn't throw your life away like that. Instead of being killed, what happens if you're wounded, disabled in combat, or arrested for fighting with a terrorist organisation, however worthy it might be? Years in jail would be misery.

Think about an eternity in a wheelchair, which would definitely expose your secret. You'd be better off sitting back and watching the world change through the decades. It would be interesting.'

'It would, but unless the world does something to curb population growth, all I'll be watching will be man's final destruction of the planet.'

Our drinks arrived and we smiled at each other as the waiter took care to place the glasses in precisely the right position. He cracked the bottle tops, but I shooed him away and poured the zero-alcohol beer myself. Kirsten was working that afternoon.

'Something about you has intrigued me since we first met,' I said. 'It worried me at first, because I couldn't believe someone so inexperienced could do a good job of representing me, but you proved me wrong. You were a year ahead of Mitch at school, and he's at least forty. You look as if you're less than thirty, but your knowledge and behaviour are of a much more mature person. How old are you?'

Her eyes crinkled with amusement. 'Forty-five.'

'Fifteen years is a big difference to hide. You, er … you are ageing, aren't you?'

She laughed and nodded. 'Regrettably. It's slow, partly because I keep fit, but age is still eating away at me: deeper wrinkles, muscles not as toned as they used to be. I feel it more than look it, which has some advantages. I don't have your condition, if that's your question.'

'I must admit I have wondered. It takes many years before it becomes apparent, you know.'

'I'm sure it does, but I promise you I'm getting older. Andrew, whatever you do, whoever you decide to become – I would like to remain in touch. When you've decided your immediate future, will you tell me?'

'Will the information fall under the umbrella of lawyer-client privilege?'

She laughed. 'No, but I won't tell anyone unless you need to be rescued.'

'Why are you so interested?'

'Because you're unique. You're a very interesting person and worth following, although there's more to it than that. In some ways I'm just like you. I don't suffer fools, I don't care about people who don't do anything to help themselves, and I have few friends. I think you and I are on the same wavelength, and I'd like to hold on to that.'

'I'm not much of a friend, I've been accused of having sociopathic tendencies.'

'Nonsense. I'd be willing to give it a try.' Then, with a wicked smile, 'Having the same rare blood group should count for something.'

'That's if we had the same condition, but we don't.' This was embarrassing. My natural mode of escape was to be facetious. 'Of course, over the long term you could reincarn-ate. For me, that's not an option.'

'Right now, I have nothing of substance in my life. I'm sick of acting the ice maiden in court and playing tough with all sorts of contemptible people. I want something or someone outside my profession to provide some normality.'

'I'm hardly normal.'

She ignored that. Have you been away since you've had Lupus?'

'To Kenya a couple of times. Alex looked after him.'

'Of course. What will you do with him now?'

'I haven't given it much thought with everything that's been going on.'

'I'll look after him.'

'I told you once before not to steal my dog.'

She laughed. 'I'm serious. I could also act as a home base for you if you need some local help while you're overseas. Before you ask: it's because I believe you and I believe in you and what you're concerned about – you're right, and I want to help.'

I studied her unwavering gaze for a long time without answering. She had floored me, frankly. For the first time, I had someone on my side who understood. She had given me a sense of anticipation, that something could be achieved. It was as if I was standing in a very long tunnel at the far end of which was a tiny bright threshold to a whole new chapter in my eternal life.

'I've never considered having help here in England. I've always managed perfectly well on my own wherever I've been. But I've achieved nothing in doing that. If I am to take my cause further, then I will need assistance. Thank you.'

'This is pure selfishness, I can assure you. I too need a cause.'

'Do you have to work this afternoon? Lupus would like to visit Mrs Fothergill and see how those girls are getting along. He's a bit nervous of going on his own: they might be scared of him.'

Kirsten laughed, reached up and pulled her bun apart. She shook her head to let her hair cascade over her shoulders. 'Suddenly, there's nothing for me in the office that can't wait until tomorrow. You do realise what you've just done, don't you?'

'What?'

'No antisocial person would care about how abused young girls are coping.'

'They struck a chord somehow: about being around for each other. I have it on good authority that Lupus will miss you if you disappear.'

She gave me another brilliant smile and leant down to stroke my dog. 'I won't.'

***

Before You Go

Thank you for reading *Thirty-Four*. Hopefully you enjoyed it. If you did and have a moment to spare, writing a short review on your favourite site would be greatly appreciated. Authors depend on reader opinions in order to produce enjoyable works. Reviews help authors to further their careers.

To find out more about the author and his works please visit: https://www.helifish.co.uk where you have the option to subscribe to his mailing list.

You can also find him on Facebook: http://www.facebook.com/casole74

Also by CA Sole

In *Scott's Choice* Cuthbert Jonathan Scott is a young man with a dominant adventurous spirit. He grew up being indoctrinated by his father into an approach to life that was completely at odds with his nature: take no risks, caution in everything, settle down while young, save your money, on and on. A random event results in a decisive moment. He is torn between two options: following his father's teaching or being himself.

Two personae emerge. One, Jonathan, begins a life following his natural instincts. His spirit of adventure predominates. His choice has consequences which bring several life-threatening events but also great rewards.

Jonathan's alter ego, Cuff, is the brainwashed youth who tries to adopt the more cautious approach. But his nature conflicts with this and leads him on a dangerous path to escape the mundane existence which was the consequence of his choice. It seems he cannot avoid risk. Indeed, danger appears to seek him out.

Two independent stories develop in *Scott's Choice*. The tales are linked only by his friends and enemies who continue to influence and react to events in Cuff's life in one way, and in Jonathan's life in another. However, certain events are common to both and fixed in the calendar.

Nature's Justice is the first sequel to *Scott's Choice*.

It traces Jonathan's life as he and Gudrun experience a horrific event in Southern Africa. Witnesses to the killing of a rhino and the sighting of the person responsible for the trade in horns, they are chased and hounded over a thousand kilometres from the Kruger Park through South Africa and Botswana to the Victoria Falls.

The Pilot is the second sequel to *Scott's Choice*. Cuff Scott tries to follow a career to become an airline pilot, but his attempts to lead a stable and prosperous life are ruined by events.

At the flying school where he instructs, he becomes aware of someone smuggling illegal immigrants into the country by night. That's not his only problem. His student is being stalked by an increasingly dangerous man, and she thinks it's him.

It seems that trouble seeks him out and brings his inherent instinct for adventure to the fore. He is forced to question if he's really the persona he's trying to be.

#

A Fitting Revenge is a thriller about extraordinary events that happen to ordinary people.

Your friends are in deep trouble. What if you take a step too far in avenging them?

In southern rural England, Alastair is helping his close friend to avoid a punishing divorce from Sandra. But Sandra is ruthless, merciless and determined to win.

As Alastair is drawn into a situation which he battles to control, the love binding him and Juliet is ripped apart. With the common goal of rescuing their friend, they strive to work together, but the tension between them only widens the rift as Alastair faces the ruination of his life.

Fighting his way out of the turmoil, Alastair stretches reason to exact a terrible revenge for the extortion and assault that has affected his friends. In doing so, he discovers a side to himself which he never knew existed.

Revenge must be taken, but is Alastair's 'eye for an eye' concept too extreme? Will Juliet remain a love lost?

The Author

CA Sole began writing in 1990 with a thriller titled Zahak's Breath. An agent took it on and, after a few not insignificant changes, submitted it to a publisher. The first rejection dented his ego and left its mark! Colin took the extraordinary and foolish step of giving up his full-time job to write in 1995. His confidence took another hit, and he had to return to work for enough money to buy beer. He persevered, wrote a couple of short stories and about half a novel. That short manuscript has been incorporated into one of the sequels of the Scott series.

Colin's first published novel, *A Fitting Revenge*, came out in 2016 and quickly received 4- and 5-star reviews. His second book, CJ, was done through a small publisher and also received a small number of 4- and 5-star reviews. However, Colin's lack of enthusiasm (and plain laziness) over marketing resulted in poor sales. CJ has been rewritten and published in the summer of 2019 as *Scott's Choice*. It has two sequels: *Nature's Justice* and *The Pilot*.

Having been in the British Army, a professional helicopter pilot and an aviation consultant, his work has taken him all over the world to some 66 countries. He lived and worked in Africa – North, South, East and West – for 43 years before returning to England for good. It's therefore not surprising that the background to Colin's books is travel.

There is far too much of the less trodden world left to see.

To find out more about CA Sole's works and future projects, please visit: https://www.helifish.co.uk

Printed in Great Britain
by Amazon

77848910R00164